RE~~~~~ FAITH

"Loved it! I kept turning pages and could not put down *Rescued Faith* until I finished. A traumatic past, action, suspense, the witness of people of faith, family, and second chances. I highly recommend *Rescued Faith* if you love inspirational romantic suspense!"

—Jeanne, GOODREADS

"Michelle Sass Aleckson did a great job intertwining faith throughout the book. I thoroughly enjoyed the reminder that God is at the center, and God can redeem us. Packed full of suspense, rekindled romance, and faith, it was better than a movie."

—Emily, GOODREADS

"I loved being back in Last Chance County and reading about familiar characters. The level of suspense was perfect as the team seems to determine who is behind the criminal activity. There is lots of fingernail biting throughout the story!"

—Laura, GOODREADS

"Buckle up, my reading friends! Michelle Sass Aleckson and Lisa Phillips have put their crafty heads together and written a barn burner of a book!"

—Deena, GOODREADS

RESCUED FAITH

LAST CHANCE
· FIRE AND RESCUE ·

MICHELLE SASS ALECKSON
LISA PHILLIPS

PUBLISHING

Rescued Faith: A Last Chance County Novel
Published by Sunrise Media Group LLC
Copyright © 2025 Sunrise Media Group LLC
Print ISBN: 978-1-963372-53-3

All rights reserved. No part of this publication may be reproduced or transmitted in any form or by any means without written permission of the publisher.

This book is a work of fiction. Names, characters, places, and incidents are either products of the author's imagination or used fictitiously. Any similarity to actual people, organizations, and/or events is purely coincidental.

Scriptures taken from the Holy Bible, New International Version®, NIV®. Copyright © 1973, 1978, 1984, 2011 by Biblica, Inc.™ Used by permission of Zondervan. All rights reserved worldwide. www.zondervan.com. The "NIV" and "New International Version" are trademarks registered in the United States Patent and Trademark Office by Biblica, Inc.™

For more information about Lisa Phillips and Michelle Sass Aleckson please access the authors' websites at the following addresses: https://www.authorlisaphillips.com www.michellealeckson.com.

Published in the United States of America.
Cover Design: Ana Grigoriu-Voicu, Books-Design

LAST CHANCE
· FIRE AND RESCUE ·

To the memory of Linda Lee Day
September 25, 1967-June 12, 2024

Even in the darkest of days you reflected His light. As we
adjust to the dimness of a world without you, may you bask
in His presence and soak in the warmth of the eternal Son.
Love you, Hooch.

"But to all who did receive him, who believed in his name,
he gave the right to become children of God,
who were born, not of blood nor of the will of the flesh
nor of the will of man, but of God."

JOHN 1:12-13 ESV

ONE

FAVORS WERE A DANGEROUS CURRENCY TO DEAL in. Too many hidden costs. As a private investigator, Penny Mitchell knew better. People got sucked into all kinds of trouble from helping out a friend. Which was why she liked her solitary life back in Denver. Less blowback. Less entanglements. Less complications.

And yet, here she was, in the last place on earth she wanted to be, all because a former coworker had given her those Bronco tickets for her nephew's birthday and now he was cashing in the favor.

Man, she needed to get this job done and get out. Before anyone knew she was in town.

She killed the engine of her Ford Edge, reached over the almost-empty coffee cup and half-eaten bag of sunflower seeds for her camera in the passenger seat. She held it to her eye, focused across the street at the red Nissan Rogue and the woman behind the wheel. The curly dark hair and round face with glasses came into sharp focus. Penny snapped a few pictures.

She should've turned down the job ATF agent Ben Freeman had begged her to take as soon as her target had headed west from Denver. He'd assured her that Emma Kemper wasn't a criminal mastermind like her bomb-making brother Vince. Which meant tailing her and snapping some photos should be an easy assignment.

But there was nothing easy about being *here*. The sooner she could get the heck out of here the better. Because if Penny didn't run into someone she knew, the memories themselves would drive her away.

All right, Emma. What are you doing here?

Last Chance County's little warehouse district wasn't a travel destination. There was no hotel in this part of town. No Airbnbs or cute rentals. Just some old metal-sided buildings and dilapidated brick storefronts from an era gone by. And Emma was simply sitting in her driver's seat. This felt more like a purposeful destination. Like she might be here awhile.

Penny used voice commands to make a call.

"Freeman here. Whatcha got, Mitchell?"

"Does Emma Kemper have connections to Last Chance County?" If he knew, he was cunning to have kept it from her when he'd asked for this "itty bitty favor."

"We haven't been able to find much about her. That's why we hired you. Why? Is that where she is?"

"Believe me, I wouldn't be here if she wasn't," Penny ground out. She shouldn't be so snippy. But . . . Last Chance. Really?

"Huh. I woulda thought she was heading for Nevada or Arizona, where she grew up. But that's good that it's Last Chance. With Jude Brooks there, you'll have some backup if you need it."

"I don't need backup." She needed to get out of here as soon as possible. "Are you sure she doesn't have known associates here? I could capture her tonight and bring her in." Then the job would be done. Favor fulfilled and she could move on with her life and not worry about running into her past.

"Nice try. Emma flew under the radar while we focused on her brother. She has no record, but she might have been sent by Vince to do some of his dirty work. I need you to keep your distance and gather intel, Ms. Private Investigator. No formal charges yet."

Penny switched the camera to one hand and downed a swig from her cup.

Ugh. She almost spat out the cold dregs of her gas-station coffee. Instead, she forced herself to swallow it. She needed the caffeine.

"You *still* haven't gotten anything out of Vince Kemper?" Ben Freeman was sharp and had a rather intimidating presence with his tall, beefy frame. The scrawny explosives expert hardly seemed like a formidable opponent. "I would've thought by now you would've cracked him."

"He may be a pasty scrap of a man, but he's not saying a thing. And he covered his tracks well. We haven't been able to untangle much here. It's up to you now to make sure Emma isn't involved in his bomb-making agenda. And if she is, then maybe we'll be able to figure out what the endgame is, cuz we're getting a whole lot of nothing."

Gee, no pressure. Penny blew out a long breath. This meant staying longer.

"What's the matter? She get away from the great Penny Mitchell?" He chuckled.

But there was nothing funny about this. Penny was barreling straight toward a disaster if she spent any more time in the area than absolutely necessary.

"I have her in my sights. I just didn't think this job would bring me to Last Chance County." She snapped a few more pictures as Emma turned toward the window, giving Penny a better angle of her face.

"Jude can bring her in for questioning or take over if you want to be done. Which, by the way, if you get tired of the wandering lifestyle, he's requested more staff for the satellite ATF office there in Last Chance."

"You suggesting I come back to the dark side?" Jude Brooks, her former coworker, had followed a case to LCC, where he'd spent his childhood summers, and reunited with Andi Crawford two years ago. Little had he known then, when he brought Penny in on the case to help capture Diego Ruiz Sosa, the series of events he would kick off. It had been nice to be a part of a case for a while, the thrill and adventure of tracking down a cartel leader. Something different than finding cheating spouses or gathering intel on criminals for the lawyers, or the private security she did for the rich and entitled. Now Sosa was dead, and Jude and Andi were married.

She, on the other hand, was still single—just the way she liked it—and in danger of getting sucked down a rabbit hole if she stayed any longer than necessary.

"Being a federal agent isn't all bad. Jude has a great thing going there."

And Jude deserved all the good things life had to offer. Including the tightly knit family he'd recently married into and a place like Last Chance to put down some roots.

So yeah, she'd given up a few things for the sake of being in business by herself. And at times like now, it would be really convenient to have the authority to bring Emma Kemper in. But no way did she want to give control over to someone else. Because those jobs came with bosses. Bosses who led people on, made promises they didn't intend to keep.

No, thank you.

"That's great for Jude, but I'm happy where I'm at. Charging the big bucks. You sure this is worth my hourly rate?" Because she wasn't sure there was any compensation worth the risk to her heart of being back here.

Maybe she *should* let Jude pick it up from here. He could keep an eye on things. She could get back to the open road. Freedom.

But her bank account balance flashed through her mind. She might not be in dire straits yet, but she needed the work. And she did have a professional reputation to consider. If she couldn't complete this job, who knew if Ben would give her another? She liked to stay near Denver so she could see Libby and the kids more often.

Of course, she always talked her sister into coming to see *her* so she could avoid this kind of thing. But with Libby's family living here, Penny should be the one to make sure there was nothing dangerous going on. She groaned again.

"Do you want me to contact Jude? If you really don't want this job—"

Her father's voice echoed from the past. *Buck up, Pen.*

"Nah, no need to bother the newlyweds. I'm just whining."

"Hey, that reminds me. Why didn't you make it to the wedding? You missed seeing Jude do the Macarena. Those Crawfords sure know how to throw a party."

Yes, they did. Memories of country music, learning how to two-step, and a certain masculine beachy fragrance floated through her mind.

"I . . . had a job I couldn't get out of in time. But I sent Jude and Andi an obnoxiously expensive gift, so all was forgiven."

The hefty price tag hadn't made *her* feel any better though. No one had to know that she'd specifically taken a job that'd meant she would be gone that day. And no need for Jude or *any* of his in-laws to know she was in the vicinity now.

Especially Bryce.

The handsome rescue firefighter, one of Andi's brothers, probably hadn't given her a second thought since the last time she'd hightailed it out of the county a year and a half ago.

And it was better for everyone if it stayed that way. Even if there wasn't a day that went by that she didn't see something that reminded her of him. Try as she might, it was hard to forget those passionate brown eyes.

"You missed a good reception." Freeman obviously wasn't going to let it drop.

Movement on the sidewalk across the street grabbed Penny's attention.

"I need to go. Someone else is coming. I'll let you know when I find anything."

"If Emma ends up sticking around, contact Jude."

Not unless she absolutely had to. "Bye."

The high desert sunset softened to a lavender haze behind the mountains outside of town. She had to give it to Jude, he'd picked a beautiful place to live. Something like a sigh escaped as she watched the street. Some things just weren't meant to be.

She sat up and watched two men park a truck and approach Emma's car. One stocky and tall, the other average height and thin. Penny took pictures as they came closer. Both had darker hair and olive skin tones that could be from a variety of ethnicities. The lighting wasn't great, but hopefully she could still identify them later.

Emma got out and opened the back of the SUV. She pulled a couple duffel bags out and handed them to the men. Then she grabbed another. They turned down an alley between two of the buildings and were out of sight.

Penny checked her Smith & Wesson Equalizer and quickly ran across the street to follow them just as the streetlights turned on. Her black leather jacket helped fight off the spring chill in the air and blend her into the night shadows. Too bad it didn't have a hood to hide her blonde head. She picked up her pace and approached the alley between the warehouse and the empty store next to it. She peered around the corner.

Empty. Just scraggly weeds growing in the cracks of the asphalt between the buildings, and trash scattered against the wall.

They had to be close. Penny jogged down the alley. There. A door in the warehouse hadn't quite closed.

With gun in hand, she toed the door open a smidge, testing it to see if the rusty hinges would squeak. It opened quietly.

Good. She peeked in first, then slipped into the dark building, letting her eyes adjust. Voices carried from deeper within the space. Penny crouched by a pile of pallets just inside the doorway and scoped out the area. Tall metal shelves were mostly empty, although some held boxes. An old forklift off to the side looked like it hadn't been started in decades. But the tables in the middle were bright white plastic, like the kind one could find at the nearest Costco. Those must be new. And the folding chairs didn't look too worn either.

There was nowhere else to hide in the cavernous space. Emma spoke to a tall man, but in the dark there was no way Penny could distinguish any features. Not even the color of his hair. His bright flashlight shone down at the table between them. Where had the other two guys gone?

"Did you bring them?" the new man asked.

"I've got them here." She dropped the duffel bag on the table and wrapped her arms around the man's neck. "I've missed you." Pulling him close she gave him a lingering kiss.

"Me too." He kissed her back. "But everything is in place now. So let's see what you brought."

She opened the duffel to show him.

"Good." The man reached in and grabbed a smaller bag out of the duffel. "And your brother? He was able to finish his work?"

"Of course. The devices are here." She unzipped a different pocket. "He showed me how to set them."

So much for the theory that Emma wasn't involved with Vincent's agenda.

Penny tried to move closer and get a better look, but there was no cover. She used her phone to get a couple of pictures. However, she couldn't see one distinguishing feature of Emma's boyfriend in the dark. The hooded sweatshirt he wore kept his face shadowed.

"And you're sure he won't—"

Emma huffed. "He's not going to rat us out. My brother understands how important this is. Now, can we get out of here? I want to see the new—"

"Boss, we're set." The thin guy from out front jogged over from a door on the wall across from Penny. It must've been an office of some sort. "We need to go."

Boss handed the duffel with the hidden device to his cohort. "You know where to put it." The man snatched the bag and ran up the metal stairs in the back of the warehouse while Emma and her guy headed straight toward Penny and the alley door.

Penny quickly moved to the back of the pile of pallets. If she opened the door now, they'd see her. As soon as they left she could follow and find out who—

"What do you think you're doing?" A dark and ominous voice sounded behind her. But it was the click of the safety being switched off that immediately put Penny on edge.

Cold metal pressed into the back of her head. "Drop the gun now."

"Who's there?" Boss Man asked.

Penny tensed her grip on the gun. She could make a move and take out the guy behind her, but the boss pulled out a gun of his own. If he came closer, maybe she could ID him, but it was still too dark.

She needed more time. She tried a little chuckle. "I was lost, I was just looking for—"

"I said drop it. I have no problem putting a bullet in you," the man behind her said.

And from the hardness in his voice, Penny didn't doubt it.

"Al, get outta here. I'll take care of her." The man spoke to Emma's boyfriend.

"Stick to the plan. Let the blast take care of her and get out." He led Emma out of the warehouse.

Clearly Emma was no innocent bystander. That girl was in this up to her eyeballs and apparently didn't care about leaving a fellow female to the mercy of whoever had a gun to her head.

Penny was on her own. "Look, I was just trying to find—"

"This is your last chance. Put. Down. The. Gun."

She slowly lowered her gun to the ground. The pressure of the man's weapon against her skull didn't give her a choice. Before she could stand up, he yanked her arms behind her and dragged her toward the back. He had to be tall. And big.

Penny was no lightweight, but his grip had no give to it whatsoever. She fought, pulling away from him, but her shoulders screamed as they were trapped against his chest.

Trapped. Again. With no one to rely on for a rescue but herself. No surprise there. If she believed like she did when she was a little girl, she might've prayed. But that never changed anything.

Buck up, Pen.

Penny tried throwing her head back, driving it into what she hoped was his nose or another soft body part. Nope. His chin was as hard as her head.

He shook her and squeezed tighter. "You're feisty, I'll give you that. But this will not end well for you."

Not if she had anything to say about it. "People are looking for me. They'll be here any—"

The other minion came barreling down the metal stairs. "It's set. We have two min—who's that?"

Two minutes? Penny's mind raced.

"Doesn't matter. We gotta go." The hulk man dragged her farther.

"Shoot her and let's get." The skinny twerp said it like it was no big deal. Real upstanding friends Emma had.

"Shooting leaves a bullet in her. A bullet they can trace. We should find out who she is, but we don't have time. Help me get her to that closet back there."

Closet? No way!

The man in front of her went for her legs. Penny kicked and flailed. Her black combat boot connected with his jaw. He staggered away for a moment but then shook his head and came back. He wrapped two vise-like arms around her thighs while the brute behind her picked her up, squeezing her arms against her chest.

"Let me go! I can help you." She tried to use her weight to throw them off-balance.

It was useless. They dragged her to the back of the room as Penny's mental countdown kept going.

The guy holding her legs let go and opened a door. She was thrown in, and her head bounced off the cement. The door shut before she could even open her eyes. No!

Her head swam, waves of agony pounded. Thoughts jumbled together except for one clear truth. She was trapped.

"It's not a basement. I'm fine." Her voice wasn't very convincing, even to her own ears. Too breathy. Too small. But if it tricked her brain into forgetting that she was alone, she would keep talking to herself. "Not a basement."

She crawled to the door in the pitch black, too dizzy to stand. The knob didn't budge. Her fingers felt the lock. Maybe she could pick it. But her pulse quickened. Her hands trembled. She couldn't see a thing in the thick darkness, and her gas-station coffee and sunflower seeds were about to make another appearance.

Penny pounded on the door. "Let me out of here. I'm serious. I can help!"

One of the men laughed. Footsteps on the concrete floor grew quieter as they moved away. And then . . . silence.

They'd left her here to die. In the dark. Alone.

Penny tried the knob again, but it was useless. Her scream of frustration ripped through the darkness.

Her phone!

With shaky hands she pulled it out of her pocket. No reception. But she could use the flashlight. Maybe—

A huge boom shook the building. Dust rained down. A paint can from the shelf above the door fell.

This was why she didn't do favors.

She never should've come back to Last Chance County.

TWO

FINALLY, SOME ACTION. THE RESCUE 5 TRUCK
sped down the road, sirens blaring. Firefighter Bryce Crawford
welcomed the sound, itching to get out and do something after a
long shift of sitting around. Sitting around and talking.

A guy could only handle so much of that. Especially when he
had very little of interest to contribute to the conversation. Life
had settled into a very dull routine lately. And he didn't know how
to shake loose from it.

"Yo, Lieutenant, you gonna tell us about your hot date last night
or what?" Ridge called from the driver's seat. They sped past the
downtown stores.

"Wouldn't you like to know." Bryce tinkered with the device
in his hands. Hopefully the hint of something that wasn't there
would keep Ridge from asking for more details. They had a job to
do and a fire to put out. One disaster was enough to worry about.
The call couldn't be any worse than his dinner with Sarai Green
last night.

His mother wanted him to date a "good Christian girl." But
Sarai had been about as interesting as oatmeal. Plain oatmeal. No

brown sugar and cream. No cinnamon or apple. No taste whatsoever.

The whole date had been a flop. She'd declined dessert and asked for him to take her home as soon as the server brought the check. Dating used to be fun. Easy. Dance a little, drink a little, show a girl a good time. But since coming to faith almost a year ago, Bryce didn't know how to navigate that world anymore. And all the old haunts felt weirdly empty. Wasn't this faith thing supposed to make things easier? Clearer?

He was supposed to be a new man.

If so, Sarai was obviously *not* impressed with the new Bryce Crawford.

Not that he could blame her. The old Bryce had been so much more interesting. And that's who people expected. So, guess he should just focus on the job once more and forget about his social life for the time being.

Bryce checked his thermal imaging camera.

"The TIC working?" Zack Stephens asked. Ridge parked the truck among the other rescue vehicles in the warehouse district.

"Yup. Let's go." They hopped out of the truck.

"So you're really not gonna tell us about the date?" Eddie Rice asked as he shouldered his air tank. The chaos of multiple sirens, crews running around trucks and setting up hoses, and bystanders gawking surrounded them.

"Dude, have I ever gone into detail about my dates?"

"I just wanna learn from a master. How do you do it?" Rice asked.

Zack chuckled as he jammed his hands into his gloves. "You're on a roll now. Third date this week. I thought you were losing your game for a while there. What was it, nine months without a date?"

"That was, like, a year ago. And it was just a little dry spell." Back when he'd hoped he could find Penny Mitchell after she'd left town without a word. But she'd cut him out of her life. Eventually he'd gotten the hint and had to move on. And what these guys didn't need to know was that most of those "dates" were Bryce sitting with his dad watching his favorite fishing show, playing chess, or taking him to the men's discipleship group at his church.

He'd tried telling the guys the truth the first time. Of course, they hadn't believed him. It'd become a joke around the firehouse. "Playing chess" was now code for "hot date." After that he hadn't even attempted to explain. He'd let the guys draw their own conclusions.

But no other woman had gotten to him like Penny had. He kept trying. He must've been desperate to think it would be sweet, straightlaced Sarai that would get him out of this funk. Her idea of a good time was knitting and watching British period dramas.

Everyone was settling down though. His brother Logan seemed to have found his purpose fighting fires out in Montana. His mother was a steady rock for his father. Now his sister Andi was married to Jude, and here he was. Alone.

At least he had his team.

The guys approached the warehouse engulfed in flames. Truck 14 was already busy hooking hoses up. Bryce checked in with the other lieutenant, Amelia Patterson.

"What's the call?" Bryce asked her, talking loudly over the noise of the trucks and sirens.

"Truck 14 has water on. Need you and your guys to clear the building. The main entrance is too hot. Looks like two side entrances you can use."

"You got it." Bryce jogged over to Rice, Ridge, and Stephens. "We're up. We need to find access and clear the building from the inside. Stephens and Rice go around the other way. Ridge, you're with me. We'll take this alley."

Flames shot out the transom windows above their heads.

"The front of the building is too hot. Let's go around the side."

Using the TIC, Bryce checked for hotspots from the outside. "The south wall is our best access point."

Bryce led Ridge to the side door and shoved his irons, fork side first, into the seam. "Hit!"

Ridge hit the pike end with his ax. The door swung open. Smoke poured out, blocking visibility, but with the imaging screen, they stayed low and navigated through the big open area. Most of the heat and damage seemed to be in the front of the building.

"I thought this place was abandoned." Ridge spoke through the microphone in his helmet.

"Like Bryce's love life." Zack busted up laughing from somewhere on the other side of the building.

Bryce ignored it. He and Ridge stepped around a pile of pallets right inside the doorway and entered the main part of the warehouse. "We can't assume anything. Let's clear it out quickly. It's chili night and I'm hungry."

Through the smoke, tall metal shelves, some full of boxes, towered over them, creating aisles. They cleared each one, then met up with Rice and Stephens in the middle of the warehouse. Flames from the front moved closer toward them.

"What about that office up there?" Rice pointed up a metal staircase. A bank of glass windows would've allowed someone to watch from above and see the whole warehouse.

"We better check." Bryce yanked on the railing. No give. He went behind the staircase and hung from one of the treads above his head. It didn't budge.

"How are we doing in there, Lieutenant?" Chief James's voice came through the speakers.

"So far it's clear. We have one more section of upper offices." Bryce pointed for the others to start up the stairs.

"The water's not doing much. You boys better get a move on it."

"Yes, sir," Bryce answered the chief, then followed the others.

"Looks like the stairs will hold. But we gotta be fast. Let's go."
They began to climb up.

A scream from somewhere deeper in the building stopped them
mid-step.

"Did you hear that?" Ridge asked.

Bryce nodded, the hair on his neck standing on end. Through
the smoke and flames, he couldn't see the floor anymore. Fires
had an assortment of strange sounds. Animal-like roars. Groans
and screeches were common as building materials warped and
collapsed.

After another three count, Rice resumed climbing. "Guess it
was nothing."

But Bryce couldn't leave it. Not if someone needed rescuing.
"You three clear that office. I'll check it out and meet you back
down on the floor."

Zack paused. "You sure? Maybe I should—"

"Go ahead. We'll see who finishes first. Winner gets the biggest
piece of cornbread."

"You're the boss." Zack chuckled.

"Stick close together. Be quick but thorough in that office. Got
it?"

"Sure thing." Stephens continued climbing behind Eddie. Bryce
quickly descended the steps and made it back to the concrete floor.
He wouldn't let any of his men go at it alone. If someone were to
take that risk, it would be him.

"Hello? Anyone here? This is the Last Chance County Fire and
Rescue." He bellowed as loud as he could and stopped to listen.
No response. Bryce jogged down the last aisle. Fire already chewed
through the front offices and headed toward the open warehouse
floor. The cardboard boxes alone would be instant fuel.

He spoke into the radio. "Anything in the office?"

"Almost clear. Nothing so far. But catching heat imaging from
the vents. It's in the walls," Eddie answered him.

Heat from the vents? Bryce's gut lurched. "Get out of there! The fire is below you."

"But Stephens is clearing the inner off—"

"Grab him and get out! You hear me, Rice?"

"Yeah—" His voice cut out.

Bryce spun and ran back toward the stairs. Zack, Ridge, and Eddie burst out of the office door and started clambering down. When they reached the concrete floor, Bryce breathed easier. But that had been close. "All right, there's no one here. Let's get out of—"

The ground shook. Bryce fell to the floor, knocked down by a blast of hot force. The windows from the upper floor office shattered, raining down glass. A high-pitched note rang in his ears.

Dizzy and disoriented, Bryce tried to stand, only making it to his knees before he had to stop and catch his breath. He tried to shake the ringing away as he searched through the smoke and dust for the others.

"Rice! Stephens!" He stood up. One of the metal shelves teetered. Fell toward them. Bryce leaped away, skidded across the cement floor, and collapsed against a door. He coughed and tried to stand. Pushing off the ground, his hand came up sticky. He wiped it on his pants, leaving a red smear.

Wait. Was that blood?

"Bryce, we gotta get out of here!" Stephens's voice came through the comms. "Where are you?"

Bryce looked around. The wall of crumbled shelving must've cut him off from the other three. The whole room was on fire now. The roof in the front of the building groaned. Sections of ceiling fell.

"I'm fine. Where's Eddie and Ridge?"

"I'm fine." Eddie's voice came through the speaker. "I think Ridge is hurt."

Bryce lifted a section of metal from the pile. More fell. A flaming piece of insulation dropped from the ceiling, forcing Bryce back against the wall again.

"Talk to me! What's going on?" Bryce tried to keep the panic out of his voice.

"Ridge is pinned. He's not moving."

Bryce had to get over there. Help them. But a wave of dizziness hit him. He leaned on the door in the wall to catch his balance. His eye caught on the dark-red puddle under his boots. Was he injured? Bleeding somewhere?

Everything hurt, but nothing felt like an open wound. He kneeled down and peered closer. The puddle seeped out from under the door. Maybe some kind of storage area. And was that blonde hair?

Someone was in there!

"Ridge! Wake up, man." Zack sounded panicked. "I think he's got a broken leg. And he's knocked out."

Chief James's voice came through the intercom. "What's going on?"

"We got a man down. We need help." Eddie coughed and gave their location.

How was Bryce going to get his guys out of this?

"I've got an injured civilian too." Bryce looked around for his pry bar and ax.

They needed to get Ridge out. Now. And whoever was caught behind this door. Bryce spotted his tools. Grabbed them off the floor as he listened through the comms. Sounded like Izan Collins and Amelia Patterson were already there, stabilizing Ridge's leg and lifting him out on a backboard. They must've entered from the other side of the building.

Bryce moved back to the door with his irons in hand. Jamming the pike end in the seam between the door and the frame, he torqued the tool up and popped the lock. The door swung out. On the ground lay a female, long blonde hair splayed over her face and the floor. Her black leather jacket was covered in dust and debris. A paint can rolled near her head. She moaned.

Good. She was still alive. But the fire was moving closer, already eating up the mountain of shelving and boxes.

"Ma'am, can you hear me?" Bryce asked.

"Roof is caving in! Crawford, get out of there!" the chief yelled over the radio.

Without another thought, Bryce scooped her up in his arms. No time to stabilize her, so hopefully they weren't dealing with a spine or neck injury. He ran out of the closet and headed for the side door. A pile of wood pallets fueled the flames, almost cutting off their exit.

With a loud screech, a section of the metal stairs fell and clanged as it hit the cement, sending up a shower of sparks. More of the ceiling fell.

He was going to have to make a run for it. He adjusted his hold on the woman in his arms. She moaned again, starting to rouse.

Bryce kept his back to the flames and ran for the open door he had come through with Ridge. They spilled into the alley just as the roof collapsed.

Bryce jogged with the woman out to the front of the warehouse, where the ambulance and other trucks were parked on the street.

"We need a medic!"

Maybe it was his yelling, but the woman stiffened in his arms, lifted her head. The hair that had covered her face fell away, allowing big green eyes to stare back at him. Green eyes he knew well. Bryce stopped moving.

"Penny?"

Her jaw dropped open. "What are you doing here?" Her voice cracked. She must be able to see him through the mask.

"Rescuing you, apparently." Because maybe God *did* answer prayers. Here she was, back in his arms.

Penny winced, eyelids slamming shut tight as if she were in pain. "You can put me down now."

Or maybe not.

"What are *you* doing here?" Bryce asked her.

Before she could say anything, Kianna Russell rushed over to them with a cot. Bryce carefully laid Penny down. She immediately pushed herself up.

Kianna tried holding her down. "Ma'am, you need to lie still. You were—"

"I'm fine. I need to sit up."

"You really shouldn't sit right now. You have a head injury and could make it worse—"

"You want a head injury yourself? I told you, I'm fine." There was that mix of fierceness and fire that was all Penny Mitchell. "I don't need treatment. I need to go."

Kianna huffed. "You shouldn't—"

"Don't even try, Russell. You won't get through to her." Bryce stepped up to the cot, removing his mask and helmet, his gaze tracing the lines of Penny's beautiful face. Even now, with ash and blood smeared across her cheek, long blonde hair tangled and matted, she could stop his heart with one look. She was gorgeous and dangerous.

Why was that combination so appealing?

But when it came down to it, it didn't matter. He looked down at her, the first time he'd seen her in well over a year. "Guess it's time for you to run away again, huh."

She stared at him.

Bryce said, "Won't be so easy this time."

THREE

THIS WAS *EXACTLY* WHY SHE HADN'T WANTED TO come back here and why she needed to leave. Penny's head pounded enough to tell her she wasn't imagining things. She wasn't dreaming. And it wasn't a hallucination brought on by a head injury.

Bryce Crawford really *had* rescued her from a burning building. He stood at the foot of her cot looking way better than any man had a right to look when covered with soot and sweat under the glaring red and blue lights of the emergency vehicles.

The concern in those brown eyes was like a kick in the gut.

"Penny, what are you doing here?" he asked.

Good question. Where was she again? Her thoughts didn't quite come together at first. Then everything crystallized. "My job." Emma. She'd escaped with the mystery man.

But across the street behind Bryce, the red Nissan was still parked on the curb. Penny climbed off the cot.

The medic reached for her. Penny kind of recognized her but couldn't come up with a name.

"Ma'am, please. You're bleeding. You were knocked out. Let us examine—"

"I have to search that car." Her feet hit the ground, but everything swayed the second she stood. She didn't want to be a jerk, but some things were more important than taking the time to make someone feel better.

Bryce caught her arm and righted her. "Whoa. You should—"

"Don't tell me what I should do. I lost her."

"Lost who?"

"Emma Kemper. That's her car."

It took more strength than she'd ever want to admit in order to pull out of Bryce's grip.

His brows furrowed as he looked down at her. "Penny, Kianna is right. You're bleeding. You need to be checked out."

Kianna. Right. She should've known that. But why waste time letting a paramedic tell her what she already knew. She had a raging headache. Probably a concussion.

"I need to figure out what she had. Her car."

"Fine. I'll help you over there. Then will you agree to let these guys take care of you?"

She didn't need someone taking care of her. But if nodding meant he'd get out of her way, then fine. Emma had bombs. In Last Chance County. And Penny had let her get away. She had to fix this.

Every step sent a shock of pain through her skull. Her vision blurred for a moment and then cleared. She could do this. She *had* to do this. If she stayed focused on the job, she could forget all over again what it was like to be in Bryce's arms.

She had to.

Okay, so she hadn't been able to forget over the last year and a half, but still. It gave her something to cling to. She couldn't let her emotions cloud her judgment again. It was too dangerous. She'd already lost so much.

She bit down hard on her molars as a wave of nausea rolled over her, but she made it to Emma's car.

Penny pulled the sleeves over her fingers and yanked on the

handle. It was unlocked. Thank goodness for some miracles. Jude would probably call it an answered prayer. She wasn't sure about that, but she'd take what she could get.

She leaned on the frame of the car and opened the driver's side door. Wrappers and loose papers littered the passenger side. Penny couldn't touch anything, but a brief look over the mess found nothing helpful.

The trunk. That's where she'd grabbed the duffel bag from. Penny looked for a lever or button to open it.

"What are you looking for? Can I help?"

Bryce was still there. Hovering.

Penny shook her head and immediately regretted it. Light flashed behind her eyes for a second. Bad idea, Pen. She collapsed into the driver's seat. Hopefully it looked more graceful than it felt.

"Penny, seriously, let someone help you for once. What are you looking for?"

She leaned over again, just to catch her breath.

She needed Bryce to leave. In this state, she was bound to make more poor decisions based on feelings she had no business feeling. She needed to pull it together.

Her hand felt along the panel by the door. Aha. There. She pressed a button, and the trunk popped open.

Trying not to make it obvious she needed the car for support, she stood and made her way to the trunk.

Bryce followed.

"Come on, Penny. Let me help. You look awful."

"Gee, thanks."

She scanned the gray interior of the trunk.

"That's not what I meant. You look like you're going to pass out. Let me—"

"There!"

"What?" He leaned over. Even masked in the scent of smoke,

she caught a whiff of his aftershave, the clean beachy scent she hadn't been able to get out of her head.

She didn't let herself look at him. Instead, she focused on the small black object in the corner of the trunk. She took out her phone and snapped a picture of it.

"What's that?" Bryce peered at it.

"Evidence."

A police officer walked past.

"Excuse me, do you have gloves? And an evidence bag?"

"You can't dig around in this car. It's an active crime scene." The police officer's badge read Thomas.

"I'm a private investigator assigned by the ATF to follow this woman and find out what she's doing. I'm trying to help." She dug out her license to show him and gave him Ben Freeman's number.

The officer studied her face, then the license. "I'll make a call and be back."

He wasn't gone long before he came back with the items. "I'm Anthony Thomas. We'll need your statement, Ms. Mitchell, when we're done here. Sounds like you know the drill." He handed her the gloves.

It took her longer than it should've to slide her fingers into them, but once she had, she picked up the object and looked at it under the streetlight.

This was bad. Really bad. "We have a problem."

Bryce scowled. "Obviously. But I really think you should—"

"She met someone here. She's not alone." Penny swung her head, searching the street for a sign of where Emma and her posse would've gone. A wave of nausea hit her. She held her breath, biting down hard until it passed.

"Do you think they'll come after you?" Bryce actually looked concerned. Even with the way she'd left? How was that possible?

But his question hung, and the less concern—or anything—he felt for her, the better.

"That's not the problem. They think I'm dead."

"That's how you ended up in the closet with a head injury?" Bryce asked.

"You were the woman they found in the fire?" Officer Thomas asked.

"Yes. My head hit the concrete floor, and during the explosion, something fell on me." Not that the rest of her body hadn't already been sore from trying to fight off the guys who'd thrown her in the closet. And yes, she'd been on the verge of an outright panic attack. But with Bryce and this other man, she needed to appear strong. Like she had everything together.

She needed to keep it professional.

"I'll grab one of the medics." The handsome officer jogged away.

Bryce, on the other hand, moved closer. He gently swept a lock of hair behind her ear. He sent her a flirty kind of smile. The typical Bryce life-of-the-party smile. "I still can't believe you're here."

Oh boy. Pull it together. She dug for something to keep him back. She might need snark, or she'd resort to flirting back. And that only got her into trouble.

So much trouble.

"Don't worry. I'll be gone before you know it."

He winced. "Could you at least stick around long enough to talk? I'd hoped you'd come to the wedding."

Talk?

What was there to talk about?

She still remembered the scene in crystal-clear color. Even with a head injury.

The sight of Ashlee Featherwood in Bryce's arms wasn't one she would soon forget.

She should probably thank Ashlee at some point. It'd been the wake-up call Penny had needed. She never should've let it go so far with Bryce. So really . . . there was nothing they needed to "talk" about now.

"I was on a job. Couldn't get back here in time." Penny dropped the object into the evidence bag and sealed it.

"You need to be careful." The smile faded. "You could've died in there."

She looked back at the warehouse still engulfed in flames. She was keeping Bryce from his job. No need to focus on the fact that it'd included rescuing her tonight.

Why did it have to be him?

She had to get back to her own job too.

Keep it professional. She should make it her new mantra.

"I know you have to get back to it, and I—" She tried to take a step but everything buckled.

Bryce caught her around the waist. "Don't tell me you're fine. You're coming with me."

He swept her into his arms and carried her to the cot again. "You're getting a ride to the hospital."

She must've really rattled her brain. This time she didn't fight it. And when the medic started assessing her vitals, she didn't stop Bryce Crawford from walking away.

Back in Last Chance County, and in less than an hour she'd almost died, then run into her extremely handsome ex. She needed to get out of town fast.

FOUR

R IDGE HAD BROKEN HIS LEG LAST NIGHT BUT
otherwise would be fine.

Bryce, not so much.

Penny was back.

Was that good or bad? An answer to prayer or a test?

"Dude, what are you doing?" Izan Collins walked out the door
of the firehall with his duffel bag.

Bryce fumbled with his truck keys, barely catching them before
they fell. "Just trying to decide where to grab some grub."

Bryce looked over the hood of his truck, still parked outside
the firehouse, at the mountains glowing in the early morning light.
Too bad he couldn't find answers there.

But wait. Pastor talked about a verse like that.

I lift up my eyes to the mountains;
Where does my help come from?

My help comes from the Lord,

The Maker of heaven and earth.

So maybe it wasn't so crazy that he was staring at the morning
sky, looking for answers.

Wouldn't Penny get a kick out of that? The fact that he went to church, read his Bible now, and even remembered a couple of verses. Maybe this was all part of being a new guy.

Penny was part of his past. So probably best if he just let it go and moved on.

But something inside didn't *want* to let it go. It clung to some minuscule, impossible hope. Which was crazy. Maybe he just needed to figure out why she'd left him so he could move on.

"She rattled your cage, didn't she?" Izan's question snapped Bryce back into the moment.

"Huh?"

"Penny. You haven't been the same since she first showed up, back with all that Sosa stuff a couple years ago."

Bryce blew him off. "Nah, haven't given her much thought."

"Right, cuz you're too busy with all the other ladies, huh?" He dropped his duffel and leaned against Bryce's truck. "Sure it's not Penny that had you tossing all night long? I heard they kept her overnight at the hospital. You worried about her?"

No need to tell Izan he'd already found out she was still at Last Chance County Hospital on the second floor. "I had too much caffeine. That's all."

"Really?"

"Who are you? My mom?" Bryce opened his door. "I'm fine."

"So Penny Mitchell showing up is no big deal? You were pretty serious about her two years ago. Never saw you like that with anyone before."

Bryce shrugged. "That was then. If I'm off my game, it's probably because of your snoring keeping me awake."

Izan shook his head and laughed. "I got you. You don't wanna get serious."

Bryce's back snapped straight and rigid. "I'm plenty serious. About a lot of things."

"Yo, didn't mean to offend." Izan raised his hands in surrender fashion.

Bryce released a long breath. Why was he so cranky? "Sorry. I'm just out of it. And hangry." He flashed a breezy grin to his friend. "I better go find something to eat."

"You do that." Izan picked his duffel up once more. "And for the record, I thought you and Penny were a good match back in the day. Ain't no shame in falling for a good woman. They're hard to find." He got into his own car and left.

Izan was right. Bryce had fallen all right. At least back then he'd been completely serious about Penny. Not that anybody ever *took* him seriously, but he wasn't nearly as reckless and shallow as people thought. They just never thought to look past the surface. And he made sure they didn't have a reason to. Better to not set high expectations only to fail.

Bryce climbed into the cab of his truck. Penny being here was... weird. How could it not be? But that was because of the way she'd left. She'd never let him explain. She'd just . . . gone. And left him with questions. Had *she* not taken their relationship seriously?

But again, what did he know? Everyone else had their lives figured out. Where did that leave him?

It left him with a sleepless night worrying about whether Penny Mitchell was okay or not. And why she'd come back right now. It was probably best that they both leave everything in the past.

Then again, he could maybe find out with one little visit—

His ringtone cut through the quiet morning. Bryce didn't recognize the number, but he answered.

"Am I speaking to Bryce Crawford?"

"This is him."

"This is Jason Woods. Not sure if you remember me, but we went to school together."

Jason Woods? When Bryce had played football as a freshman, he'd looked up to Woods and some of his buddies. They'd been skilled players. Seniors. But they'd messed with his friend Iggy, who had a slight limp. After seeing that side of them, Bryce hadn't had much to do with the group. So why was Woods calling now?

"Yeah, I remember you. What do you need?"

"I work at the governor's office, and we want your help."

"Help how?" Bryce started the truck's engine.

"I'm here prepping for Governor Noble's visit to Last Chance County. We're putting together a task force to address this recent spike of arson and explosions happening. Your chief recommended you. Do you have time to swing by city hall?"

Macon had suggested him? A warmth built in Bryce's chest. Huh. "When would you need me?"

"Now. We need to be on top of this before the governor comes. His wife and son will be here in a few days. He'll be arriving later."

Guess that answered his question about going to see Penny at the hospital. "I'll be right there."

At city hall, Bryce was ushered into a plush conference room. The long table polished to a high shine took up most of the space. His new brother-in-law, Jude Brooks, looked up from where he sat in one of the cushy chairs. A couple of cops and Allen Frees and Chief James from the fire department were already there.

Quick introductions were made, then the lanky man in the suit took command of the room and asked everyone to sit. It had to be Jason. He'd changed since high school. The once-thick brown hair had thinned significantly. The suit looked expensive, so different from the jeans and letterman jacket he used to wear.

"I'm Jason Woods with the governor's office. You were all called here today because we have a problem, and we need to get to the bottom of it. Last night's warehouse fire was the third explosion in this city in the last week. I understand the fire department will do their own arson investigation, but the governor wants extra effort put into collaborating to make sure we deal with this quickly."

"Sure, we all want it dealt with, but why is the governor getting involved?" Chief James said.

"The big Memorial Day celebration is coming up with Governor Noble and his family to help kick off the event. It wouldn't look good to have this threat causing problems for their visit. So, work together and get to the bottom of it. Let us know what you need, and we will do our best to expedite anything we can. Working at the capital with the governor myself, I can pull strings to get state resources if needed. Brooks, I'm assuming with the ATF you have access to the federal databases. Whatever it takes, folks." He waited for nods of acknowledgment before looking directly at Bryce. "Crawford, come with me for a minute."

Woods straightened his tie and left the room.

Bryce followed him out to the hall.

Woods held out a hand. "I just wanted to put aside whatever past we had and start fresh. I know we weren't exactly friends back in the day, but I'm hoping for your cooperation."

Bryce shook his hand. "I guess we all had a little growing up to do since then."

"A lot has changed. What do you say? Shall we let bygones be bygones?"

"Sure." Who was he to hold it against the man when it had been over a decade ago? Besides, he wanted to get to the bottom of whatever was going on just as much as the state. This was his hometown, and he wanted to keep it safe. It was a big deal to have this visit from the governor. Posters were plastered everywhere around town about the Governor's Ball and other activities. His own mother, who had once met Governor Noble and his wife, was on the celebration committee. They'd been planning this for two years.

"Good. Let me know if you need anything." Woods left, and Bryce walked back into the conference room.

Chief James stood at the end of the table. "So the explosions took place at three locations, all in different parts of town. One was a house out in the boonies. The other an electronics store, and then the warehouse last night. I'm not seeing an obvious connection between all three. Do you guys on the force know anything?"

"That warehouse block has been known to be a hangout for a Puerto Rican gang. It's possible they used the store too." Olivia Tazwell, with the police department, swiveled back and forth in her chair.

"But no idea where the house comes into it?" Bryce asked.

She shook her head.

"So far we haven't had any deaths due to these explosions, but one of my men was injured in the secondary explosion in the warehouse, and a woman almost died. They're escalating." The chief leaned over the table. "We need to end this now."

Allen spoke up. "Can we talk to this woman? Did she see anything? Or is she a suspect?"

Bryce sat up in his chair. "She's not a suspect."

Everyone looked at him. Okay, so maybe that came out a little stronger than necessary. Bryce cleared his throat. "She almost died in that fire. She's a private investigator."

"Then we need to talk to her and see what she knows. What do you say, Crawford?" Frees asked. "Can you go talk to her?"

Talk to her? A big part of him wanted to. Wanted it badly. But Bryce had seen her last night, and all it had done was bring up a lot of things in him that should've stayed buried. Maybe he really wasn't ready for this. Because now that they were literally handing him the chance to see her, it sounded like a horrible idea. Like sending an alcoholic to a booze convention. He needed more time to shore up his resolve before he could see her.

"Uh, maybe you should talk to her, Jude." Bryce's thumb tapped the table.

"Why me?" His brother-in-law looked up from his notepad. "Oh. She must be married. Meaning you can't flirt, huh?"

"Since when did that stop Fire and Rescue's playboy?" Olivia grinned from across the table. "More likely she's too old or something. What's the matter, Casanova? Not your type?"

Oh, she was very much his type, and that was the problem. One minute with her and he'd probably be falling fast, while she would be counting down the seconds till she could leave. "She's not married. But Jude knows her best. And I'll go work with the chief and look at the fire scenes again."

His *job* was fire. He'd already established he sucked at relationships. And yes, he was almost desperate to know Penny was okay, but if Jude went, Bryce could satisfy his curiosity about her well-being and avoid a re-emergence of his old self.

"Who is it?" Jude asked.

"Penny." Bryce straightened up the papers in front of him and shoved them into the file folder someone had passed out. He stood, ready to leave.

"Penny Mitchell?" Jude stopped him. "What is she doing here?"

Bryce lifted his hands. "Thought you would know. She's investigating something. Isn't she working with your office again?"

Jude shook his head. "Haven't heard from her in over a year except to get her regrets that she couldn't make the wedding. But I'm slammed at work. You always got along great with Penny. Why can't you talk to her?"

Why? Maybe because just when he'd started to think he'd found "the one," she'd left him in the dust without a word. Because she'd gotten to him more than any woman ever had. And—fine—he was still sorting through the aftermath of it all. He didn't have a chance at staying professional with her. And he didn't want to mess this up. Being on a task force was a big deal. Something to show this town he was serious. He was more than a good-time guy.

"I . . . just thought since you and Penny worked together and know each other on a professional level, it would be best if you talked to her."

"I actually took her statement last night." Police officer Anthony

Thomas perked right up. "I wouldn't mind talking to her again. Getting more details to see if anything would help us."

Of course he wouldn't mind. Bryce bit back a growl.

Jude glanced at Bryce, then at the others gathered around the table. "I'll talk to her."

Good. That's what Bryce wanted, after all.

So why did he feel so deflated?

FIVE

THE ALARM ON THE IV PUMP BLARED AGAIN. And again. Where was the nurse? The bag of saline solution was empty and Penny needed to leave.

Now.

The door opened, a rush of cooler air sweeping in. Final—

Nope. Not the nurse. Penny was in for it now. Libby walked into the hospital room. She didn't even have to say anything. She just had that look of someone who had life figured out, staring down at someone who couldn't pull it together.

She stood by Penny's bed and folded her arms. Her crisp blouse was tucked neatly into her navy slacks, and every strand of caramel-brown hair was pulled back into a sleek bun. Nothing was out of place.

"So, were you even going to tell me you were in town, or am I only an emergency contact now?"

Penny held back a groan as she sat up. "It's about time you got here."

"What else are sisters for?" Libby set a bag on the bed and pulled out a hairbrush, toothbrush, and toothpaste. She handed them all to Penny. "Before I take you anywhere, you might wanna take care of a few things. I don't want you scaring the kids when they see you."

"I look that bad?" Penny stood slowly and picked up the items.

"No comment." Libby sniffed. "You sure smell like you were caught in a fire. But I suppose a shower will have to wait until we get you home."

Home. What would that be like? Libby and Dan and their two kids had settled into a new house in Last Chance right before Penny had left. Penny only knew what it looked like from video chatting with the kids. Guess she would be seeing it firsthand now.

The nurse walked in. "Ready to go?"

For the love of all that is holy . . . "Yes!"

"Let me get this IV out of you and you can get dressed." She made quick work of removing the cannula and bandaging the site. "I'll be back later with discharge instructions."

Free at last from the tubes and infernal beeping, Penny made her way to the bathroom. Yikes. Libby hadn't been exaggerating. She looked awful. Felt worse. Her head screamed, her whole body was sore. No wonder Bryce hadn't come to see her.

Not that she wanted him to. It would make it easier to pass this case off to Jude if she could avoid Bryce altogether.

After signing discharge papers and half listening to the nurse giving her instructions, Penny slid into Libby's minivan.

"How are the kids?" Penny asked.

"How about we get down to the real issue." Instead of starting the ignition, Libby turned to her. "I left California and moved here because *you* were here. And then *you* up and left. No rhyme or reason. Now, I don't regret making that move, because it has been good for Dan and the kids and me. But you—I don't hear from you for months, and then you wind up back in Last Chance without telling me, and it's the *hospital* that I get a call from? What's that about?"

"I missed you too." Penny gave her a fake smile. "But you know my job takes me all over. Besides, I thought you and Dan weren't doing so well. When you moved out here, you weren't even sure if he was coming with you."

"I'm serious." The older-sister scowl grew.

Penny pulled down the visor mirror. This was worse in daylight. Penny pulled out the hairbrush again. "For the record, I never asked you to move here."

"I thought you left the ATF because it was dangerous. You seriously could've died, Penny."

That fact was well established by the pain that ricocheted through every part of her. But dwelling on it never got her anywhere. She could only rely on one person. Herself. "But I didn't die. I'm fine."

And Libby had no clue why Penny had left the ATF. No one did.

"Well, thank God for that! He must be watching out for you, but still—"

Penny dropped the brush. "Whoa. Did you just mention God?" And watching out for her? Was she kidding?

"Just because Dad didn't believe in anything doesn't mean we have to follow his example. And what's the big deal? The kids and I have started going to church. Dan and I are attending a Bible study."

"Are you sure *you're* not the one with a head injury? I can't believe Dan is going along with this."

"Well, he is. Even though at the moment he's on a work trip in Germany. But if he was here, he'd be the first to tell you that he's completely on board with it. And you know what? It's good. There's a lot of evidence that I wasn't aware of. Christianity isn't some social club of brainwashed people. There's actually a lot of evidence about the Bible. About . . . well, everything."

Yeah, and when Penny had been seven years old, she'd prayed at Vacation Bible School, but at some point, people had to grow up and stop believing in fairy tales.

"Good for you. But if you don't mind, you can take me to my car and I'll find a hotel. Hopefully I'll be out of your hair by the end of the day."

"Out of my hair? Have you heard anything I said?"

"Yup. You found religion. Whereas I, on the other hand, screwed up . . . again."

Had gotten trapped. Again. Where was God then?

"That's not what I'm saying, Pen. I mean . . . you didn't call."

"Because I'm on a *job*. I didn't realize I was even heading in this direction until the person I was following exited the interstate late last night. I didn't have a chance to call you. But I'm passing the case off to someone else and I'll be out of your hair."

"I don't want you out of my hair!" Libby dropped a hand on Penny's arm. Libby touching her? That was weird.

"Ugh. Can't you see? I'm only upset because—" Libby looked away a moment. When her gaze met Penny's, tears shimmered in her eyes. "I was really worried. I don't want to lose you."

Aw . . . "Lib . . . you're not going to lose me."

"Well, we miss you. The kids and I do. Even Dan has asked about when we'll see you next. You've been gone for over a year."

Seeing real emotion in her big sister brought a tightness in Penny's own throat. "I'm sorry. I've been busy."

"Too busy. You're running from one case to the next. Have you stopped to even think about your family?"

"Of course I have. And I miss you guys too." Especially the kids. But yes, her sister also. Maybe it wasn't so bad to have someone with whom she could drop the professionalism, the masks she needed to wear to go undercover and get the job done.

"So you'll stay?"

A day to recover and see the kids wouldn't necessarily be a bad thing.

As long as she didn't run into Bryce Crawford or fall back into his extremely capable and strong arms again, she'd be fine.

She hated to leave a job undone, but she could pass this off to Jude and see what other work was out there. That was the beauty of being her own boss. And, being licensed in multiple states, hopefully she wouldn't have to try hard to find another case.

"Maybe I could crash on your couch for a day and see my favorite niece and nephew before I head out? I'm pretty sure Hazel owes me my own personal dance recital."

"I'd like it if you'd stay longer. I'm not even sure you should be driving."

And there she went, back into big-sister mode. At least this didn't throw Penny off-kilter like the God-talk did. Or the lovey dovey stuff. She always left that to their younger sister Tori, who as a kid, used to switch from Penny's to Libby's bed any given night because she hated sleeping alone. Now she was out in Alaska wanting to jump out of planes and fight wildfires.

"We'll see how it goes. But for tonight, I'll stay with you."

"Thank you."

She almost looked like she wanted a hug or something, but eventually Libby just smiled and started the car. She drove them to where Penny's SUV was still parked on the street. Only because she could follow her did Libby even allow Penny to drive her own vehicle to their house. But when they pulled up to the three-story family home in a cul-de-sac neighborhood, another car was waiting in the driveway. A man with dark hair, wearing a shirt and tie, leaned against it.

"Jude! What are you doing here? Bible study is next week, right?" Libby asked as they got out of the minivan.

"It is. I'm here to see Penny, actually."

"Of course. Why don't I run and get some coffee going. After that, I need to run to work, if you two are okay."

"Do what you need to do, Lib. I can take care of myself." Penny waved her on.

Her sister nodded and then walked inside the front door.

Jude took the weekend bag out of Penny's hands and carried it for her.

"Always the gentleman, Book."

"Looks like you had a rough night."

"I've been through worse." She led Jude to the living room. Sounds of cabinets opening and closing and the clink of dishes came from the kitchen. "So, what's up?"

"Denver office looped me in after I called them this morning. Emma Kemper?"

"Yeah, so much for this being a 'follow-and-report-in case.' And I'm glad you're here. I was hoping I could pass off what I've got so far and you could take over." She sent him a bright smile.

Jude just looked at her for a moment. "You're done?"

"If Emma was going to keep heading west, I'd follow, but knowing whatever she has going on is right here in Last Chance, I don't want to intrude."

"Penny, I'm swamped. You wouldn't be intruding. In fact, I have to leave for work for a couple days. I won't be here, so I couldn't take the case on my own even if I wanted to."

"Maybe Denver could send someone else to help you."

"Who? They're up to their eyeballs in caseloads too. Why are you in such a hurry to leave?"

She grew warm under his stare.

Why? Because the one person that was so good at blurring the lines between her professional life and personal life was here. Because she needed to be free, not tied down. Bryce was her kryptonite.

"Look, Jude, I have other cases too. I'm—"

"Scared."

"What? No. That's not it. I'm busy. I have things to do."

"I never pegged you for coward, Mitchell." Jude smirked. He was totally egging her on.

"I'm not. I'm *busy*."

Oooh. That did sound a little defensive.

"You take your job seriously. That's why I brought you in on the Sosa case. So what's going on now that's changed that? I've never seen you leave something undone like this."

She didn't have a reply.

"The governor's office created a task force this morning to get to the bottom of a series of explosions that have happened in the last month. And then last night's fire, we almost lost you and another firefighter. We have no witnesses. No leads. Except you. You've researched Emma and have more information on this case than anyone else. You can help us ID some of the players. You should stay and finish it. I have to leave for Denver tonight. I was hoping you'd take my place on the task force."

What was she supposed to say to that? She wasn't the kind of person who could dump a burden on someone else. Jude knew that.

But she wasn't going to cave so easily.

"I'll think about it. I have other work as well." She sat down. "But maybe I can help for a day or two. That's all I can commit to."

"I'll take all the help I can get."

Libby walked in with a tray full of two steaming mugs, creamer, and sugar. "Did I just hear you convince my sister to stay for a while?" She looked like she was holding back a grin, probably excited for a little free babysitting, especially if Dan was gone.

Penny grabbed her mug and poured creamer into it. "I said a day or two."

"We'll take it." Libby let the grin loose.

Jude sipped his black coffee. "Thanks for the help. I'll have Bryce contact you."

Penny coughed as her own drink went down the wrong pipe. "Bryce?"

"He's on the task force too."

Of course he was.

She set her mug down and speared Jude with a weighty look of her own. "But if I do this, I need to be hired. No more favors. I want a contract."

"Shouldn't be a problem to hire you officially. We're desperate for leads."

"All right. Get me the paperwork and I'll get started."

"I know I'm leaving the task force in good hands if you take my place."

If God wanted to shine on her, someone would say no to hiring her on. Then she'd be able to leave this town behind with a clear conscience and not look back.

SIX

BRYCE TAPPED HIS THUMB ON THE STEERING wheel of his truck, Jude's text message running through his mind. *Penny will meet you at the police station.*

No big deal. Not even sure why Jude thought to tell him. Bryce could walk into that police station and treat Penny just like any other person. Seeing each other in a work context might help him keep his head.

He killed the engine and hopped out of his truck. She was probably only there to help ID the guys that tried to kill her last night. She'd update them on what she knew, then she'd be on her merry way. Again.

And he would learn to move on with his life. Not let this rattle him. Because he wasn't the same guy anymore.

He turned his head to the side to crack his neck as he walked through the front doors. It would be fine. Busy chatter and the smell of coffee and copy-machine toner surrounded him. Men and women in dark-blue uniforms were scattered throughout the area behind the main counter.

And there in the middle of it all sat Penny, her blonde hair clean and curled, the black boots and skinny jeans giving her that nod to the biker look that she pulled off really well. Her smile brought back a wave of good memories. Bryce couldn't help but meet it with a grin of his own. They'd had a lot of fun together.

A *lot* of fun.

He tried to cover the hitch in his step as he walked up to Penny, who sat with Olivia Tazwell at a desk in the bullpen.

"You okay?" Olivia raised an eyebrow as she studied him.

"Sure thing." He swiped a pen off her desk and twirled it through his fingers. "Well, if it isn't Penny Mitchell. PI extraordinaire. I thought you would've been long gone by now." He winked, hoping a playful vibe would cover up anything else that might leak out.

"Looks like you guys can't handle things without me." She gave him a sassy look she'd given him a million times before.

Obviously she knew how to play this game too. Just like old times.

And just like old times, he slipped into the role. See? He would be fine.

"I suppose you're trying to ID those guys that threw you in the closet. Any luck?"

"As a matter of fact, we found them. I got pictures of them outside before I went into the warehouse. Olivia and I just ran them through facial recognition and got our matches."

Olivia pointed at the computer screen. "Meet DaNeal Gomez and Arturo Hernandez."

"They both have rap sheets?" Bryce asked.

Penny nodded. "Yup. A little aggravated assault, larceny, theft. Drug possession. And skipping bail. Don't want to forget that."

"Guess we got us a regular pair of thugs." Bryce leaned casually on the desk. A whiff of Penny's usual vanilla scent, sweet but mixed with something earthy that had always driven him a little wild, wrapped around him. He cleared his throat. "Where are they from?"

"Why don't you come with us now, and we'll only have to go

over it once. We're going to meet Allen Frees, Sergeant Donaldson, and the others in the conference room." Olivia gathered the file and laptop off the desk.

"I guess you're heading out then?" Bryce looked down at Penny.

"You're not getting rid of me that fast, cowboy. The governor's office hired me to be on the task force." She stood, the breezy smile slipping a little. "That won't be a problem, will it?"

At this height, she was almost eye to eye with him. Bryce scrambled for words. "Uh, yes. I mean, no." He dropped the pen. He scooped it up off the floor and combed back the hair off his forehead. "It'll be fine. Great!"

She was staying.

Hopefully his overly bright grin didn't display the inner turmoil those words set off in him.

"Good." She didn't break eye contact.

"Good."

It would be fine. She'd help them. Maybe he'd even get a little closure on their past. And *then* she'd leave.

Out of the corner of his eye, Bryce caught Olivia snickering and walking away. "I'll see you both in the conference room."

Penny spun and followed her.

He jogged after the women, down the hall and into the room. Sitting around the long table were Allen Frees in his wheelchair, Anthony Thomas, and Sergeant Donaldson. The freestanding white board and a large-screen TV took up most of the space along one wall. Penny helped herself to the coffee carafe in the middle of the table.

"All right. Looks like everyone is here. Let's get down to business." Frees tossed the dry erase marker to Bryce. Good. Something to keep his hands busy.

"Let's start by recapping what we've got." Bryce tapped on the board with the marker.

"Perfect." Penny sat in one of the office chairs and leaned toward the board. "Read me in."

"Four weeks ago we were called out to a fire in an electronics store. We thought it was a fluke, maybe some kids playing around with fireworks, since that's what ignited the blaze in the back of the store." Bryce wrote *electronics store* on the board. "Then last week we had a shed blow up on an abandoned property right outside of town. But I'm not so sure it was abandoned. There were a lot of tire tracks and signs of use even though the house was like something out of a horror movie. An accelerant was used in that fire. We also found fragments of PVC."

"So we're thinking pipe bomb." Allen Frees spoke up. "I already met with the arson investigator. Residue is being analyzed."

"Which brings us to last night." Bryce wrote the word *warehouse*. "We were called to the warehouse fire, but there was a secondary explosion. We're still not sure what caused it. It might've been that the fire reacted with a flammable substance—"

"It was a bomb," Penny said. Gone was the playful smile and tossing of the blonde curls. She was all business. Bryce liked this side of her too. That precision and focus.

"How do you know? We haven't been out there yet to investigate." Allen said.

"Because I saw it." The room hushed.

"That's why Jude called you in. This is part of your case?" Olivia asked.

Penny nodded. "Like I told Officer Thomas last night in my statement"—she looked over at him and smiled—"I followed a woman named Emma Kemper here from Denver. The ATF office there arrested her brother, Vincent. He's a bomb expert. They haven't figured out his endgame or who he's working with. Emma was a person of interest. They didn't think she was directly involved but wanted to be sure. I followed her around for a few days in

Glenwood Springs while she laid low. Stuck a tracker on her car. Yesterday, she packed up and left."

"And ended up here? In that warehouse?" Bryce asked.

"Yeah. She met up with the two men we identified and someone else. A guy with whom she seems to be romantically involved. I don't know who he is, but he's running the show here, from what I can tell."

"How'd you wind up in that closet?" Bryce asked.

Surprise flashed across her features for a quick moment, then she cleared her throat. "They spotted me."

Knowing how tough Penny was, he would bet she put up one heck of a fight. "They had to be pretty big to get the best of you." Bryce tried lightening the mood. For himself as much as the others. He didn't want to think about how close she'd come to death.

"Big and sneaky. They're both sporting some bruises themselves." The slight smirk on Penny's face faded. "But there's more than just a bomb maker's sister we have to worry about. They hinted at plans here, something beyond last night's warehouse fire. And it has to do with this." She held up a small piece of plastic, as big as the tip of her thumb.

"That's the thing you found in her car. What is it?" Bryce asked.

"It's not the exact same one, since that's in evidence." She sent Anthony another smile, and dang it if it didn't send a bolt of something hot right through Bryce.

Penny continued. "But it does the same thing. This little hunk of plastic turns a regular ol' Glock 19 into an automatic weapon capable of firing thirty rounds in two seconds."

"Whoa." Olivia's brow furrowed. "A Glock clip?"

Penny nodded. "Emma had a whole bag of them."

"Sounds like someone is arming for war. Here in Last Chance?" Sergeant Donaldson asked.

"I think so." Penny set the clip on the table. "I don't know who Emma's boyfriend is, but they have an agenda. And it sounded like it was to take place here. This isn't a random string of explosions. I'm not sure where the Glock clips come in, but somehow they must fit into the picture too."

"Can you track the clip and see where it came from?" Officer Thomas asked.

"Unfortunately, anyone with a 3D printer can make these. It's illegal, but when has that stopped a criminal?" Penny folded her hands on her lap.

Olivia started tapping on her laptop. "We need to look into Arturo and DaNeal."

Their pictures flashed up on the television screen next to the white board. In the mug shots, Arturo Hernandez was a stocky six foot three inches, his mean glare made more menacing by a scar from the corner of his mouth down to his chin. DaNeal Gomez seemed more like a pretty-boy type. Lanky, smooth skin, dark hair slicked back. "Penny ID'd these two bottom feeders from California as the ones Emma met with last night."

"DaNeal set the bomb in that upper office of the warehouse. The bomb Emma brought with her. Unfortunately, I think there were more in the duffel bag she had."

"So they aren't done creating havoc." The sergeant leaned back in his chair with a sigh.

"Who are the big shots around town now, Liv?" Penny asked.

"We've got a few dealers we keep tabs on—still not sure where their supply is coming from. A gang from Honduras that's on our radar, as well as another group from Puerto Rico that causes some trouble, and they use that warehouse area sometimes. We've also got some pimps that keep us busy. Beyond that we have the whackos that say the world is ending and some militia types that seem to keep to themselves. Nothing like a well-organized criminal effort, though that warehouse district has seen drugs and the gangs in that area."

"Could there be a turf war with the Puerto Ricans or another gang?" Bryce asked.

Olivia tapped her pen on the notebook in front of her. "It's possible."

"Emma and her brother aren't either ethnicity. So why would they be involved in something like that?" Penny asked. "Although, Arturo and DaNeal are Latinos. Do they have any known associates here?"

Olivia scrolled down the list. "Nothing on the rap sheets that I can see. Everything we have on them is from Arizona and California."

"So what brought them here?" Bryce asked.

"Good question." Allen Frees rolled back from the table in his wheelchair. "For now, why don't we all go back and look at any other case files with explosions or firearms for the last couple of years. Maybe they've been here longer than we realize. We can reconvene later."

"We're processing Emma's car. I'll see where they're at on it." The sergeant stood.

Bryce didn't have cases to look at if Allen was going to do so, but he wouldn't mind a look through the warehouse in the light of day. "I'll go check out the warehouse."

"Then I'm coming with you." Penny stood. "I need to see if there's any other clues."

Oh, that shouldn't make his hopes soar like this. Or account for the way he wanted to puff up his chest at Anthony.

Penny and Bryce were coworkers now. That was it. But maybe he'd get his own questions answered after all.

Then again, he might not like those answers either.

SEVEN

ENNY FOLLOWED THE FAMILIAR RED TRUCK IN front of her through town. They passed her favorite coffee shop, a new bookstore, and the Backdraft Bar & Grill, where she'd spent many an evening in one of their booths or the bar top. A nostalgic pang rolled through her. She and Bryce had spent some time cuddled up in that truck bed, in the cab driving around, and . . . doing other things she shouldn't be recalling. Not that she'd ever let it go too far physically. It was the emotional entanglements that worried her more.

Oh, this was such a bad idea for her to come with him. Her phone rang, jarring her from the memories. She stared at the name flashing on her dashboard caller ID.

Great. And now this. If she didn't answer, Libby would keep calling.

Better get it over with.

Penny hit the answer icon. "Hey. I don't have a lot of time right now. Did you need something, sis?"

"Did you take your meds?"

"That's why you're calling?" Penny had pretty much lived on a steady diet of over-the-counter pain killers and caffeine since leaving the hospital. She couldn't afford to take anything stronger. She cranked the wheel to make the left-hand turn.

"I wanted to see how you were doing. Is that so bad?"

"No . . ." But it was strange for them. Did all oldest siblings feel the need to keep tabs on younger sisters? And why was it springing up now?

"So, what are you doing?" Libby's voice sounded a little breathy.

"Driving."

"Are you sure you should be—"

"Lib, I'm in the middle of an investigation. I promise you, I'm fine. Besides, I'm following Bryce, so not like I'm all alone."

"Bryce Crawford? You're working with your ex?"

"Yeah. Not a big deal. We're both adults." And she knew better than to get involved with someone from work.

But she only had the ten-minute drive to the warehouse to figure out what to *say* to Bryce and get ahold of herself.

Funny how after just seconds in his presence, all the feels had rushed back, as if they'd grown in her absence instead of diminishing. How was that possible? Especially after what he'd done.

"So, what happened to you two anyway? You never said."

"How we got together? Or how it . . . ended?"

"Both."

"I dunno. From the first moment we met when I came here to work the Sosa case, there was something there." It'd been more than just his handsome face that'd drawn her. That charisma. That intensity that was all Bryce. "He was easy to be with. Fun."

He enjoyed life, but beneath that party exterior was a man who would do anything for his family. Someone you didn't want to mess with, either. Many people probably didn't look past the extrovert persona, but she couldn't help but see the protective side of him too. Sure, he was impulsive and didn't mind pushing the line. But she liked that. She'd never wanted to be with a guy that would fall apart at the first sign of danger. Bryce had guts. He'd jump in and ask questions later.

"So why did you break up with him?"

"How did you know I was the one who did the breaking up?"

"Just a hunch. Thanks for confirming it though. So spill. Why'd you run this time?"

"He cheated on me."

"Really? Did he try justifying it? I hate when guys do that."

"Uh, no. He didn't." Because she'd never given him the chance. The second she'd seen Ashlee in his arms, it was over. She'd packed up and was gone within the hour. "I ended it and left."

So why couldn't she get over Bryce just as quickly? Because she *needed* to get over him. She was here strictly for the job. She couldn't afford to let things get personal. Especially now that they were working together.

But he still had some kind of pull on her. She would put up her nonchalant mask, flirt a little just to show everyone there was nothing there. But it was already getting harder and harder to wear.

And she couldn't deny there was a part of her that wondered. What if what she'd seen hadn't been the whole picture?

She'd never let him explain. And he had begged her—with numerous voicemail and text messages—to let him explain.

But it didn't matter. She should thank Ashlee for bringing her back to her senses. Because Penny never should've let him get that close in the first place. She'd known better.

"Is he the reason you won't come visit us here? Why you always want us to come to you?"

"Maybe."

Libby paused. "I see."

"Look, I'm sorry, Lib, but I need to go. We'll talk later, 'kay?" Because time had just run out. Penny followed Bryce as he turned onto the street lined with industrial buildings and abandoned stores.

"Sure. Be careful out there, Penny."

"You know I will."

Penny parked at the curb by the warehouse. The blackened shell of a building was almost unrecognizable. She stood on the sidewalk, taking it all in. Through the gaping hole in the cinderblock structure, the inside looked like a giant game of steel-beam pickup sticks. Smoke still curled up from the piles of debris. The air smelled of burnt plastic and chemicals.

"It's still too hot to get in there, but what do you see?" Bryce asked her as he walked up to her from his truck. The sun glinted off his dark-blond hair, scruff lining his squared jaw. She couldn't see his eyes behind his aviator sunglasses, but she knew they were zeroed in on her. Intense as always.

She needed to get to work, focus on the job, but the opening to the building was blocked with a mountain of debris and ash. "I can't see much. Let's take a look from that side alley."

"Ladies first." He gestured for her to go ahead of him. But she slowed and waited until he caught up with her. They walked side by side around the corner of the building, their hands brushing against each other as they squeezed into the narrow alley. The contact immediately sent a jolt through her.

"Trying to hold my hand again?" Bryce winked.

She laughed, releasing the pent-up energy that swirled at his touch. Leave it to him to make a joke of it. "Old habits die hard." She flipped her hair over her shoulder. See? She could totally handle this. Keep it light. Keep it simple.

"So that's all I am, huh? A bad habit?" His grin was playful, teasing.

She tried to match it. "I didn't say it was bad." She gave him a pointed, hopefully flirty look, something that told him this was no big deal.

"So why did you leave?" He kept the playful smirk, but there was something behind it she didn't like. Something that looked a lot like she'd inflicted pain.

"You know why. Besides, I can never stay in one place long. And I told you from the beginning I wasn't looking for anything serious. I thought you agre—"

"Wait." He cupped her elbow and tugged her to a stop before she could step into a mysterious pile of goo. He led her around, not letting go of her arm until they passed it. When he dropped his hand, the loss of contact was noticeable.

Ok. Fine. She'd missed this. That rare sense of chivalry, like someone was looking out for her. It had been a long time since she'd experienced that.

And maybe she had taken the coward's way out by leaving town and ghosting him. Acid pooled in her stomach.

She could've talked to him before she'd left. But even if there was a perfectly good explanation, it was for the best that she'd left. It was never supposed to be serious.

Thankfully, it didn't look like she'd caused permanent damage. But she did owe him an apology, at least.

"Hey, Bry—whoa." They stopped at what had been the door she'd gone through last night.

The doorway had caved in, but the huge hole in the wall showed them the inside damage. A steel beam leaned precariously on the outer wall. A mountain of blocks and ash stood where she'd been thrown into that closet. She'd almost been buried in it.

If it hadn't been for Bryce rescuing her.

She swallowed hard.

"You okay?" Bryce looked at her, concerned.

"Of course."

He nodded, seemingly satisfied for the moment. "So, you're the explosives expert. What do you see?"

"Oh, uh, over there, in that upper office, look at that smoke pattern. I think that was where one of the explosions originated from." She pointed at the far wall.

"Makes sense. And they used an accelerant. The place smelled like gasoline last night. I'm guessing they started the original fire in that front part of the building, gave themselves time to escape."

She should've been more aware of what was going on. "They had to know first responders and firefighters would be on the scene, though, when that secondary explosion hit." Bryce and his team had walked right into their trap. And she'd been helpless to do anything about it.

"Then they wanted more than a damaged building. I think someone is trying to get our attention. And they didn't mind leaving you to die either." Bryce's brow furrowed. "We need to get to the bottom of this."

"Is there anyone who has a beef with the crew?" Penny turned away from the rubble and watched Bryce.

"Dunno. But I'm gonna find out."

And with that pure determination etched in every line and angle of his face, she had no doubt he would. He was never one to back down from a fight.

They took pictures where they could without stepping into the building. Wavy heat lines still rose from the smoldering remains. "Once it's cooled off, I need to get in there and investigate more."

"Your boots will melt or catch on fire if you step in there now."

He was right, but she hated having to wait. They turned and headed back to the street. A car engine somewhere revved. They shooed a pigeon out of the alley as they walked back to the sidewalk where they'd parked their vehicles.

"Do you want—"

"Hey, could I—" They spoke at the exact same time.

Penny chuckled. "Sorry. What were you saying?"

"Like I said before, ladies first." That twinkle in his eye was so irresistible. He smirked, leaning against the hood of his truck.

She cleared her throat and stared down at her boots. It was too distracting to trace the outline of his jaw or try to read his eyes. She could lose herself so easily.

Hold it together, Pen. He's just another handsome face. And he cheated on you. Didn't want you.

A loud noise sounded. Bryce popped up and spun to face a low-riding black car as it sped toward them. She caught the glint of metal sticking out of the windows before Bryce knocked her to the ground.

Gunshots rang.

The engine of the car roared. Sharp sounds of metal hitting metal filled her ears. Her breath stopped as Bryce held her, cradling her head off the cold sidewalk. He sheltered her body as shards of cement, cinderblock, and dust rained down. Within a matter of seconds, it was over. The gunshots stopped. The sound of the car engine faded as it sped away.

Penny searched the brown eyes hovering over her.

"Are you okay?" His voice caught.

She took quick stock of herself. No more pain than she'd had when she'd woken up earlier. She couldn't find her voice, so she nodded.

The relief in his gaze was palpable. He dropped a light kiss on her forehead. "Thank God." His breath shuddered near her ear. "I thought I'd lost you again."

To be there in his arms, held, cherished, safe for just a moment, quieted the ringing in her head. He was protecting her even now.

"I'm sorry." Even to her own ears she sounded a little broken.

"Sorry? For what?"

"I'm sorry I left without saying anything."

EIGHT

I'M SORRY I LEFT WITHOUT SAYING ANYTHING.

Bryce could've kissed her right there. Really kissed her. Too bad someone had just tried to kill them.

But Penny was alive. Having her back in his arms felt right. True. No one else fit there like she did.

But . . . she'd left once. And sure, he blew it off to anyone else, but the truth of what she'd taken when she'd left was very evident in this moment, now filling the hollow spaces her absence had created.

She had taken a good chunk of his heart. And it felt like it'd just started beating again. But for how long?

And here she was lying on the cold, hard sidewalk. He was probably crushing her.

He rolled off and gently helped her up. They dusted the dirt off themselves.

He wanted to brush off her words just as easily. Pretend he wasn't lapping them up like a dog lost in a desert finding water.

"Sure you're okay? I didn't hurt you?" he asked.

She shook her head. "I'm fine." She offered a wobbly smile, a hint of vulnerability he had never witnessed in her before.

"Good." He slowly nodded. "Good."

He combed his fingers through his hair, tangling them up for a moment. He should say something. Acknowledge her admission. "And, uh . . . thanks. For the apology."

"Yeah. Of course. It's . . . long overdue." She brushed more dirt off her sleeve.

"Then will you finally let me explain what—"

She slashed the air with her hand. "There's no need to hash out what happened back then. It's been over a year. We've both moved on."

He stepped closer to her. "Maybe so, but we never discussed what happened."

"We were just involved in a drive-by shooting. I don't know that this is the best time."

"Okay, so maybe not right at this moment, but we should sit down and talk. Soon."

"Fine." She blew out a long breath and muttered, "My sister is going to kill me."

"Why?"

"She thinks my job is too dangerous. How am I gonna tell her about this? And if I don't tell her, she'll find out some other way, and it will be even worse."

"Sounds like she cares about you."

"Maybe, but she's gotten weird all of the sudden. She's talking about God and praying and . . . hugging."

"And that's a bad thing?"

Penny shrugged and rolled her eyes. "I dunno. It's weird."

Great. What would she say if she knew about Bryce's recent faith journey?

Before he could consider that, she faced him, hands on her hips. "So, any idea who just tried to mow us down with bullets?" Her chin tilted up like she was ready to face whoever it was and teach them a lesson. Maybe also wanting to move on from the awkwardness of the moment.

Right. The shooting. He'd follow her lead.

For now.

"I didn't get anything off that Chevy Camaro's license plate. You?"

"Not when someone knocked me to the ground." She offered him a light smile. "Thank you for protecting me."

Was it crazy that he loved being there to protect her? If he had his way, he would always be there to watch her back and keep her safe, but considering what she'd just said about her sister, he'd better keep that to himself and play this cool. "We couldn't have them putting holes in that pretty head of yours."

"Right." She chuckled and pulled out her phone. "I better call this in."

And now she was already on the phone with dispatch.

Within minutes, Olivia Tazwell pulled up in her squad car. "You two can't stay out of trouble, huh?" She looked at the building behind them. "This is the burning building you barely escaped from?" Her jaw dropped as she stared at the mess behind them. "Penny, you must have nine lives."

"I think she's down to seven. Maybe six." Bryce bent down and picked up one of the casings from the bullets.

"All right, so walk me through what happened."

After they'd both given statements to Olivia, Bryce debated his next move. Should he leave? Part of him wanted more time with Penny. Maybe she'd elaborate on that apology from earlier. Because maybe if he figured out why she'd left, he could change that part of himself, figure out what it took to be this new creation he was supposed to be. Not that there was a future with Penny.

It would probably be wiser to let the tempting woman go her own way, but when had he ever been considered wise?

"Are you hungry?" he asked her after Olivia had left.

"I should probably go—"

"Come on. We're investigating together. Might as well take a lunch break and get back to it."

She scrunched up her nose as she thought. "I suppose it would save us time to grab something together. As long as there's an understanding that it's a work thing, right?"

"Of course. A working lunch." And if they happened to get into a more personal frame of mind, so be it. Because they still had a lot to sort out about their past.

They settled in a little café tucked in next to a bakery downtown. The collection of random cookie jars on shelves all over gave the place an eclectic, homey feel. The servers still wore uniforms with aprons, and the chalkboard with the day's specials was hand-drawn. Bryce slid into one of the red vinyl booths across from Penny. The server brought menus and placed water glasses on the Formica tabletop.

Penny looked around. "I don't remember this place."

"Been here forever. My grandpa used to bring Logan, Andi, and me here for malts. They're famous for them."

"That sounds delicious. I think I know what I'm ordering." She set the menu down.

As she did, Bryce looked up to see John McClelland, a retired plumber and one of the guys he'd met at a Bible study, walking toward them. He carried his tattered Bible and wore one of his many Christian T-shirts.

"Bryce! How's it going?"

"Hey, John."

"Who do you have here?" He smiled brightly down at Penny and held out his hand, which she graciously shook, although Bryce didn't miss the hesitancy in her own smile.

"This is my . . . friend, Penny Mitchell," Bryce said.

"Hi, Penny. I'm John. Nice to meet you. I'd love to stay and chat, but I'm on my way to the food shelf for my shift. Will we see you Thursday night, Bryce?"

"Uh, I think so. Unless I get called into work. We've been busy lately."

"Right. Take care and I'll see you when I see you." He left with a wave, the little bell above the door jingling at his exit.

Penny stared at Bryce, one eyebrow quirked. "So . . . how do you know him?"

Her words about her sister earlier came back to him. *She's gotten weird all of the sudden. She's talking about God and praying and . . . hugging.*

So maybe this wasn't the best time to get into his own rather new relationship with God. "I met John at a function with my mom. There's a group of guys that meets up weekly, and I bring my dad sometimes. John's a nice guy."

She seemed to accept his explanation. The waitress took their orders and left. They kept the conversation light while waiting for their food. It wasn't long before the same waitress plopped a plate of thick, shiny french fries and a chocolate malt in front of Penny, and Bryce's cheeseburger and onion rings in front of him.

Penny a took a sip from her glass. "Wow. I can see why they're famous for their malts. This is amazing."

Bryce grinned and took a big bite of his burger. Penny laughed and pointed at his face. "You've got ketchup on you."

He swiped his napkin across his cheek. She laughed harder. "You just smeared it. Hand it over." He passed his napkin over to her. She gently dabbed the corner of his mouth. "You always did wear your food."

The whiff of her vanilla perfume swirled around him, evoking memory after memory.

So many good times they'd shared. And he hated that she thought the worst of him. That he'd pushed her away. So after swallowing his bite he blurted out, "I want you to know that I *didn't* cheat on you."

Penny's hand immediately fell away. "What?"

"That night you left. I know what you saw, and it probably looked bad. Ashlee showed up at my door. Drunk. She came on to me, and I was trying to let her down. She kept tripping and falling—"

"I get the picture." She shoved a fry in her mouth.

"Do you? Because I swear, that's all you saw when you showed up. I had Logan help me take her home. She got sick all over her living room, and we helped clean up the mess and made sure she was okay before we left. But nothing more happened. And as soon as I left, I went directly to your apartment. But you were already gone."

"Oh."

He waited for her to say more. Ask questions. Demand answers of her own. But she stayed silent.

"Oh? That's all you have to say?"

"Look, Bryce, I'm . . . glad you weren't cheating—"

"So you believe me?"

With her arms wrapped around herself, she shrugged and looked up at him through her lashes. "Yeah, I do."

Okay then. That was all he wanted. Right? For her to know he hadn't cheated on her.

But it felt unfinished still.

"You don't have any questions for me?"

"Not really." She dragged another one of her fries through a pile of ketchup and took a bite.

Huh. Well, that'd been a heck of a lot easier than he'd expected. But why didn't that seem to fix the gulf between them?

Why *had* she left?

"I think I'm going to take the malt to go." She stood and took her glass to the counter. Guess that was the end of that.

Her words from earlier echoed back.

I told you from the beginning I wasn't looking for anything serious.
Of course. Because people didn't take *him* seriously. Why would
it be any different with her?

And why did it matter? He'd said his piece. And like she'd said,
they'd moved on. If he was going to get serious about someone,
she probably should be the kind of girl that didn't balk at going to
church or reading the Bible. Obviously, that wasn't Penny.

But as he watched a little red-headed kid bump into her and
caught her wince, that surge of protectiveness rose within him
again. She'd been caught by thugs, trapped in a fire, knocked out by
a bomb blast, and then shot at. All in less than twenty-four hours.
The woman needed backup and a league of angels to surround her.

He was certainly no angel. And she most likely would leave as
soon as this case wrapped up. But while they were doing this job,
he would do everything in his power to protect her from getting
hurt any more.

It was the least he could do.

When she came back, Penny's phone rang.

"Mitchell here." Her eyes widened. "Really? Yeah, give me that
address." She gestured for a pen. As soon as Bryce handed it to
her, she scribbled on a napkin. "That's great. Thanks!" She ended
the call and looked at him. "We've got a lead. Tony ran down the
license plate from the truck I saw last night parked near the warehouse. Gomez and Hernandez drove it. The name on the license
came back. Doreen Van Kerk."

"Who's that?"

"A woman who died three years ago. She still has a house under
her name though. Tony gave me the address. He and Olivia are
already there."

Since when did the guy go by Tony? "Then we should check
that address out. Mind if I ride with you?" She always did like

being in the driver's seat, and there was no better way to keep her safe than by sticking close.

And hopefully she'd forget all about *Tony*.

NINE

PENNY WASN'T SURE WHAT WAS MORE BATTERED: her body or her heart. Every muscle movement and bump in the road brought more pain. But to have Bryce back in the passenger seat of her car again was a different kind of torture.

And yet part of her soaked it in, begging for more. More of the way he protected her from bullets and shrapnel with his own body. More of the dark chocolate-brown stare that pulled her in. More of the way he focused so intently on her when she had something to say.

"Hey, is that the penny I gave you?" He pointed at the one dangling from her keychain. Yes, the very one he'd pulled out of his pocket when he'd taken her up in the mountains to watch the stars. They'd lain on a sleeping bag in the bed of his truck, a velvet night sky and the Milky Way stretching above them with stars so bright she could almost touch them.

"Penny for your thoughts," he'd said as he'd handed over the copper coin.

"I think this is about as close to heaven on earth as a person can get." Even her voice had sounded small in the vastness and glory displayed in that sky. And she remembered the contentment of that moment. Her mother had felt close. The ache of missing her dulled to almost nothing.

Almost.

Bryce had looked at her then. She could've sworn he saw all of her, down to her soul. And he'd smiled, happy with whatever it was he'd found. "I think you're right."

But he wasn't looking up at the stars or the tiny sliver of a moon. He was looking at her.

And she'd kept the penny to remember that feeling. She wanted to get back to that place of contentment. Of feeling close to her mom. Of feeling seen.

She hadn't found it yet, but surely she would eventually. She just had to keep searching.

Instead of answering Bryce's question, she looked at the navigation screen on her dashboard. "Looks like we're here."

They pulled up to an old farmhouse with a sagging porch. The yellow paint was peeling away from the siding. Weeds grew in the flower beds that lined the front. Two cop cars took up the short driveway, but no one was in the front yard. They followed the pavers around to the side of the house. Bryce hung behind to take a phone call while Penny continued to the backyard. An old red shed meant to look like a miniature barn stood in one corner against a tree line. One of the officers she hadn't met was studying it. She heard Tony's voice and turned to look for him.

Her gaze locked on to the little ramp against the back wall of the house and the gaping doors opening up to cement stairs.

A cellar.

The smell of damp, musty earth hit her.

Penny stood frozen halfway across the yard. Despite the hot sun beating down on them, she shivered.

She didn't move. She couldn't. Her breathing was too fast, but it wasn't nearly enough oxygen. What was happening? A shadow came up the steps toward her.

The voices she'd heard so clearly now sounded muffled and far away. Her vision blurred.

"Penny?"

Bryce touched her arm. "Pen?"

She tried to speak but couldn't.

"Hey, maybe you should sit down. You're white as a ghost." He looked worried, but all she could focus on was pulling enough air into her suddenly shrunken lungs.

He helped her sit in the grass. "Try resting your head on your knees."

The warmth of his hand helped ground her.

She couldn't tell if it had been a few seconds or hours, but eventually her lungs cooperated and relaxed enough to get a full breath.

"That's right. Take it nice and slow." Bryce knelt in front of her, rubbing her arms, fighting off the chill that overtook her.

The spotty vision cleared. It wasn't just Bryce with her. Tony and Olivia stood behind him, obvious concern in their gazes.

"Hey, girl, are you okay?" Olivia squatted down. She handed Penny a bottle of water.

Was she? Penny tried to open the cap, but her hand was too weak. Bryce opened it, even held the bottle to her lips. After a few sips, the fuzzy thoughts sharpened back into words.

"I'm sorry. I'm fine now. I just . . . spaced out or something."

Bryce searched her face. "Is it the concussion? Do you feel like you're going to black out?"

She shook her head. Slowly. "I don't know. This has never happened before. But I'm okay now." But something inside told her it wasn't the head injury throwing her into a tailspin.

She started to stand. He was right there, gently pulling her to her feet but not letting go of her arms until she stepped away. Even then his brow furrowed.

"I'm fine, Bryce. I promise."

Tony and Olivia stared too. "So, where were we?" she asked them. "We have investigating to do."

"You wanna check out this storm cellar with me?" Tony asked.

Absolutely not. Her lungs seized again at the thought. She backed away. "How about I check another part of the house?"

"We already checked everything else," Olivia said. "There's nothing here. There's evidence of boxes of some sort in that shed, dust patterns on the floor, but they're gone now. We'll wait for the lab guys to collect samples and see if they can find anything, but our initial sweep is almost done."

"Okay if I poke around the main level?" Penny asked.

"Go for it." Tony turned toward the cellar doors. "If this place is as empty as the rest of it, this won't take us long. Tazwell, why don't you come with me?"

Penny couldn't watch as he and Olivia started down the stairs.

Bryce didn't say anything, but he stuck close to her side as she walked to the back door that was still propped open. The kitchen was straight out of the eighties with almond-colored appliances and a dusty blue-and-pink wallpaper border. An old farmhouse table stood off to the side. The honey-oak cabinets were open, revealing bare shelves. They walked into the equally empty living room and followed the blue shag carpet down the hall to the bedrooms and bathroom. Nothing but an old bed in one room and a big table lamp on the floor in the other. So much for this lead.

Tony and Olivia found them as they walked back to the kitchen.

"Nothing in the storm cellar either, but like that shed, there had been something recently moved. The dust pattern suggests more boxes." Olivia leaned against the counter.

"Guess this place is a bust." Tony led them all back outside.

"They might find trace evidence we can use." Olivia held the door open. Once Bryce and Penny walked through, she closed it up. "But for now, we'll have to wait. I'll go back to the station and start digging into Gomez and Hernandez more."

"I'll see what I can get from my sources too," Penny said. She gave the storm cellar a wide berth as they passed it to walk around to the front of the house.

"Do you want me to drive?" Bryce asked as they approached her car.

He asked it so gently, not demanding or fussy, no implication that she couldn't do it herself. Just a simple request. And as drained as her body was from whatever that had been on the back lawn and the beginning of what was sure to be a major headache, she couldn't deny the relief of letting someone else take the wheel.

"Sure." She dug the keys out of her pocket and handed them over.

Penny sank into her own passenger seat. A residue of unease she couldn't shake still filled her. Bryce pulled out of the driveway and back onto the road.

She closed her eyes.

Suddenly, she was there. That horrible musty place. The cold floor seeping through her clothes and turning her bones to ice. The spiders. The smell.

Nope! Better to keep her eyes wide open.

It had been years.

So why was it all coming back now?

Sure, she avoided basements at all costs, but she'd never had an episode like whatever had just happened on the Van Kerk back lawn. She forced steadiness into her fingers as she pulled out her phone and swiped across the screen. Anything to look busy and focused so Bryce wouldn't ask her more questions. Or stare at her with those all-too-knowing eyes. And since when did he have that kind of power over her? He was Fun Bryce. A good time. Nothing more.

But it'd been his steady gaze, helping her slow down her breathing, that'd brought her out of that darkness that'd almost swallowed her.

And sure, on the lonely nights, he was her favorite thing to reminisce about. The nights they'd gone out dancing. Of course, it'd been country music, but the man had looked good in those tight Levis and cowboy boots. And he sure could two-step. They'd always agreed to keep it light. Casual.

And that was over. Now it was time to stay professional. No more personal moments or emotional breakdowns.

Pull it together, Pen.

Shaking off the chill, she breathed in deep and concentrated on reading her email. Nothing super important.

"Here we are," he said.

Looking up, she caught sight of the Crawford home.

"What are we doing here?"

"Mom heard you were here. She invited us over for coffee. And dinner. And I don't know if you noticed, but our lunch was cut short."

"Really, Bryce, you don't need to bug your family. I'm sure they're all busy. I have plenty—"

He didn't let her finish. Instead he got out of the car and walked around to open her door. *Infuriating man!*

"You gotta try my mom's coffee cake. She's been taking more time to be at home with Dad and took some baking classes."

"I have so much to do right now. I can't be taking hour-long coffee breaks."

He held out his hand to her. "Andi wants to see you. And I happen to know she's here." He gave her that "come on" gesture and didn't move.

She shook her head. "I have work. You stay. I'll go."

He leaned in closer—close enough she could smell his after-shave. The one that reminded her of rugged coastlines of a wild sea. "You missed her wedding. You can come have dinner with my sister and the family." He wiggled the penny keychain with her fob on it. "Besides, I have your keys."

His pointed look, that hint of a smirk. He was relentless.

"Fine. But I'm warning you now. I can't stay long."

She ignored his hand as she hopped out of the passenger side of her SUV, but the warmth on the small of her back as he guided her inside was equally as powerful. Why couldn't she pull away?

"Mom, we're here," Bryce called out from the entryway.

"Penny!" Before she could come up with another excuse to leave, she was engulfed in a hug by Elizabeth Crawford.

As soon as she was released, Andi claimed her own embrace. "It's about time!"

Jude lifted his can in greeting as he walked into the entry. The smell of savory meat wafted in from deeper in the house.

"I thought you were leaving town," Penny said.

"I was. Just got back and leaving again tonight."

Andi claimed Penny's arm and dragged her through, into the kitchen.

She was as relentless as her brother. Poor Jude never had a chance. Not that it looked like he cared as he stared adoringly at his bride from across the room.

It was sickening and . . . sweet. Maybe the sooner they finished the meal, the sooner she could make her excuses to leave. Someone else could take Bryce to get his truck.

"So, did you finish your big case?" Andi asked.

Cases. Yes! That, she could talk about and keep it professional.

"Yeah, what case was that again?" Jude lifted one dark brow.

"The one that kept you busy last month."

The one that'd kept her away from their wedding was what he meant. "It wasn't big as much as it was time sensitive."

"Did you have to find a missing kid or something?" Andi asked as she set a tall glass of iced tea in front of Penny on the granite countertop.

"Uh, no." She didn't take those kinds of cases anymore. "Just tracking down a suspect. So, tell me, how was the wedding?"

Bryce hung his head back and moaned. "Don't get her started. Next thing you know, we'll be forced to watch the wedding video. Again."

Elizabeth laughed and steered Bryce away. "Go get your father and let him know it's time for dinner."

Bryce left, which somehow made the room feel a little bigger. But she couldn't decide if that was a good thing or not. Jude grabbed the stack of plates on the counter and started setting the table.

Good idea. Stay busy. "Can I help?" She reached for the pile of silverware someone had set on the counter.

"Oh no you don't." Bryce's mother scooped the utensils up and handed them to her daughter. "That's Andi's job."

"Surely there's something I can do." She always hated not doing her share.

"Do you mind slicing a few veggies for our salad?"

"Not at all." Penny settled at the counter, where Elizabeth passed over a cutting board with some tomatoes and cucumbers. They all settled into an easy rhythm as they prepped for the meal. Elizabeth went on about the governor's family, his wife and son who were arriving in a couple days. Apparently, she was part of the welcoming committee.

Soon they were seated together, Bryce's father at one end, Elizabeth at the other, with Andi and Jude across the table from Penny and Bryce.

Before she realized what was happening, Bryce and Elizabeth both grabbed her hands, and they were joined in a circle. Elizabeth asked Jude to pray.

Penny tried not to squirm as everyone bowed their heads. Bryce sent her a playful shrug, like he played along but didn't necessarily put a lot of stock in what they were doing.

"Lord, thank You for Your provision and protection. Bless us as we gather here. May this meal bring nourishment to our bodies, and may the conversation be encouraging and uplifting. Amen."

Elizabeth gave Penny's hand a light squeeze before letting go. "It's so nice to have a full table again."

"A full table?"

Andi speared her salad. "You're sitting in Logan's spot. It's been vacant since he left for Montana last year."

"Oh, right. How does he like it out there?"

"He seems to enjoy it. And with the dry spring they had, it sounds like their fire season is supposed to be a bad one." One didn't have to be an observant PI to recognize the lines of worry in his mother's eyes. "So, dear, tell us what you've been up to."

"Oh, not much. Tracking down bad guys. You'll never guess how I found the last one."

"How?" Bryce asked.

"I did a face search and found him on a dating app."

Everyone laughed.

Andi batted her eyes at Jude. "I guess even criminals are looking for love."

Bryce leaned into Penny's side. "I told you not to bring it up. Now they'll be staring moon-eyed at each other over the rest of dinner."

"Oh, let them be, Bryce." Elizabeth stared him down for a moment, then turned her blue eyes Penny's direction. "Don't you have a sister in Last Chance now?"

Elizabeth probably meant to steer the conversation to safer waters. But the only thing more personal than romance was family.

Penny nodded as she took a sip of her tea. "Yeah, Libby and her husband moved out here over a year ago."

"Is it just the two of them?"

"They have two kids too."

"Is your sister Libby Lawson?" Elizabeth tilted her head.

Penny's fork froze, the cucumber on it hanging in the air. "Yes. How did you know?"

"I just met her at the women's Bible study at our church. What a small world!"

Some might say too small. She still couldn't get over the fact that her sister darkened the doors of a church in the first place. Of course it would be the one Jude and Andi attended, and apparently Elizabeth too. At least she didn't have to worry about Bryce joining the club. He'd never had much time for church.

"Does this mean you'll settle down here in Last Chance too?" Elizabeth's face brightened up way too much. "That would be nice, Bryce, wouldn't it?"

He tried to hide his surprise behind his too-handsome grin. "Sure."

"You could join us for Sunday dinners! You know you're always welcome. You saved our lives bringing down Diego Ruiz Sosa, so like it or not, you're one of us."

One of us.

It sounded a lot like belonging.

Elizabeth's warm smile bored a small but piercing hole straight to Penny's heart—a motherly gesture that Penny hadn't experienced in so long. That was the only reason she'd reacted so strongly, right?

But as nice as belonging sounded, it came with entanglements, expectations.

And it made her vulnerable.

Vulnerability could be exploited. She'd seen it with the Sosa case. Diego Ruiz Sosa had used Elizabeth's own family, caused a car accident that had forever altered her husband's brain and personality, another car accident that'd injured Logan, and Andi had almost been killed too. All so he could force Elizabeth to give up the identity of Izan Collins, who he'd thought was his son. And he'd probably wanted the millions of dollars his accountant—Izan's true father—had stolen. Evil people went to a lot of trouble to get what they wanted, and they didn't tend to care who they hurt to get it.

And Penny tracked down such people.

Could she really bring danger to the doorstep of nice people who had already been through so much?

Penny had already lost her mother. How in the world would she handle it if anything happened to someone else she loved? She needed to settle this now.

"I'm not much of one for settling down. Anywhere. Ask my sister." Penny chuckled. "She blames our dad for my wanderlust."

"Oh? And where do your parents live?" Elizabeth took a sip from her glass.

Penny could've smacked herself on the forehead. "Uh, my mom died when I was young, and Dad passed away a few years ago."

"I'm sorry to hear that." The compassion welling in Elizabeth's eyes had Penny squirming.

"I'm fine. It's been a while."

"Well, please know you have a standing invitation. And we have a guest room if you ever need it. Do you have any other family?"

"My sister, Tori. She's been out in Alaska as part of a hotshot crew the last few years. She's hoping to be a smokejumper this year. Speaking of which, how is Logan liking being a smokejumper in Montana?" She stuffed her mouth with a big bite of pasta.

Anything to get the attention off her fractured family.

"He loves it. I shouldn't be surprised he stayed. I don't know where *his* thirst for adventure comes from. I wish he could've found it closer to home though."

"Aw, Mom, don't be too down on him. He needed a change of scenery." Bryce grabbed a roll from the basket in the middle of the table. "At least it's not Australia."

"I know. I just miss him."

Andi smirked. "Don't pretend like you don't miss him too, Bryce. You two talk all the time."

Penny looked over at Bryce. How could he not miss his brother? His twin brother, no less. Didn't twins have special bonds?

"It's not like I'm crying over him or anything. But Mom here is practically tearing up just talking about it."

"Oh, just wait till you have your own children. Let's see how you like it when you do everything you can to give them the world and then they up and leave you to live their own lives!" Elizabeth speared her two kids with a pointed look.

"Mom, we've already talked about this. You're not going to pressure us for grandkids. We just got married." Andi put her fork down, ready for battle.

"Who said I was pressuring?"

Probably no one at the table believed the innocent look on Elizabeth's face. The familial banter made Penny want to laugh and run away at the same time. It would be so easy to be swept up in the love and loyalty around this table. The way they enveloped her so easily, talked to her like she was one of them.

But she wasn't. She couldn't be. She was already committed to taking this case, but she'd need to stay focused or she'd find herself putting down roots where she had no business doing so. Last time she was here, Bryce had too easily slid past her guarded heart.

The scene with Ashlee had made it obvious. Deep down, it wasn't the idea of Bryce cheating on her that shook her to the core. It was how much it hurt that clued her in she was already in too deep. Once she'd realized what was happening, she'd hightailed it out of there so fast she'd left pieces of herself behind.

He was easy to be with. Easy to fall for. But they both knew how it would end. Bryce was only a coworker now. No more family dinners. The lines too easily blurred.

She'd better get out while she could and solve this case quickly.

TEN

BRYCE MADE A CHECK MARK ON THE CLIPBOARD. Nothing like the monotony of inventory checks to help shake Penny from his mind. He needed to be able to work this task force without her tying him up in knots.

Only, monotony wasn't working all that well.

He could still feel the way her body had tensed when Mom had asked about her mother. Her father. Both were gone. She didn't even seem that close to her sisters. Why hadn't he noticed that before?

Back then he'd been all about the good times he and Penny enjoyed. How had he never noticed that hint of sadness, how uncomfortable she was talking about her past and her family?

John had said something in their discipleship group a while back.

As a new believer, you might notice things you never noticed before. Care about things you didn't think mattered before. That's God changing you from the inside.

Was that what this was?

Logan's ringtone sounded from the phone in his pocket.

"Hey, little brother. How's Montana?" Bryce asked.

"Awesome. When are you going to come out here and see for yourself? Not to mention stop holding it over my head that you were born, like, seven minutes before me?"

"Someone has to be the oldest. Apparently that means *someone* also has to stick around and watch over Mom and Dad."

"Mom and Dad are fine. Sure it's not because Penny Mitchell showed up in town?"

"How did you know she was back?" It had been two days since their family dinner. And yeah, his life was hardly recognizable from last week, what with the near-death experiences and all the shake-up Penny had brought with her, but that wasn't why he was sticking closer to home lately. Logan was gone. Andi married. Who was left to protect his family?

"Dude. I moved away. It's not like I don't talk to anyone anymore."

"Andi told you." Pesky little sisters.

"The important thing is, what are you doing about your lady love being back?" Logan's taunting tone didn't improve Bryce's mood.

"Not doing anything but my job. It doesn't matter to me at all that she's here." He set the air tank he'd been checking back on the shelf.

"We shared a womb. I think I know you well enough to know when you're lying. Maybe even to yourself."

"Don't know what you're talking about." He reached for another tank.

"Nice try. She messed you up."

Logan would know. He'd been there in the aftermath. Trying to keep Bryce in line when he went on a wild spree doing things he shouldn't do to forget her. Driving him home when he was too drunk to drive. Helping him find the truth and the light when everything went so very dark.

He let the weight of the tank fall and set it on the floor. "Look,

I thought we had a good thing going." Really good. He'd been picturing them together, considering something long-term. Permanent even. "And then she left. End of story."

"You let her go. Without a fight."

"Do you know how many times I tried to call or text her? She blocked me. I never heard from her again. After a month of that, I got the hint. She'd moved on. And I did too." He checked the air pressure, wrote it down.

"Funny. I remember it differently. But you know, I'm not sure that you would've come to faith if she hadn't left. Maybe there was a reason for all of this."

"Then why is she back now? Is this supposed to be some kind of test? See if I've really changed?"

"I don't think God works like that. Why did she say she's back?"

The air tank clanked as he set it back on the shelf. "She's working a case. Staying with her sister who moved out here."

"Think you'll give it another go?"

"No way. I mean, she's great. But obviously whatever we had is long gone. But I do have to work with her. We were both recruited for this task force. Trying to figure out why we have a string of explosions and why some girl Penny is chasing down brought a bag of Glock clips to Last Chance."

"So you have to investigate with her?"

"Yup."

"And how's that going?"

Bryce leaned against the truck. "I don't know. I'm trying to play it cool. And she did apologize for leaving without a word. I even explained about Ashlee."

"What did she say?"

"Not much. She said she believed me."

"So maybe this is all about you getting some closure. And you can move on."

"Yeah. Maybe."

Closure. Moving on. Bryce didn't like the sound of those words at all. But they made sense. Did that mean he was destined to spend the rest of his life with someone like Sarai? Someone bland and boring? And . . . wait. He needed to tell Logan.

"Speaking of old flames, you should hear about Jamie Winters."

"What about her?" Logan's voice was strained.

Bryce could practically see the hackles rising on his twin.

If Logan wanted to talk about broken hearts and past relationships, Bryce at least had a little ammunition of his own. "You sure you wanna know? You two are ancient history, right?"

"Spill it. Now." Bryce pictured Logan, hands probably fisted, mouth tight, brown eyes drawn.

"Touchy, touchy. Relax. It's not even that big of a deal. I ran into her the other night. She told me she's leaving Last Chance. I thought you'd wanna know."

"For good?"

"Sounds like she's heading for Alaska. Trying to find some long-lost brother or something." Bryce sat on the back bumper of the rescue truck.

"Wait. What? Alaska?"

"Yeah, Land of the Midnight Sun and all that. I think she mentioned Copper Mountain area. Guess someone saw her brother up there and she's gonna go find him."

The silence on Logan's end was very telling. They may be twin brothers, but they didn't share everything. Jamie had been one of those unspoken things. Penny too. It was only fair that if Bryce was going to have to bare his wounds for others to poke, Logan did too.

"Well . . . good for her." He sniffed. "Not that it means anything to me."

Right. Like he believed a word of that. But he would let Logan hold on to his pride. "So, you gonna get out here for the big Memorial Day bash?"

"I wish. But I don't have the time off."

"That's too bad. Not sure why, but I get the feeling Mom misses ya."

"Just Mom, huh?"

"She's the only one. Me? I'm just glad to have the apartment to myself." Sometimes.

Because he did kinda miss having a built-in buddy to spot him on the weight bench or to share a sausage-and-olive pizza with. Missed co-coaching the Backdraft Bar & Grill community baseball team of third and fourth graders together. "Although, I could clear off the couch for you when you need a place to crash."

"Miss you too." Logan chuckled.

Izan Collins walked in.

"I gotta go." Bryce said into the phone.

"Yeah, get back to work, slacker. Talk to you soon."

"Later, bro." Bryce pocketed his cell and nodded a greeting to Izan. "What's up? Are you just getting in?"

"Yeah, I called the chief. I had a break-in at my place and had to wait for the cops."

Bryce stood, looked Izan over. "You okay?"

"I'm good. It just took a while."

"Did Officer Olivia Tazwell come to your rescue?" Bryce wagged his eyebrows.

"Shut up." Izan grabbed the clipboard out of Bryce's hand. "What was stolen?"

"Nothing." Izan shrugged. "They made a mess of the place, but I couldn't find anything missing."

"Weird. Someone trying to send you a message or something?"

"Dunno, but are you ready for the school?"

"You're coming with me?"

"Yup."

"Sweet. Let's go."

They packed their gear and soon parked the rescue truck in front of the Theodore Roosevelt Elementary School. A woman in a pencil skirt and blazer met them on the curb. "Thanks for coming today. I'm Principal Haywood. We have a lot of excited kids."

"I'm Bryce Crawford. This is Izan Collins. We're excited too."

He might not admit it to the other guys, but this was one of his favorite parts of the job. He loved seeing the awe in the kids' faces when they took in the shiny red truck, tried picking up the hoses, and their laughter when he told them a funny story. He and Izan grabbed a few of their tools and one set of turnout gear and followed the principal into the school and down a wide hallway into a media center.

Principal Haywood clapped her hands, settling the chatter in the room instantly. "All right, third graders. Let's be kind and respectful to our guests today. I expect you to be on your best behavior."

"Yes, Mrs. Haywood," they said in unison.

She turned to Bryce. "They're all yours."

"Hi, Coach!" a little voice called from the middle of the group of kids sitting on the floor.

Bryce scanned the crowd. A tow-headed boy gave him a gap-toothed grin and waved. "Harry! Nice to see you, buddy. These are your friends?"

The boy nodded. "And Ty and Hayden are here too. But Charlotte is sick today. So she prob'ly won't be at practice tonight."

"Good to know." Bryce winked at his toss ball player. "So." He rubbed his hands together. "You guys are in third grade?"

Most of the kids nodded.

"Wow, third grade. Do you remember third grade, Izan?"

"Sure I do. Best four years of my life."

The kids laughed.

"I remember in third grade I got to start staying home alone for a little bit. But we had to prove to my parents that we could be safe." Bryce gave his usual safety spiel, reminding kids to stay away from fireworks, incendiary devices, and chemicals. Izan showed the kids the turnout gear, mask, and air tank. They asked for a volunteer. Harry waved his hand so hard he almost pulled his arm out of its socket.

Bryce chuckled. "Okay, Harry. Come on up."

They dressed Harry in the coat and gloves, then plopped the helmet on his head.

The kids giggled to see the yellow sleeves on Harry hanging down to the floor and the helmet go sideways.

Bryce picked up the air tank. "Ready for this?" he asked. "It's only twenty-eight more pounds."

"What?" Some of the kids' jaws dropped.

Bryce set the tank on the ground. "Go ahead and put it on, Harry."

Harry picked it up and lifted it a few inches off the ground. "Ugh. This is soooo heavy!"

"I wanna try!" One of the other boys jumped up.

"First, we're going to go see the fire truck outside. I'll have the tank out there, and you can take turns picking it up—"

Emergency tones for the fire department sounded from Bryce's and Izan's phones. The kids covered their ears at the piercing sound. Bryce froze, listening for his crew's tones. He wasn't technically on duty, and they'd brought the extra truck used only on occasion.

"Fire department, please respond to a confirmed fire at—" Nope. Just the fire crew. Bryce turned down the volume of his radio. The dispatcher called out an address on Broadway. Sounded like a restaurant.

"Do you have to go?" one of the girls in front asked. "Is there a fire?"

"There is, but—" Bryce's phone buzzed. He ignored it and faced the kids for his last message, probably one of the most important things for them to hear. "Remember, Izan and I are firefighters, but you can be safety experts too. If you see anything dangerous or unsafe, or *anyone* who needs help, make sure you tell an adult who you trust."

The phone buzzed again. Bryce leaned over to Izan and whispered, "I better take this call. You got this?"

He nodded and Bryce left the room. He pulled out the phone. Allen Frees? What did the fire department community liaison want? "Hey, you should get down here."

"Are you at the restaurant fire they just paged out?" Bryce asked.

"Yeah. One casualty. They cleared out the rest of the strip mall."

"So why do you need me?"

"It's a known hangout for the Honduran gang, the one that came up in the task force meeting."

Oh. "So they think this has to do with our case?"

"I'll fill you in when you get here. Bring Collins with you."

Izan and Bryce quickly said goodbye to the kids and threw everything back on the truck before they headed to the scene of the fire.

It was a busy area of town, the strip housing a variety of stores. The other crews were still fighting the fire when they arrived, multiple trucks and hoses clogging the parking lot. The front display windows of the restaurant were busted, the glass door covered in black soot and ash. Thankfully, the restaurant was on the end, but the small nutrition store right next to it had probably suffered damage.

Bryce walked up to Allen Frees. "What do we know? More explosions?"

"Kind of. Molotov cocktails through the front window started the fire. There was also a hail of gunfire according to witnesses. A black Camaro in a drive-by shooting."

"That's the same car that tried to take out Penny and me the other day. Anyone hit?"

"The restaurant hadn't opened yet, so only the cook and some employees were in the building. But one of the hostesses was setting tables and died on the scene."

"So now we have a casualty." Izan frowned.

"Not only that, but the way the witnesses described the gunfire made it sound like automatic weapons. Look at the brass in the parking lot."

Empty casings scattered on the ground glinted in the sun.

"You thinking they had those Glock clips like Penny talked about?" Bryce asked.

"These are nine millimeter casings. It's a reasonable explanation."

Bryce tensed. "You think this is a gang war now?"

"Not sure, but we better get Penny and the others down here." So much for trying to keep her off his mind.

ELEVEN

ALL PENNY HAD TO DO WAS FIND EMMA, SOLVE this case, and not get involved personally. As she studied the mug shots on the board, she paced the conference room. She'd finished her energy drink hours ago. The caffeine must be wearing off. The stale air forced into the room through the vents helped a little to keep her from nodding off, but she could use some more pain killers.

Or better yet, a break in this case. Tony stroked his chin as he studied the same board.

Officer Anthony Thomas was the kind of guy she'd have gone out with . . . before Bryce. He was fun. Flirtatious. Handsome, no doubt. The clean-cut kind of handsome, always clean-shaven and well-dressed. Polished even. So different from Bryce's rugged version of the word, with his perpetually scruffy jawline and worn jeans.

But working with someone like Tony was safe, and she'd take that any day over sitting in the conference room with Bryce, his presence and beachy scent filling the space.

They looked over the mug photos again.

"So these are the main players with the Honduran gang?" she asked him.

"Yup. We've got Beto Cordez here trying to run the show. He's been here since he was a kid, and his dad transported migrant workers and drugs here illegally. Dad is now in prison. We haven't got enough to put Beto there yet. Beto relies on Parker and Guillermo here to keep his dealers and thugs in line." Anthony tapped their respective pictures.

"And the Puerto Rican gang?"

"Relatively new. Moved up here after Hurricane Maria caused all that chaos in 2017. Most of the islanders are law-abiding citizens and stay clean. But Hernando Fuentes seems bent on defying that trend and giving the Hondurans a run for their money."

Penny looked at her screen where she'd been digging even deeper into Emma Kemper's past and few known associates. "I can't find a connection to Emma with either group. If there is one, they've worked hard to keep it quiet."

"And none of them look like Emma's boyfriend?" Anthony leaned closer to her as he asked.

Penny shook her head. Not that she'd gotten a good look at the man. It still galled her that they'd gotten the jump on her. She refused to believe that niggle of doubt that said her instincts were slipping. She had just been tired after the long drive.

"I didn't see him, but I could identify Emma's boyfriend's voice if I had to. It did sound like he had a slight accent." And she couldn't sit here and look at any more pictures. She needed to get out and start pounding some pavement and kicking up answers. "If we can't figure out a gang relationship, any CI's that have a pulse on the drug scene in general?"

Anthony leaned back in the office chair and propped his ankle up on his opposite knee. "I put out feelers yesterday. I'm waiting for one to contact me."

"Why wait? Let's go to—"

Her phone rang. "Hey, Olivia. What's up?"

"We need you down here at the restaurant fire. It's connected to the case."

Finally, a break! "Be right there."

"I'll text you the address."

Penny ended the call and looked over to Anthony. "Looks like we're wanted." She told him what Olivia had said.

"That restaurant is owned by a Honduran family."

"You think the Puerto Rican gang is sending a message?"

"Better go find out. Why don't we take my service vehicle, and we'll get there faster."

Considering she was parked over on the next block, it *would* be faster. "Sure."

They pulled up to an active scene. Firefighters in full gear had to be sweltering in the afternoon sun as they directed water from their hoses to the flames still shooting out of the roof. Bystanders circled the edge of the scene, many with phones out, probably live-streaming the drama unfolding.

Penny and Tony walked over to where Olivia, Bryce, and Izan lingered in the parking lot.

"What'd you find?" Penny asked.

"Look at the casings and the gunshot pattern on the building, and tell us what you think," Bryce said. He moved his gaze to Anthony and frowned.

What was that about?

Not that she had time to ponder that. She had a job to do. Penny looked down. Casings littered the parking lot. She studied the front of the restaurant. She could've painted an elaborate dot-to-dot picture with all the bullet holes piercing the stucco siding of the building under the busted-up window.

"Automatic weapons." She bent over and picked up one of the casings. "Definitely 9mm Luger rounds. Like from a Glock 19 with a clip."

"You think Emma and her boyfriend armed Fuentes and the

Puerto Ricans with the clips?" Bryce folded his arms across his chest, his gaze direct, intense as it always was.

"With this pattern"—she pointed to the building—"it definitely looks like a possibility."

Olivia tapped a pen on her small notebook. "They want you to take a look at the woman who died on scene too, make sure it's not Emma Kemper."

Anthony pulled evidence bags and gloves out. "We can test these and see if ballistics matches anything on file." He carefully bagged some of the brass. He paused when his phone buzzed.

"Looks like my CI is up to meeting." He stood and sealed the bag. "Would you like to join me, Penny? You're at my mercy for a ride anyway."

Bryce actually bristled.

"I need to make sure the deceased isn't Emma." Penny nodded toward the coroner's van off to the side.

"I can wait." Tony looked at her, voice almost husky, even with Bryce, Izan, and Olivia right here with them.

Oh brother. Penny spun and headed toward the van.

She wasn't too surprised when footsteps sounded behind her.

"No need to depend on Thomas for a ride. I can take you anywhere you want to go." Bryce caught up to her.

His brown eyes turned cold when he glanced behind them at Officer Thomas. But when he turned them back on her, she felt warmth spiral through her. What was it about that dark-chocolate stare that made her so weak?

Focus, Penny! The case.

She approached the vehicle. The young guy in a jumpsuit held a tablet. She gave him her ID and explained the situation.

"We already had a positive identification made. This is Juana Silvio."

"Can I take a quick look, just to be sure?"

"It's not a pretty sight. Sure you don't want to wait until we can clean her—"

"I'll be fast. I just need to know."

"Fine."

Penny followed him as he stepped into the van and unzipped the black bag on the cot.

It wasn't Emma.

Penny's chest squeezed. To witness the violence, the loss of such a vibrant young life, only firmed her resolve to get to the bottom of what was happening. She thanked the man and turned. Bryce was right there at the back of the van to help her down.

"It's not her," she told him.

If he heard the catch in her voice, he didn't show it. He simply nodded. "So we keep looking."

And he would. Bryce Crawford had a tenacity that wouldn't quit.

They headed back to the others. "You sure I can't take you anywhere? I can come up with an explanation. If it has to do with the case, Frees will let me off duty."

He was right about having options, but riding in a confined place with Bryce would only cause more distraction, and she had a case to solve.

"I've got to find Emma. Tony's CI might have a lead."

"So? If it's about the case, I should go."

She almost laughed at the scowl on his face. He might look ferocious when upset, but she knew the big heart that beat inside him. "We don't want you scaring the CI away." She stopped and rested a hand on his arm. For some dumb reason, she wanted to soothe the worry creasing his eyebrows. "I'll talk to you later, 'kay?"

"Fine."

They approached the others. "It's not her. Let's go see what your CI has to say, Tony."

As they walked away, she could've sworn she heard a growl from

Bryce, which was rather humorous. Tony wasn't a threat. She'd learned her lesson the first time. No more dating in Last Chance. She needed to keep her relationships to a minimum and scoot out as soon as this case was done.

Tony, thankfully, was already dressed in street clothes. White athletic shoes without a scuff or scratch. Jeans with a designer label—even his pristine T-shirt looked expertly tailored and expensive without a wrinkle to be seen. They pulled up to a 24-hour truck stop/café and slid into a booth. Penny took the bench that faced the door. Rather than taking the spot across from her, Anthony slid in next to her.

A lanky teen boy with greasy hair, torn jeans, and a dark hoodie, despite the summer-like temperatures, slid in across from them. "You're paying, right?"

Tony nodded. The server brought glasses of water and took their order. Once she left, the kid frowned at Penny. "Who's she?"

"None of your business. What do you have for me?" Tony tapped the menu on the table.

"Not much. But I'm leaving."

"Why?"

The kid stared out the window, brows furrowed, chewing on his lip. His eyes shifted. Jumpy little guy.

"Koby, what's going on? What do you know?" Tony kept his voice low.

"You'll look after my mom if I go?"

"You know how this works. It's a give and take. You want something, you have to give me something first. But yeah, if your intel is good, I'll keep an eye out for her."

"How do I know I can trust you?"

"I could ask you the same. But I think we've had a good thing going here. Why do you want to leave?"

"It's not like I want to." The frown only enhanced the whole angsty-teenager vibe. But he seemed genuinely worried about his mother.

"Then who's forcing your hand?" Tony asked.

The boy clammed up.

The server set steaming hot plates in front of them. "Anything else I can get you?"

They shook their heads. Once she walked away again, Tony took a bite of his burger. Penny followed his lead and nibbled on a hot, salty french fry.

The kid lost some of his nervousness as he scarfed down his meal.

Tony, on the other hand, leaned back leisurely like he had all the time in the world. "So, what's it gonna be, Koby?"

Koby swallowed his bite and wiped his mouth with his sleeve. "Look, I don't have a choice. I owe . . . someone. And he's calling in favors."

"Your dealer?"

"Maybe. All I know is that they're picking up and moving the whole operation. Someone bigger has taken over and is forcing them out."

"One of the Hispanic gangs?"

Koby swallowed another bite. "Someone else. A cartel."

"It's not the Puerto Ricans?"

"No way Ray-Ray would run from them."

Penny pulled up a picture of Emma on her phone. "Have you seen her around here?"

Koby studied the picture. "She seems kinda familiar."

"Where have you seen her?" Penny asked.

The kid shrugged and stuffed a handful of fries into his mouth.

Tony stared him down. "Tell the lady what you know."

"I think I saw her at the biker place once."

"What were you doing there?" Tony's gaze narrowed.

"I had a meeting is all."

A drug delivery most likely.

"And Ray-Ray? You got anything on him?"

"He just told me the competition is getting crowded and we're setting up somewhere else."

Now they were getting somewhere.

"You sure it's the competition and not the feds or something?" Tony asked.

"Like he's gonna tell me jack. I just do what I'm told. We're heading out as soon as we get the call." He took a gulp of his pop. "So will you do it? Look after my mom?"

"I'll do what I can. But she's gotta stay clean too."

"She is."

"Okay. We have a deal." Tony stuck out a hand and the kid shook it. He finished the last of his food and was gone.

"So . . . what are you up to tonight?" Tony turned to her.

Penny knew that tone, had used it herself many times. But better squelch whatever kind of flirtation he was hoping for at the start. "I've got work to do."

"We're on the same team. Shouldn't we be working together?"

"Nice try, Officer Thomas, but I've got more than just this case right now. So if you don't mind taking me back to the police station, I'll grab my car and get back to it."

She gave him a practiced smile. The one that was friendly and light but not too encouraging.

"Please, call me Tony. And I think we could be pretty good together. Sure I can't help you on your other cases?"

She chuckled. "I have to give you props for your persistence, but believe me, I'm sure."

"All right. Can't blame a guy for trying, right?"

No, she really couldn't. And she couldn't account for the lack of attraction to him. He was exactly her type, he wouldn't expect much more than a fun time. But she had a case to solve, and the less people involved the better. It was surprisingly easy to down his second offer to compare notes later once she reached her car.

"Thanks, but I've got my own leads to pursue. Keep me in the loop?"

"Sure thing." He paused a moment. "So, you and Bryce. Is that like . . . an official thing? Is that why you're busy?"

"Bryce and I have a past." A past that still took up too much room in her head, but Tony didn't need to know that. "That's all it is. I'm here to work this case and then I'm gone. Believe me, Tony, you're better off with someone else. I won't be here long."

It was the only way to keep her heart in one piece.

"Then I'll see you around." He waved before riding off.

Now, time to make some progress on this case so she could get out of Last Chance herself.

TWELVE

BRYCE FINISHED TIGHTENING THE SCREW ON HIS
mother's kitchen sink faucet.

"There you go. No more leaky drips."

"Honey, are you sure you're okay?" His mother seemed a lot
more homey these days with her silver hair pulled back in a low
ponytail and an apron on instead of the business suits she always
dressed in as a lawyer. She leaned against the counter, her concerned gaze unmistakable.

He barely refrained from rolling his eyes. "Mom, I'm fine. Why
do you keep asking?"

"I heard about the case and this task force you're on. You're already in a dangerous profession, and now we have to worry about
drive-by shootings? Not to mention the woman who broke your
heart—"

"Whoa, whoa, whoa. Penny Mitchell did *not* break my heart."

His mother raised one eyebrow and stared him down.

"What?! She didn't. And no need to get all worked up about
my job. I know how to handle myself."

"I'm your mother. I'm supposed to worry. It's bad enough we
got through all that upheaval with the Sosa craziness, then Logan

goes back to being a smokejumper and moves away. Andi has Jude looking after her. Who else do you have to look after you?"

"You make it sound like I need a babysitter, when in reality I'm a grown man. And I have my crew. It's not like I rush into burning buildings by myself. Besides, Sosa is dead. End of story."

His mother sighed and pulled a glass out of the cupboard. "I know. But one of my sons jumps out of planes into fires. I don't need you putting yourself recklessly in danger. We've been through more than our fair share of trouble in the last decade." She filled the glass with cold tap water.

Bryce wasn't about to change careers or anything, but maybe he could help smooth some of those worry lines he was responsible for.

"I know what I'm doing when it comes to my job."

"And your love life?" She set the glass on the counter and turned to face him.

"Ma! I'm not gonna go into that with you. Besides, don't you have a meeting to go to? I thought you were giving the governor's wife and son a tour of the courthouse."

"Nice try. That's tomorrow." She stepped closer. "You were serious about Penny back then. I saw it. The way you looked at her."

Bryce tossed the wrench and screwdriver into the open toolbox on the floor. "Then she thought I cheated on her and she left."

"I thought you explained that to her. The whole Ashlee debacle."

"I did. It doesn't change anything. We're just working together now. Nothing else."

"Maybe there should be a 'something else.' She's strong. Smart. Beautiful. She challenges you."

"She doesn't want to settle down. And I don't think she wants anything to do with God."

"And you do?"

"How can you ask me that? I'm going to church with you every Sunday I don't work. Going to discipleship group. I'm trying." He slammed the toolbox closed and returned it to its place under the sink.

"I ran into Izan last week when you took Dad to your men's discipleship group. He thought you were out on date. He made it sound like you went out a lot. Like he had no clue you were actually at a Bible study. Or watching a show with your father most nights."

Bryce's neck grew hot. But he knew enough to keep his mouth shut.

His mother folded her arms, a bright red fingernail tapping against her white blouse sleeve. "Why do you let people believe you're still that guy? Because I don't think Penny is the only one you need to show who you are now. You've changed. So why are you so afraid to show that?"

There was the question. And he didn't know how to answer it. Maybe it was because everyone at church kept talking about being this new creation now, but he felt very much the same. Struggling with the same temptations and doubts. And the few times he tried to bring the conversation around to something like faith, his buddies gawked at him and thought he was joking.

"People see what they want to see. Penny thought she saw a cheater and left. Izan and the others see what they think I am too. It's not like I lie to them. They have their assumptions."

His mother tilted her head, leaned closer. "There's a lot more to you, Bryce, than the wild-child persona you put out there. There always has been. And I think Penny is one of the few people you let get close. One of the few who might know that."

"And she still left." Bryce held her stare and pushed back with his own.

"Maybe it's not you she's running from."

Huh? "What else would it be?"

"I suspect it's her own past. Losing both parents already couldn't have been easy. I wonder if always moving, never settling down, is her modus operandi, a way to keep herself from being hurt again."

Well, that was something he hadn't thought of. "But what do I do about that? And besides, I thought you wanted me with someone like Sarai Green. A good Christian girl that would help me 'settle down.'" He made air quotes.

His mother laughed. "Sarai Green? Why would you think that? She would bore you to tears."

"I thought that's what you wanted! And for the record, I'm pretty sure I bored her, too, on our one and only date."

"Of course you did. You two have nothing in common."

"But she goes to church."

"Honey, there's a lot more to a good relationship than that. You need someone you enjoy being with. Can't get enough of, in fact. You're a passionate man. You should be passionate about the woman you love too. I don't see that happening with someone like Sarai. But I could see it with Penny."

"And what if there's too much passion? Temptation, even. I thought I was supposed to be a different guy now. But with Penny, all the old feelings are right there."

"Maybe that's not a bad thing. Just don't hide yourself. Be honest with her. See what happens."

"Don't expect much, Mom. We're working together. But at the end of this case, I have a feeling she'll be gone. I'm only here to keep her safe."

His mother smirked. "Maybe she just needs a good reason to stay. Give her one."

Yeah right. Like that was so easy. He'd stick with his decision to keep Penny out of trouble and guard his heart. But why explain?

Instead, Bryce swiped the glass off the counter. "I'll take this to Dad, but then I've gotta go. Community ball tonight."

He would take all the chaos of coaching third and fourth graders any day over talking about relationships. He popped a quick kiss on his mother's cheek. "Love ya."

She sighed as he left the kitchen and went into the living room, where Dad's favorite fishing show played on the television.

Bryce set the glass of water down by his father's chair. "Here you go, Pops."

The man barely acknowledged his presence. His father was nothing like the guy he'd been when Bryce was a kid, but Bryce couldn't think about that too much. At least Dad was still alive. Sosa's cartel may have wanted to intimidate Elizabeth Crawford by targeting her husband and running him off the road, causing a traumatic brain injury, but they didn't know the Crawfords very well. It only fueled their intentions to make sure justice was done. Sosa may have wanted for them to cower in fear, and his cohorts had almost killed Andi, but they'd completely underestimated how far family would go to protect their own.

And yeah, he felt the loss with Logan having left town. But his mother didn't need to worry. As much as Bryce loved the thrills and adrenaline, he wasn't going anywhere. They'd gotten too close last time. And even though Sosa had been eliminated and was no longer a threat, the lesson had been learned. Bryce would stay close to his parents and make sure they were protected. Besides, he liked Last Chance. He'd traveled a little, but nothing was quite like his hometown. He could make a difference here. Keep people safe. Prevent tragedies.

And sure, maybe it would be nice to find someone to share life with. Penny was the only person he could see that happening with, but she definitely wasn't on board. So no matter what his mother thought she saw, he needed to play it easy when it came to Penny.

Bryce drove to the practice fields and pulled out the bases from the storage shed. It was a perfect spring evening—a slight breeze to keep the bugs away and freshly cut grass scenting the air. The mountains in the distance stood guard over the town.

"Need some help?" Izan grabbed one of the bases in his arm before it could fall.

"Hey! You made it. You really gonna help coach these rugrats?"

"Sure. I love baseball. Got nothing better going on Tuesday nights anyway."

"Right. And that has nothing to do with Olivia Tazwell's work schedule at all, huh?"

Izan shrugged. "She barely gives me the time of day. But enough about her. What do you need me to do?"

Kids began arriving. Bryce introduced them to Izan as they came up. They split the kids into two groups and had them warm up with light tosses.

"Coach, where do I go again?" A little hand tugged on Bryce's arm.

"You're going to go practice with Jadyn."

"Okay." The little girl in braids jogged over the grass to her friend.

"You sure you're okay?" Izan walked up to Bryce.

"Of course."

Izan narrowed his eyes. "What's got you brooding?"

"I'm not brooding."

"Uh, yeah you are. Ever since we showed up at the shootout at the restaurant, you've been . . . quieter."

"Don't know what you're talking about." Bryce jammed the extra glove he'd picked up back in the bag.

"Sorry I'm late, Coach. My aunt didn't know where to park."

Bryce looked up. Harry was running toward them with a familiar blonde walking behind him.

"She's your aunt?" Bryce asked the little boy with freckles and blond hair.

He nodded. "Uh-huh. And she said after practice we get to go get ice cream!"

What was it with Penny Mitchell showing up everywhere this week?

"I'll go get Harry set up. Give you some…privacy." Izan chuckled as he jogged away.

"So, you're Harry's coach I've heard so much about." Penny grinned. With her hair pulled back and a ball cap on, she looked like she belonged here on the baseball field. And since when did she wear shorts and sandals? He'd rarely seen her in anything besides jeans and her boots.

And he had to admit, she looked good like this.

"And you're the aunt. The one who's taking him out to ice cream."

"Don't want to shirk my auntie responsibilities." She looked down at the equipment. "Need any help? I'll be here for the whole practice. I promised Harry I would stay and watch."

"How are you at pitching?"

"I'm decent."

Which probably meant she was a real ace. "Great. You can work with them on batting. Take it easy on them though. They're just kids." He couldn't help but lean in closer to her, taking in every fleck of blue-green in her eyes.

"I don't take it easy on anyone." She lifted her chin as if to say *challenge accepted.*

And didn't he know it. A chuckle escaped.

He tried not to sneak too many glances at her as she took seven kids to work on their batting while he had a group in the field catching grounders and pop flies.

Keeping himself from falling right back in love with her was going to be harder than he'd thought.

THIRTEEN

PENNY RELAXED IN THE DRIVER'S SEAT OF THE car. Might as well get comfortable if she was going to be here a while. She pulled out her telephoto lens camera and set it on the dash. She popped a piece of minty fresh gum in her mouth and settled in.

Situated on the edge of town, out on the state highway, the biker gang bar across the street from her was one of the last things on this road before people hit the interstate. The rusty metal siding gave the building the appearance of an old warehouse, while the colorful neon signs for various brands of beer beckoned people in. A few Harleys leaned heavily on their kickstands near the door while a semitruck without a trailer shaded them from its parking space at the edge of the lot.

"Come on, Emma. Give me something here."

As she lifted the camera up, her phone rang. Jude.

"Hey, how's Denver?" she asked him on speaker phone.

"I'm in Georgia now. Leading some training. How are things going there?"

"Well, I'm outside the Highway to He—"

"Lemme guess, the biker bar?"

"Yeah. Tony's CI said he saw Emma here. I've been scoping it out the last few nights."

"Must be getting impatient, huh?"

"You know me well. So what do *you* know about this place?"

"There's a group of people very concerned about their Second Amendment rights that frequents the place, but they tend to go a little radical. They call themselves Soldiers in Arms. I haven't had any specific run-ins, since they keep to themselves, but they made quite the fuss over the last DA election."

"Why was that?" Penny blew a bubble with her gum and let it pop.

"They thought the guy who won was too soft on criminals."

"Enough to want to take justice into their own hands?"

"They have some strongly worded social media posts about driving out gangbangers and drug dealers, but they're not dumb. No real names or pictures. I just know they frequent the bar there."

"Good to know. If I go in, I'll try to look the part."

"Is your CI a biker?"

"No, just a kid, really. I'm not sure how trustworthy he is. But I'm drawing a blank on ways to track down Emma. If she doesn't show in the next hour or so, I'll go scope things out."

"Good luck with that."

"When are you back in town?"

"Taking the red-eye tonight. Let me tell ya, it's not soon enough. I miss my wife."

"TMI, Brooks. So, back to Emma, nothing I saw in her background sounds like she would come to this kind of place. What do you think she'd be doing here?"

"What do you know?"

Penny snapped a few pictures of a couple of guys going into the bar. "She's a ghost, really. A ghost without much of a past. She and her brother bounced around from family member to foster care after their parents died when they were young. But still. How did they get from California to way the heck out here in the middle of nowhere?"

There was a reason they called this place Last Chance County. "No clue. Guess you get to find out. Just be careful out there. Maybe you should have one of the officers on the task force go in with you. You seemed to hit it off with Anthony."

"Stick to the ATF and not matchmaking."

"That's not what I'm doing. I just think it would be safer if you had backup."

"You know I can take care of myself."

"But maybe you shouldn't have to."

"I'm leaving now. Call me if you find anything or if Emma's brother finally talks."

"Doubtful. Stay safe though."

"You know it."

Penny continued to take pictures of anyone going into or out of the club, but there weren't that many. A couple hours into her stakeout, she had a few pictures of people and a growing pile of pistachio shells, but no sign of Emma. Time to go inside. And hopefully the establishment had a restroom.

Penny slipped a black crop top with an eagle on it over her tank top. She'd have worn the black leather jacket to hide her gun if it weren't torn and still reeking of smoke. The light-wash denim jacket would have to do. She tied a red bandana around her head as the finishing touch and walked in.

The light was dim despite the bright afternoon sun outside. Smoke from the kitchen grill hovered over the bar. Penny could easily picture the place filled with cigarette smoke back in the day. Rusted license plates covered one wall, a big elk head surrounded by smaller deer mounts graced another. Classy. She refrained from grimacing at the decor as she quickly used the bathroom and approached the bar. A wiry woman with big hair and a gray tank top filled a mug with beer from a tap and handed it to the big man at the end, perched on a stool. The legs of the stool creaked every time he moved. Hopefully the thing held.

"What can I get you?" the bartender asked without looking at her. She continued to stack clean mugs from a rack into a cooler. Penny ordered a drink she could sip slowly without standing out. "Got a food menu to go with it?"

The woman slapped a laminated paper menu in front of Penny and then turned to the guys at the billiard table off to the side. "If you're gonna order something, get it now before Hank closes down the grill."

Penny ordered a burger and fries when the bartender came back and plopped her drink in front of her.

"Have you seen Emma Kemper around lately?"

"Don't know that name."

Penny showed her a picture off her phone. "She's my cousin. My mom was worried about—"

"Look, just because I'm behind the bar doesn't mean I have time for people's sob stories. I don't know the chick." She spun on her heel and pushed through the door leading to the kitchen.

Whoa-kay. That was a bust.

"Don't mind Mo." The big guy at the end of the bar slid closer.

"Mo?" Penny asked.

"Short for Moira. She's ornery, but she keeps her beer cold and is generous with her shots. I'm Bobby, by the way."

Penny gave him a flirty smile. She could definitely get further with this guy than the bartender. "Good to know. Well then, have you seen Emma?" She showed her phone to him. "We think she's out here with a guy, but we never met him. We're just worried about her, ya know?" Penny twirled her hair around her finger and conjured a worried look.

"Don't know that I've seen her, but I'm on the road a lot. Only come around here every few weeks."

"Oh, are you from Last Chance?"

"Born and raised."

"And you think it's safe here? I mean, I heard about gangs moving in. I'm wondering if Emma got caught up in one of them."

Bobby's brows furrowed. "Them gangbangers don't stand a chance."

"How do you know? I mean, I heard there was a drive-by shooting last week. And then I saw that restaurant fire in the news. I'm worried."

He moved in closer, puffed out his chest a bit. "No need to be, doll. We got us a concerned group of citizens that's gonna make sure they don't settle here."

"The police and sheriff's office?"

Bobby waved off the thought. "They don't do nothin'. These guys are selling drugs and shooting up buildings and the law don't do a thing."

Oh, this was too easy sometimes. "That's not right."

"Darn right it isn't. That's why regular folks need to wake up and do somethin' about it."

Penny took a sip of her drink. "That sounds kinda . . . noble. Something I'd like to be a part of." Penny gave him her best doe-eyed innocent look and laid a light hand on his arm.

"Oh, well, I dunno. I mean, no offense and all, but we don't know you. And we got things handled. Just you wait and see." He gave her a toothy grin. "You won't have to worry about a thing."

She tried not to cringe at the tobacco-stained teeth. "Well, I'm glad there's people brave enough to do something about a problem. But what about my cousin? What if she's in one of these gangs?"

Bobby leaned in low. "Then I suggest you find her and get the heck out of Last Chance. Soon. Real soon."

He stood, threw some bills on the bar, and saluted the guys at the pool table before he walked out.

Well, that was interesting.

The food arrived. Mo plopped a plate in front of her without a word and went back to the kitchen. Penny quickly ate her burger and left over half her drink on the bar top when she walked out into the bright sunshine again.

She ignored a call from Anthony Thomas. She had her own lead and needed to follow it. The less distractions the better.

She drove to the public library and used their free Wi-Fi to quickly type Bobby's license plate from the big rig that had been parked at the bar into the database she used. Looked like Bobby Prescot had had a few minor run-ins with the law, nothing huge. But it was another name that popped up that grabbed her attention.

Conway Prescot. His name sounded familiar. A quick public-records search showed Conway owned a good chunk of land east of town. On her navigation app, it looked like only one road led out there. Satellite feed showed a main house with a lot of outer buildings. Good places to hide things. But it would be tricky to get in there undetected. Even if it wasn't the main hub of this group, her gut said she'd find something related to the case. If Bobby was to be believed, they didn't have a whole lot of time to figure out what was going on.

Looked like she would have to move her stakeout to Conway Prescot's place and see what she could find.

FOURTEEN

BRYCE CLOSED HIS LOCKER. FINALLY, AN UN-
eventful shift. Usually he liked the action, but lately it was hitting
too close to home. So he'd take a quiet day shift and leave knowing
his crew was safe for another day after all the explosions and injuries.
They'd taken turns checking in on Ridge since he was recuperating
from his broken leg.

Izan walked in. "Hey, you doing anything right now?"

"Why? Wanna grab a bite?"

"Totally, because whatever Stephens calls that stuff he makes,
it's not food." Izan unbuttoned his uniform shirt. "But first, I was
wondering if you'd spot me on something."

"What's up?"

"Remember that break-in? I was wrong. Something *was* taken.
Some of my dad's letters."

"What letters?"

"You know, my biological dad. Those letters your mom gave me
from him that he wrote in prison before he died. Most I have at
my bank in a safety deposit box, but I kept a few at the apartment.
They're gone."

"Why would someone take those letters?"

"Before he died, Sosa was looking for his stolen money. If anyone made the connection that my real father was Sosa's accountant, they might be resuming the search where Sosa left off when he was shot. It's the only thing I can come up with, because whoever it was went through a lot of trouble to get the letters from my apartment."

Bryce's gut twisted. Sosa had caused a lot of havoc and turmoil. But he was dead. So who was this new threat? "So where are you going tonight?"

"Back when I was trying to figure out who my real father was, before I realized who Sosa was and everything, I got involved with some shady people. I had to pretend to be one of them."

"What does that mean?"

"I kinda started dating this girl. Maria. She knew who the players were."

"So you used her."

"Hey, I treated her well. Better than any of her other boyfriends. And we left on good terms. But either way, she lives in a rougher part of the city. If I'm gonna go there and see what she knows, I'd prefer to have someone watching my back."

"I'm in." 'Cause no way would he let a friend go in there unprotected. And maybe a little adrenaline rush would keep his mind busy enough that it would stop thinking about Penny Mitchell and where Bryce had gone wrong. Especially the Penny Mitchell that played catch with kids and took the whole team out for ice cream after practice.

Bryce and Izan crossed a parking lot dotted with potholes. The stairwell reeked of pot. Exiting onto the second floor, the smell wasn't much better as they knocked on a door. A television show in a different language sounded through the walls. Somewhere down the hall a baby cried. Izan pounded on the door a second time.

"'Ria! It's Izan."

Bryce kept an eye on the hallway.

Finally, the click of the locks and the knob turning sounded.

"Izan? What are you doing here? And who's that?" Dark eyes probed from the crack of the doorway.

"It's a friend. Can we come in?"

Maria stuck her head out and looked down the hallway herself before opening the door wider and letting them in. The apartment was tiny, worn, but clean. Izan's ex had long black hair pulled back in a loose ponytail. She wore jeans and a light-pink T-shirt, her arms folded across her chest. "What are you doing here?"

"This is Bryce, by the way." Izan flashed her a dimpled grin. One all the ladies at the station teased him about. "You look good. Healthy."

"I am. Over a year sober now. And I'm going back to school." She pointed to a stack of textbooks on the tiny dining room table.

"That's awesome. I always said you were smart. You're probably getting straight A's."

Maria blushed. "Enough with the flattery, Iza. What are you here for?"

"Someone broke into my place. They took letters from my biological father. I was wondering if you still ran with that crew from when we were together. If you heard anything."

She shook her head and looked worried. "I had to cut ties with all of them. You were right. They weren't great friends. I left that scene not long after we broke up."

"So you don't know what they're up to?"

"I mean, I still hear things, but it's ridiculous stuff."

"Like what?"

"Like Sasha saying Diego Ruiz Sosa is back from the dead." She rolled her eyes.

Bryce bristled at that name. "No way. I watched him get shot. Right after he had my sister kidnapped and she almost drowned."

Maria narrowed her eyes. "Who are you again?"

"Izan's friend." He took a step closer. "Who is saying Sosa is still alive?"

"My friend has a cousin who works at the Riviera Club. She said there's talk. That's all it is, right? I mean, you saw him die. So why should it matter?"

Because most of the time, rumors had a seed of truth in them. Bryce wasn't going to let any potential threat to his family go unheeded. He knew what happened when people ignored the warning signs.

"What d'ya say, Collins? Wanna go check out the Riviera Club?" Bryce asked.

"Sure thing."

Maria stepped forward and tugged at Izan's arm. "Be careful. I know Sosa is dead and all and I haven't seen you in a couple years, but . . ."

"Don't worry. We'll be careful. And you'll let me know if you hear anything else? Especially about Sosa or my letters?"

She nodded. He scribbled out his number on a slip of paper by her books. "This is my cell. If you need anything, you call. All right?"

She kissed him on the cheek and they left.

"What do you think that was all about? Sosa back from the dead?" Bryce asked as soon as they were back in the car.

"Dunno, but I'm sure as heck gonna go find out. That club is where Maria's old crew used to hang. It makes sense that if anyone knows anything, we might find out there."

They drove in Bryce's truck to the club. Dancing lights lured them in from the dark parking lot, promising fun and a good time. The loud bass thrummed through their bodies as they approached the door.

Once inside, Bryce had to practically yell in Izan's ear to be heard. "I didn't even know this place existed."

"Not surprised. This is what you call *real* music. Not that country twang you play." Izan bopped to the Latin beat of the music as they walked farther in.

They gave drink orders to the guy behind the bar. Izan's feet couldn't stay still. The man had rhythm—even if the music wasn't something Bryce would ever voluntarily play. Bryce focused on scanning the room. The dance floor strobe lights made it difficult to see faces clearly. They were going to have to do a lap around or something to get a good look at people.

"Recognize anyone?" Bryce asked as he took a long drink.

Izan shook his head. "Not yet."

They leaned against a tall table off to the side of the room. "But you better loosen up or you're gonna scare everyone away."

"What?"

"Loosen up. What's the deal? I thought this was your kind of scene. Drinks. Ladies. Dancing." Izan put his drink down and started swinging his hips to the music. A trio of girls in skintight clothing, long elaborate fingernails and their own drinks in hand, surrounded Izan and drew him out to the dance floor.

If one could call that dancing. Give Bryce a honky-tonk any day. He was pretty sure his body did not bend and flex enough for the moves Izan was putting on. Obviously his Mexican heritage was coming through despite having been raised by the Collinses, who'd adopted him at the age of four.

Besides, kinda hard to loosen up with this stupid rumor of Sosa bringing all his senses to alert. Just when his father had gotten used to a new nurse after his other one had been murdered, Andi and Jude were settling down, and now this?

But Izan might be right. Bryce probably shouldn't scowl as he studied the room. He relaxed his face, smiled at a woman off to the side who was looking his way. But it was too dark to see across the room or in the shadowed booths along one side. And was that—? The man in the opposite corner of the room stood, his back to Bryce. But he had the right build, dark hair. A bulkier guy in a suit moved behind the man and blocked the view.

No. Sosa was dead. There was no way—

Izan's phone flashed as he took a selfie with the girls. Good idea. Maybe Bryce could try taking some video, pretend he was FaceTiming or talking to someone. He took out his phone. A flash would be too obvious. He tried for video, using the settings on his phone to compensate for the low light conditions.

"Hey, wanna dance?" A woman . . . a very young woman with curly brown hair, a low-cut flowy tank, and jeans stepped in front of him, taking up the whole screen.

"Ah, I'm sorry. I'm not much of a dancer." At least, not this kind of dancing.

"That's too bad. Maybe I could keep you company? Buy you another drink?"

He stopped the recording on his phone. He hadn't even finished what was in his glass. But he was never one to turn down a lady brave enough to go after what she wanted.

Usually.

This time, it just didn't sit the same. He wasn't flattered. No rush of attraction or anything. And she was pretty.

But he didn't care.

"I'm sorry. I appreciate the offer . . . I just . . ."

She smiled. "I'm not her."

"Her who?"

"There's someone else you want to be with."

Okay, yeah. There was. Because it didn't matter how pretty this girl was or how evocatively she swayed to the music. She wasn't Penny.

He glanced down and then smiled sheepishly at her. "You're right. No offense."

"None taken." She glanced behind her toward the door and then turned a seductive eye on him. "But if you ever want to try to forget her"—she ran a finger down the length of his chest—"you know where to find me." This time she walked away, and he lost her in the crowd.

"Who was that?" Izan grinned as he grabbed his drink.

"No clue. I'm gonna walk around and see what I can see. Find anything out?"

"I don't recognize anyone from that old crew."

"You think Maria was telling the truth?"

"Why would she lie? She said it was only something she heard."

"Maybe she wanted to rile us up. Lead us on a wild-goose chase or something." The lights and music were getting to him. He tried to stretch his neck to the side and release the tension there. It didn't help. "I'll take a look around, and then I'll be ready to leave."

Bryce took the roundabout way, skirting around the dancing crowd and sticking to the edges of the room. He studied each person, but no one looked like the dead man, Sosa. By the time they left, he had a full-blown headache and not even a good time to show for it. He dropped Izan off and then went back to his own apartment.

He swallowed some painkillers and scarfed down a quick sandwich before he lay down. All he could see as he stared at the ceiling was Penny. Memories marched through his mind. Teaching her how to two-step. The way she'd throw her head back and laugh. Watching her show a little blonde girl on the team how to swing a bat. It stirred so much longing inside he could hardly breathe.

Okay, so fine, everyone was right. He'd fallen hard and fast for Penny Mitchell, and she still had some kind of hold on him.

The question was, what could he do about it?

FIFTEEN

PENNY RUBBED HER EYES AND TOOK ANOTHER swig of coffee. She was going to need so much caffeine to stay awake today after her all-night surveillance op.

She walked into Jude's office. He looked way too put together for this early in the morning in his pristine button-down shirt and impeccably knotted tie. She, on the other hand, plopped into the uncomfortable office chair in a wrinkled shirt and proceeded to scratch the pink bumps covering her arms.

Jude looked up. "It went that well last night scoping out the Prescot place?"

"Let's just say the mosquitos had a Penny Mitchell–sized feast."

"You didn't pack bug spray?" He gave her a "duh" look.

"I didn't think I'd have to hunker down in the weeds the whole time. That place is guarded like Fort Knox."

"So, what did you find?"

"Not Emma Kemper." She sighed as she pulled up photos from her phone and then emailed them to Jude. "But once things quieted down enough, I was able to sneak into the big barn. They have a whole arsenal there. Boxes of weapons with serial numbers filed off. Some short-barreled rifles and silencers. Are those registered?"

Jude typed something on his keyboard. "One Conway Wallis Prescot has a permit to run a shooting range on that premises and has one homemade SBR registered."

"I guarantee you there's more than one SBR there. What about silencers?"

"Nothing on record."

"When was their last inspection?"

"Good question." He clicked a few more keys. "Looks like it's been over five years."

"It is within normal business hours and the scope of your authority to make sure he has his paperwork in order." She gave him a cheesy forced grin.

"You want me to walk onto a suspected militia compound alone for a routine inspection so you can see if your girl Emma is there?"

"Who said you'll be alone? I'll come with you. As backup. Besides, there's something going on. Big Bobby made it sound like they had plans."

"You know you can't do a thing if you come. And what if Bobby Prescot sees you? You'll blow your cover."

"I'm okay with that."

Jude paused, studying her. "Would you come back to the ATF?"

Penny stilled. "What do you mean?"

"You're good at this, Pen. We could use the help. I know Last Chance feels like it's the middle of nowhere, but we're not far off the major routes between Denver and Salt Lake City. There's more than enough work here for the both of us. You could recertify. Be close to your family. Pick things up with Bryce."

Her stomach clenched. After everything she'd gone through? No way. She'd joined the ATF thinking she would fight for justice. She'd never expected to fall for her boss. Or what had happened later. But it had been enough to know that working with others on a permanent basis was not for her. She couldn't afford to get attached.. Because the fallout had been devastating. She'd lost her job, her heart, and her identity. She would never go through that again.

Not even for Bryce Crawford.

And the longer she stayed in town—for any reason—the more at risk she was of falling for him.

Falling for *anyone* only made her easy pickings. No more of that, thanks!

"First off, I'm not even gonna touch the whole Bryce thing. That's done. In the past. Finished. As for the job . . . I'm flattered, Book. It's high praise coming from you. But we both know I don't exactly like following the rules when they get in my way. I like calling the shots. And you would hate what I would do to this very boring and gray office." She grinned at him, trying to let him see the professional reasonings so she could continue to conceal the personal ones.

"All right. Can't say I didn't try."

Penny forced her body to relax. Jude bought her reasoning. Bryce never would've let her off with such lame excuses. He would've kept pushing for the real answer.

Good thing he wasn't here.

It had been bad enough in the downtime waiting last night. All she could think about was how sweet it had been watching him on the bottom of a doggie pile of sweaty kids on the baseball field. Or the sense of something new under all the energy and passion that drew her to Bryce Crawford.

He was still the same Bryce in most ways. But a difference she couldn't pin down piqued her curiosity. And although she didn't know what it was, obviously it was dangerous. Her guard was already slipping.

"Sooooo . . . are we going on a little field trip or what?" She leaned on the desk and batted her eyes.

Jude stood with a sigh. "Let's get this inspection over with. I'm going to loop in the police chief, though, so we have backup ready if needed."

She popped up off her seat. "Sure thing, boss."

Finally, something to get her blood pumping.

She rode with Jude out to Prescot's property. A gate barred access with a mounted camera and speaker.

A crackly voice blared through the speaker. "If you don't know the code, you're in the wrong place."

Jude held up his badge and ID to the camera. "This is Jude Brooks with the ATF. Just doing a routine inspection of the shooting range, making sure your paperwork is in order."

"We weren't given notice of no inspection."

"Don't need to. By law, as an ATF officer I can inspect without a warrant."

"You should call first or come back when we're not so busy."

"Are you refusing this inspection? Your permits won't be renewed if you are."

After a long pause, the speaker crackled again. "Wait there."

"Think they're hiding everything?" Penny kept her voice low.

"Most likely."

It took a good ten minutes for a faded red truck to meet them at the gate. The man that came out from behind the wheel wore a brown cowboy hat and a shoulder holster with a Beretta 92. With his average height and lean frame, he was pretty much the opposite of Big Bobby in build. His weathered face was wrinkled, the mustache and beard all gray.

"Don't know why you gotta bother honest folks out here just tryin' to run a business. How long is this gonna take?"

"Are you Conway Prescot?" Jude asked.

"I am the owner of this property." He stood, hands on hips, boot-clad feet spread wide.

"Good. Then as soon as you open up the gate, we can get on with this, and I'll be out of your hair."

"Let's see that identification again."

Jude pulled it out and showed the man. He studied every part of the badge and card. Silent seconds ticked by. Total power-play move. She had to give it to Jude. He started whistling and smiled like he had all the time in the world. All Penny could think about were the places Emma Kemper or her boyfriend might be hiding.

With a big sigh, Conway finally released the gate. "Follow me."

The dirt road in was bumpy and dry. The cloud of dust kicked up by the truck made it impossible to see much. They pulled into the heart of the compound, which Penny had scouted last night. Dogs—some kind of heelers or pointers—left the front porch of the big log ranch house and rushed toward them.

"Down, boys." Prescot shooed them away.

Penny'd had to wait until the dogs were penned up last night before she could sneak into the buildings. Today at least five vehicles were parked in front of the barn. A handful of men milled around. All obviously armed. Penny smiled at them, hoping to find the weakest link. No one smiled back. Thankfully, Bobby Prescot was nowhere to be seen. But neither was Emma.

That was probably just as well. If they realized who they were, they wouldn't hesitate to kill her and Jude and bury them out in the back forty.

Conway led them to the shooting range, showed Jude his store where he sold ammunition, and retrieved the one short-barreled rifle he had the permit for. While Jude waited for the paperwork, Penny milled through the little store. Through the window, she watched a couple men in camo and dirty blue jeans scramble around the corner of the barn after another drove a skid loader. What was going on out there?

"So, are we done here?" Prescot said from the counter.

Penny whipped around. They'd better not be.

"I'll need to see the rest of the premises. Where you receive deliveries and store overstock. And I'd like to see the shooting range." Jude paused. "I might even join."

Penny almost laughed at that.

Prescot didn't seem amused. He simply marched out the door, leaving it open for them to follow. They walked out back to the shooting range.

Still no sign of Emma Kemper or the men she'd been with the night of the warehouse fire.

After inspecting the shelves of ammunition in one of the sheds, Conway faced Jude and planted his feet. "There. I've complied. You're welcome to go now and let me get back to work."

"What about the barn?" Jude didn't back down at all.

"What about it?"

"I need to see it."

Prescot's eyes narrowed. "There's nothing there but animals and old tractors."

"Still, I have to be thorough if you want to keep your permits."

The crusty rancher's mustache drooped as he frowned. "I think you've seen all you're legally required to see."

"You don't want me coming back here and shutting this whole operation down for not complying with a federal agency."

It was all Penny could do to keep her mouth shut. She hated bullies like Prescot. But she and Jude were severely outnumbered if it came down to it. A muscle in Prescot's jaw twitched. He looked over at the stocky guy leaning on the barn door.

"Tray, our nosy ATF agent here wants to see the barn. Give him a tour and then escort him to the gate."

"Yes, sir."

He opened the large barn doors. The space had completely transformed since last night. Huge straw bales created a wall around the shelves of boxes of weapons Penny had seen last night. Two rusty red tractors were in the back, and a couple stalls held horses. The skid loader was nowhere to be seen, but she'd give her last dollar to bet that they'd used it to quickly move the huge bales and hide all the illegal guns and ammo.

There was nothing she could do about it without revealing that she'd been there. Penny seethed. Tray made a point of letting them see everything, even the hay loft above. They climbed down.

"I'll take you to the gate now."

Penny went over to the wall of straw bales. She wanted to punch it, tear it all down and show Jude what they were hiding. She gave the bale a small kick. Of course it didn't budge, but something black glinted in the sunlight streaming in from the open door.

"What's this?" she asked as she bent down and picked it up.

Jude looked at what rested in her palm. "That looks like a Glock clip."

Tray shrugged. "Looks like tractor parts to me."

"Do you know where this came from?" Jude asked.

"Never seen it before."

Obviously they would get nowhere now. But this might be the evidence Jude needed for a full-blown raid. Better not tip their hand yet.

They left and went back to the conference room at city hall, where the rest of the task force was already assembled, since Penny had texted them as soon as she and Jude left the compound.

"We got them." Penny set the small clip on the table.

"You found a Glock clip?" Olivia asked.

"It looks exactly like the one we found in her car. That means there's a good chance Emma Kemper is tied to this militia, which means they are part of our investigation with the explosives and fires."

"Glad someone made some progress. We wasted a night at the Riviera Club trying to track down a dead man," Bryce said.

The Riviera Club? How did Bryce wind up there? Not that Penny had a right to even care, but the thought of him at a dance club, surrounded by music and probably beautiful women, dancing the night away, left a horrible taste in her mouth. She forced herself to relax her jaw, not even aware of when she'd clenched it.

"Who's 'we?' And what dead man?" she asked.

"I was with Izan Collins last night. His ex said there's rumors that Sosa's back from the dead. We went to see what all the fuss was about and wound up empty-handed."

"Not exactly empty-handed," Olivia said.

Penny's back snapped rigid. What did that mean?

"Huh?" Bryce looked confused. Or was that guilt?

Not that it should even matter to her. They had no understanding. He could do whatever he wanted. If he went home with another woman on his arm . . . It. Didn't. Matter.

"You said you took some video footage when you thought you saw someone that *looked* like Sosa, didn't you?" Olivia asked him.

Video footage? That's what he'd had with him when he left? Tension in Penny's middle melted away.

She really shouldn't be so relieved by that. What was wrong with her?

"Yeah, but I don't think it was anything. Besides, the lights were getting to me. I was probably just seeing things. Dead end."

"Let me see the video." She wasn't likely to forget Diego Ruiz Sosa after all they'd gone through to find him.

Bryce sent it to Penny. With such a big file, it would take a while to download.

"Don't start it without me, but I'm going to run and grab a drink," Olivia said as she stood. "I'll be right back."

Jude, Allen, and Anthony all gathered on one side of the table and chatted baseball. Bryce scooted his office chair closer to her. She tried not to make it too obvious that she breathed a little deeper, wanting more of his ocean-inspired aroma. His gaze drew her in with its equally enticing spark.

"Hey, are you doing okay?" he asked.

"Of course. Why do you ask?" She broke eye contact, watching the bar on her phone showing the progress of the download.

"You look a little . . . tired. Or maybe you're still sore from everything that happened?"

He always saw too much. "I'm fine. Still on a regimen of drugstore pain meds. But I was up all night doing surveillance."

"Alone?" A muscle in his jaw twitched.

"I'm a big girl, Bryce."

"Believe me, I know. But you've also been thrown in a closet, left to die, and almost mowed down with automatic weapons. A little concern isn't completely unheard of."

But Bryce Crawford didn't do anything in "little." He cared. Deeply. It was there in his gaze—steady, intense. In the energy and warmth always radiating outward from him.

She swallowed hard, lifted her chin. "I'm good. No need to worry."

"But I do. Worry about you. Not because I think of you as incapable, but . . . uh . . ."

The wavering in his voice snagged her curiosity. Was he flushed? She stayed quiet.

"I was . . . wondering if maybe we could spend some time together."

Her heart swelled with warmth.

Stupid, stupid heart. Hadn't it learned? She checked her phone again. Still over twenty-five percent to go. "We are. Spending time, I mean. Right now, for instance." She sent him a brief smile.

"Yeah, but—" He grabbed the back of his neck. "I know you said we've both moved on. But we've both changed in the last year or so. And I'd like to get to know you more. Or again. Or . . . something."

"So you want to spend time together doing that?"

"Exactly." He picked at a crumb on the table, then looked up at her, the tenderness in his eyes unmistakable. "So what do you say?"

"Sure." Wait. What did she just agree to? Spending *more* time with him?

"Yeah?"

Hope lit up his whole face. There was no way she could back out now. Not when he looked at her like that. Like she was the one he wanted to be with. Like he would do whatever it took just to be with her.

Oh, she was in so much trouble.

But maybe he was right. Maybe they'd both changed enough that this wouldn't be so bad. Maybe she'd learned enough to not completely lose herself this time.

Before she could say more, Olivia walked in. "I'm ready. Thanks for waiting."

Right. The video. It had finished downloading. Penny cast it to the television in the room. The grainy images of people dancing played. The flickering lights made it hard to focus, but suddenly a familiar face filled the screen. Penny gasped.

"What? Is it him?" Olivia asked.

"No, but I recognize someone else." Penny studied the screen. Finally.

"Who?" Bryce leaned over to look at her phone.

"Her!" She paused the video. "That's Emma."

"The girl who came on to me is your Emma Kemper?" Bryce sat straighter in his chair.

She came on to Bryce? But she'd seemed pretty attached to her boyfr—

A sense of dread filled Penny. That little minx. "She was distracting you."

Bryce balked. "Distracting me from what? The horrible music and lighting?"

Oh, she really shouldn't be so relieved to know that Bryce hadn't enjoyed clubbing last night. But a weird sense of victory surged through her.

"The man you thought looked like Sosa. What happened to him once she approached you?"

"I . . . don't know. I didn't see him after that." Bryce shrugged.

It made sense. Bryce would stick out in a place like that, studying a crowd, searching for someone in particular. Not that women didn't throw themselves at him all the time everywhere he went, but Emma was good at acting. She was on the run. She'd be on the lookout for suspicious people trying to track her down. Or her boyfriend. Because something inside Penny told her that this Sosa lookalike was the man that had ordered her to be burned in the warehouse.

"I think we need to go clubbing tonight."

SIXTEEN

BRYCE WAS A GROWN MAN. HE SHOULDN'T SULK. But seriously.

"Isn't this fun?" Penny sipped on a huge convenience-store fountain drink as she stepped into the back of the barbecue-food truck/stakeout vehicle. She threw a bag of sunflower seeds to Anthony and a package of beef jerky to Jude in the front seat.

"This isn't exactly what I had in mind when I said I wanted to spend some more time with you," Bryce grumbled under his breath as she dropped the bag of chips he'd requested into his lap.

Crammed into a van with little air flow and five other adults was not what he wanted at all. What he wanted was a chance to show Penny that he'd changed. A chance to see if they could be together again.

Because his mother was right. He didn't belong with a sweet, quiet girl like Sarai. He belonged with Penny.

And chasing after Sosa? He was dead. There was no question about that.

Still, Penny set down her pop to help Olivia Tazwell strategically place her necklace with the hidden camera between her collar bones. Bryce averted his eyes from the tight dress she wore. In that outfit, even being blonde, Olivia would fit in with the crowd all right. And he wasn't sad that she was the one going in undercover rather than Penny.

Penny would stick out no matter what she wore. Any hot-blooded guy in the place would be all over her. But, oh darn. Emma knew what she looked like and so did her boyfriend. So Olivia was up. Izan wasn't so pleased. Not that he could do anything about it. Until the man got the guts to ask the girl out, he was in the friend zone. But Jude had let him ride along tonight since he knew the place and might recognize some of the players from Maria's old group.

"You sure you don't want me to come in with you?" Izan asked Olivia.

"He does have some pretty sweet moves," Bryce said. One less person in the van meant more breathable air. And more of Penny's attention.

"If Emma remembers Izan was with you, it might scare her off to see him again. We can't risk it." Penny stared Bryce and Izan down. "She's a cop. She'll be fine."

"I still say it would be smart to have some backup." There was no sign of his famous dimple or usual good humor as Izan spoke.

"I'll go." Tony stood.

Olivia and Penny studied Tony as he took off his jacket, as if assessing if his wardrobe was club-worthy.

"Uh, no. That's not what I meant." Izan stepped in front of Anthony so he was face-to-face with Olivia. "I'll go in separately, a few minutes after you, so Emma won't think we're together. I'll stay close to the bar and that side of the dance floor and watch your back."

Jude spoke up from the front seat. "Neither Izan nor Bryce are law enforcement. You have no weapons, no training in apprehending someone. It's not that we don't trust you guys, but we have to do this by the book. You two need to stay here."

Izan and Bryce looked at each other.

"Then, Tony, you're up. You go in first, find a spot, and we'll send Olivia in about ten minutes." Penny took his jacket from him.

"Sure thing." He grinned at her before he hopped out of the truck and headed across the street to the club entrance.

"Sorry, man. I tried," Bryce whispered to Izan as soon as everyone went back to their tasks. He could commiserate with his friend. Sitting around waiting for something to happen was not his forte.

"Okay, I'm ready. Are you getting the camera feed?" Olivia asked.

Jude came to the back area. He and Penny studied the three screens hanging on the side. Penny turned to Olivia and made some adjustments to the necklace. "Everything looks good. Give Tony a few more minutes to get situated and you're on."

Olivia stepped out of the truck, checked her mic, and was gone. Bryce glanced over to Izan. His leg bounced to a fast rhythm. The man had it bad.

"All right, let's keep our eyes peeled for Emma and her mysterious boyfriend." Penny stuck a long stick of red licorice in her mouth as she studied the screens. Bryce's focus stuck on her lips. Clearly Izan wasn't the only one pining.

Once Olivia made it into the club, everything went silent as four pairs of eyes scanned the monitors for their targets.

An hour into the stakeout, Bryce's bag of chips was long gone and his attention fading. "How long are we going to stay here? There hasn't been a hint of Emma or the Sosa lookalike." He sat between Jude and Izan on stools while Penny stood behind them all, leaning on the opposite counter.

"These things take time. Patience." Jude's eyes didn't leave the screen as he spoke. Steady and stable as ever, which was great for a man married to his little sister. But for himself, give him something tangible to do or he was going to go nuts.

"I think I'll step out and get some air." Bryce started to rise.

Penny pushed him back down. "You promised if we let you come, you'd stay in the truck. We can't risk you being seen."

Was it just him or did her hands linger a little longer than necessary on his shoulders? Either way, her touch trickled deep down inside him and ignited longing. Longing for something true. Something deep and lasting. Most of the time he could ignore it, but since Penny had come back to town it was getting harder and harder to push aside. So why fight it? His mother thought they were good together. Logan saw it too.

If only he didn't have an audience, he'd ask her if she'd be willing to give him another chance. But no—

"There! Olivia, turn toward that southwest corner." Penny spoke into the mic.

The camera angle slowly turned. Jude pointed to the screen. "That's Emma."

Bryce froze. "And that's Sosa." The man guiding Emma into a dark booth looked very much like Diego Ruiz Sosa. The man who had tried to kill his family. The man responsible for throwing Penny in that closet, expecting her to die in the fire. Bryce squeezed the empty chip bag and twisted it. If he got close enough, it would be more than a foil bag he would wrench. "Who is he?"

"He can't be Diego. This guy is too young. Really young. He's gotta be related though. Look at his nose. It's longer. He's taller . . . but there must be a DNA connection." Penny's finger traced the different features on the screen.

"That's not a point in his favor. If anything, that makes him more guilty." Bryce was ready to pounce.

"What do we do now?" Izan asked.

"Olivia, see if you can get closer, strike up a conversation. If I hear his voice, I'll know for sure if that's who Emma met with in the warehouse. Once we confirm, we'll move in and arrest them."

"You mean Olivia and Tony will arrest them." Jude looked at her.

"Yeah, yeah. You know what I mean."

The camera view moved. Olivia wound her way through the dancers and approached the table.

"Oh my goodness. Sebastian!" Olivia's voice was higher than normal. "I can't believe you're here. It's been so long!"

The Sosa twin frowned. "I'm not Sebastian." He turned away and continued talking to Emma.

"That's him!" Penny hit the counter. "Move in!"

Jude stood. "I'll go back up Olivia and Tony." He hopped out of the truck.

Bryce stood too, ready to follow, but once again Penny pushed him down. She pointed at the monitor. "You stay and watch. I need eyes until I get there."

"You two need to come with me." Olivia's voice came through the speaker.

But it was Emma's face on the screen. The same woman as last night but no seductive smiles and lingering stares. Her glare could draw blood. "This isn't Sebastian. You have the wrong person."

"No, she has the right people all right. And you two need to come with us right now." Anthony must've come up behind Olivia. The screen showed his hand holding out his badge.

Bryce couldn't quite tell what happened next. Everything on the screen went blurry. Screams sounded.

"What's going on?" Izan asked.

"She's *not* getting away." Penny lunged for the door of the truck. She jumped down to the street, Bryce right on her heels.

She spun and stopped his forward motion with a palm to his chest. "Stay. Here."

"No way! I'm coming with you."

"Bryce, I know you want to help, but you have to stay. You don't even have a weapon. Please."

He was just supposed to sit here and do nothing? Let her take all the risk?

"I don't work that way."

"Today you do. We had a deal. You were here to watch."

She turned and ran across the street. "You better stay put, Crawford!" she yelled without even looking back.

Once again, the woman he loved ran off, leaving him behind.

He could honestly say watching it happen was way worse.

SEVENTEEN

PENNY COULDN'T LET HER GET AWAY AGAIN, even if it meant she alienated Bryce forever. Emma Kemper and her boyfriend—whoever he was—would be spending the night behind bars. Penny shoved open the club doors, ignored the yells from someone at the door. She ran onto the dance floor and pushed aside anyone who got in her way. The strobe lights made it look like she was moving in slow motion as she searched the crowd for her target.

Where were they?

"He's getting away! Anyone see him?" Tony's voice called over the radio.

Jude caught her eye across a crowd of dancers. He lifted his hands as if to ask *Where did they go?*

She shook her head. She scanned the group in the southwest corner where Emma had been.

"Could use some help here! Jude! Penny! Where are you?" Tony's voice crackled through the speaker.

"We're on our way," Penny radioed back.

Seriously. Where could they have gone? There were too many people blocking the way. There. Penny finally cut through the crowd enough to see.

Olivia must've been knocked down, because she was lying on the ground with Emma sitting on top of her with a fistful of hair in one hand and the other poised to punch. Tony stood over them both, trying to yank Emma off. Dancers didn't even seem to care, though a few crowded around the spectacle cheering or laughing.

"Where's Sosa?" Penny didn't even know who was listening. She and Jude reached Olivia at the same time. Jude helped Tony contain Emma, who continued to thrash and scream.

"Get off me!"

Penny set down her radio and helped Olivia up. "Are you okay?"

She grunted. "She caught me by surprise, shoved me so hard I lost my balance and fell backward. Stupid high heels. I knocked Anthony over. The next thing I knew, Sosa was gone." She sounded mad. Probably mad at herself more than anything.

"We have to find him." Penny ground her molars together as she studied the darkest edges of the room. No Sosa. Jude and Tony had Emma secured. Finally.

"We need to move her." Tony cinched the cuffs around Emma's wrists while Jude held her. They had their hands full. She wasn't going anywhere willingly.

"Use your mic," Penny told Olivia. "See if Izan and Bryce saw anything on the monitors."

Olivia did as she asked. Paused. "Izan says they can't see anything but black screens right now. She must've broken the camera."

"Does he know the layout?"

Olivia relayed the question and waited. "He said there's a back exit by the restrooms. He didn't see Sosa out front."

"We split up. I'll go this way to the back exit. You take the front."

With a quick nod, Olivia was off. Penny studied the crowd as she quickly moved back toward the bar and the restrooms. The long dark hallway had a few women leaning against the wall, waiting in line.

"Have you seen a man come through here?" Penny asked the group.

"Honey, all the guys are out there on the dance floor. Nice try but you're not cutting in this line." A woman in a blue dress rolled her eyes and went back to picking at her nails.

Penny ran past the line and shoved open the men's restroom. Empty. Figured. She ignored the gasps and comments from the ladies as she turned the corner to a back storage area. The exit. She reached for the crash bar when her training kicked in.

Where had she put her radio? Sosa could be waiting outside to take out anyone who walked through this door. It's what she would do. She needed backup.

For the first time in a long time she could admit it might be nice to have someone watching her back. Maybe not do this alone. But she was losing time. He could be getting away. Still, better to be alive than stupid. She called Jude. As soon as he answered, she spoke over him. "Anyone have eyes on the boyfriend?"

"Negative."

"Where are you?"

"Inside still. Emma is putting up quite the scene. Screaming for an ambulance. Where are you?"

"Back exit."

"Don't go out there alone. I'll be there in twenty seconds." He ended the call.

It had to be the longest twenty seconds ever, but eventually Jude ran toward her, gun out and pointed low. Why did she wish it were Bryce instead?

She shook herself. *Buck up, Pen.* Pulled her own weapon out of the holster hidden under her jacket.

"On the count of three?" she asked him. They'd practiced this numerous times. She went low and to the right. He would sweep to the left.

At his quick nod, she counted. "One, two, three!"

She pushed the door open and swung to the right. A rush of air as Jude brushed past her. The back parking lot was still. Quiet. A handful of parked cars and a couple of streetlights were the only things in sight.

"I'll go around this way to the front," Jude said. Penny turned in the opposite direction.

Someone off to the side of the building yelled. She knew that voice. Bryce.

What was he doing? He was supposed to stay in the—

Gunshots rang out. Penny's heart lurched. The sound of an engine revving barely registered as she sprinted to the side of the building. All she could picture was Bryce Crawford sprawled on the dirty ground with a bullet in his chest.

Why hadn't he stayed like she'd asked?

Maybe he was still in the truck. Maybe it was her own imagination that heard him.

Please be in the truck.

Her own chest squeezed even tighter. She swiped at her wet cheek. Could barely see. She rounded the corner and skidded to a stop.

Bryce was on the ground, not moving.

EIGHTEEN

NOTHING ABOUT THIS NIGHT WAS GOING THE way he wanted it to. Bryce lifted his head. He'd been so close! But of course the Sosa-like guy'd had a fully loaded gun and a motorcycle stashed behind the trash bins. Bryce'd had to dive to the ground for cover as the stranger sped away in the dark.

He should've been faster. Now he was out there again.

Bryce stood up and brushed the gravel and dirt off his jeans. Who knew what—

"Bryce Crawford, if you're not dead right now I'm gonna kill you myself."

He turned to see Penny stomping toward him. She marched from the corner of the building, the wind blowing her long blonde hair off her face, her eyes snapping and full of fire as she headed right for him, heightened color in her cheeks.

Man, she was gorgeous when she was angry.

Well, she was gorgeous any time, but to see her rushing toward him all fury and storm was enough to take his breath away. This was why he couldn't find a second date. Because no other woman could compare to this. Her energy. Her drive. She was incredible. And once he'd had a taste, no one else was even close. He was stupid to even try. As she drew closer, she pulled back a fist, probably ready to drive it into him.

And that was about the best thing he could ever see.

She wouldn't be this mad if she didn't care.

But before she could let it fly, Bryce stepped forward and wrapped an arm around her waist, because now that he knew exactly what he wanted, he wasn't going to waste any more time.

She *cared*.

A moment of confusion flashed across her face before he crushed her to himself and kissed her.

For a quick second, she fought it, her mouth rigid, arms stiff.

Maybe this wasn't such a good idea. But then . . . she melted into him. The hands that had pushed against his chest a moment ago slid up around his shoulders and tangled themselves in his hair. The lips that at first had been hard and unyielding softened against his own and then took over.

And he let her.

How could he not? He was completely at her mercy. He'd go anywhere for this woman. She led him deeper, pulled him in tighter, and the kiss took on a life of its own. It grew hungry, desperate, like she couldn't get enough. Or maybe that was him. It was hard to tell where he left off and she began.

Then just as suddenly as it started, it stopped. She stepped back gasping, cold night air rushing in between them.

"Why did you do that?" Her whispered words carried a mixture of question, wonder, and maybe a little bit of disbelief. Her eyes narrowed, her hand flying to her mouth almost as if to cover up what had just happened.

He chuckled. "Seemed like a good idea."

"A good idea?"

He lifted a shoulder. "Seemed like you agreed."

Her jaw dropped.

Yup. He'd rattled her. And he couldn't help but grin. Because that meant she felt it too. She'd tried to push him away, pretend that there was nothing there between them, but he had proof now. She'd kissed him back.

And then some.

But before he could tease her about it, she slapped him across the cheek. Hard. Pain shot through the side of his head.

"Wow. I did not see that coming." He worked his jaw to loosen the sting still there.

"Well, you should've. I told you to stay in the van." Her voice went low, lethal.

"Better watch it, Slugger. The angrier you get, the prettier you are."

"Argh! You're impossible. You could've *died*!"

"So you're worried about me, is that it?" He quirked an eyebrow.

"This isn't funny, Bryce. You were supposed to stay in the truck. You don't have a gun. You—"

"I couldn't watch and do nothing." Didn't she realize that?

"It wasn't your job to go after him."

"What was I supposed to do? I saw him." He pointed toward the street. "He was getting away. And I don't know who he is, but if there is *any* connection to Diego Sosa, I'm sure as heck not going to stand by and let him run off. Not after what he did to my family."

Not that it had done a lot of good.

Penny backed away from him. "You're too impulsive. You're gonna get yourself hurt one day."

"At least I'm doing something."

"What is that supposed to mean?"

"It means I'm not gonna pretend anymore." He moved closer to her. He wasn't going to let her run again.

She swallowed. "I'm not pretending anything."

"You're pretending right now. Pretending I don't matter to you, that you don't care. But you can't fool me, Penny. There's something here between us. Something good. Something real."

The quick catch of her breath said he was onto something.

Of course, that's when Anthony, Izan, and Olivia rounded the corner.

"Did you see him?" Olivia asked. She panted like she'd been running. "He wasn't out front."

"He was here. I almost had him, but he had a gun and a motorcycle stashed. I took cover when he shot, and he got away." Bryce nodded toward the narrow alley between the neighboring buildings.

Penny released a long breath, hands planted on her hips. "You guys got Emma?"

"Jude met us out front and is taking her in right now. He told us to find you. Said we could meet him at the station and do the interrogation there," Anthony said. He glared at Bryce. Like it was his fault that the gunman had gotten away. But where had Anthony been all this time? He was the one that let the man slip by him in the first place.

The ride in the back of the food truck was quiet and tense. Penny wouldn't look at Bryce. She even let Tony drive.

That was fine. Bryce would simply bide his time. He may be impulsive like she said. But he also knew what he wanted, and he wasn't going to give up without a fight. She would see he could also be patient when it was called for.

Patient and persistent. Serious.

Mom was right. He and Penny were good together. He just had to figure out why she ran. Why, even now, she denied their connection and tried so hard to push him away.

Once they reached the police station, Tony brought them in through the back entrance.

"I'm going to change. Meet up with you in a sec." Olivia veered off from the group.

"What now?" Izan asked.

"You two should go home." Penny faced them.

Yeah, right. "What are you going to do?"

Anthony tilted his chin toward a short hall. "Jude is getting set up to interrogate Emma. There's nothing else you guys can do."

"Aw, come on. Why can't we sit in on it? We helped you guys find her." Bryce didn't know the last time he'd seen Izan so worked up.

"You're not cops. We can't have a watch party just for kicks." Anthony moved closer to Penny as if it were a showdown. If he touched her, there were going to be problems.

"She's not a cop either." Izan pointed to Penny. "No offense, Mitchell."

"I'm not a cop, but I'm working with them and hired by the ATF, who is paying the bill. I may not have authority to do anything, but she has valuable information we need for me to close this case. I have to figure out who her boyfriend is and what they're up to."

"Shouldn't being part of the city task force give us some clout here? This might affect my family." Bryce took a step closer.

"Sorry. I can't have you guys sit in on this. It's up to you if you wanna wait around, but I have a feeling it's going to be a long night. Might as well go home." Anthony escorted Penny away. He didn't seem too upset at leaving them out in the cold, either, and having Penny to himself.

"You know, I pictured tonight going a lot differently." Izan sighed and walked toward the direction of the lobby.

"You and me both." Bryce cracked his knuckles and followed. He might not be in on the interrogating, but he wasn't leaving this place until he had some answers.

NINETEEN

THIS WAS TURNING INTO A DISASTER. PENNY slipped into the room adjacent to where Jude was interrogating Emma.

"You all right?" Tony asked her.

"Of course."

His eyes narrowed, like he was studying her. "You know, Bryce Crawford might not be the guy I thought. At least, not with you. You said there was nothing between the two of you, but it sure feels like there is."

"We have a history. That's probably what you're seeing." She stared down at her boots, arms wrapped around herself to ward off the chill in the room.

"Penny, is he the one?"

Her head snapped up. At one point, she'd wondered. That night in the mountains, looking up at the stars. But then she woke up. Remembered the promise she made to herself to never give that much of her heart to anyone. One look at Ashlee Featherwood in Bryce's arms was all she needed to douse any romantic daydreams she had about settling down and happily ever afters. It wasn't only

that she'd thought he'd cheated. That had been bad enough. It was
the fact that she'd let herself go that far. Let herself *depend* on him.
She didn't say a word out loud. But Tony nodded slowly, gave
her a sad sort of smile. "I think you two need to talk." He moved
toward the door. "I've got to get some paperwork started. I'll be
back."

As soon as he left, she allowed herself the luxury of leaning
against the door for a moment.

But just a moment.

She closed her eyes and breathed deep, letting her shoulders
relax, shaking out her hands. She could do this. She could pull herself together. Finish this investigation and not let Bryce get to her.
She *had* to do this. It didn't matter that Bryce had kissed her.
That she'd kissed him back. It was only a momentary lapse of control.

A lapse like opening Pandora's box, but she could stuff it all
back to where it had been tucked nicely away and shove a lid on
it all again. She had to. Everything depended on it.

Ugh, why had she let him get to her like that?

She couldn't let her emotions get the best of her again. Letting
things get personal was what got her into trouble. She knew better.

Still, his voice haunted her.

*You're pretending right now. Pretending I don't matter to you,
that you don't care. But you can't fool me, Penny. There's something
here between us. Something good. Something real.*

How could he understand? She wasn't pretending. She was
protecting.

Obviously, they had chemistry. That was never the issue. But
when it came down to it, she could only rely on herself. Fathers
who were supposed to protect fell apart when their wives died. Big
sisters were busy with their own lives. Bosses that were supposed
to look out for their employees couldn't be counted on either. She
couldn't lose herself again. Depend on him so much that it ached

when she wasn't with him. An acute ache. A soul-deep ache that would overtake her. Weaken her. People got hurt that way.

She got hurt that way. What fool would put herself in that vulnerable position again?

Bryce was more persistent than most, she'd give him that. And working with him wasn't so bad. If she kept the personal stuff out of it. So that's what she would do. Work with Bryce. Close this case. Keep it clean.

Sure, maybe life on the road was getting old. If she could handle working with Bryce without falling for him, maybe she could look at staying around Last Chance more. Seeing her niece and nephew more. Jude's offer to stay did spark something in her. She didn't want to go back to being a fed again, but she liked it here. She could have enough work and use this as her home base.

But she couldn't let Bryce kiss her like that again. He had to have better offers out there. Someone content to keep house for him and—

Jude's voice interrupted her thoughts.

"Please state your name."

Emma, in her tight club attire and curly hair that had earlier been neatly pulled back but was now a mess from her little cat fight, answered back with an expletive.

Penny moved to the one-way glass and watched. Jude didn't react. She should be more like that. Calm, cool, and collected.

He set a bottle of water in front of Emma. She glared at him.

"Emma Renee Kemper. Born in Maricopa County, Arizona. Your brother is Vince Kemper, currently in federal custody."

"You're a bunch of pigs."

Jude continued reading off his tablet that was also recording the conversation, acting like he hadn't heard the insult at all.

"Your mother, Priscilla Kemper, died when you were ten. No known father. So you and Vince were moved into the foster care system." Jude looked up at this point. "That had to be difficult."

"What do you care?"

"Believe it or not, I do care. You're already an accessory to attempted murder and arson and a number of other charges. You're already going to prison. But we can work together and see about reducing your sentence."

"If I rat on Alonzo or my brother? Is that what you want? Lemme save you the trouble. I'm not a rodent."

Alonzo. Must be the boyfriend's name.

"You think you're being loyal to them by not saying anything? You're going to take the fall for Alonzo?"

She leaned in and sneered. "He'd do the same for me."

"You think he loves you?" Jude tilted his head, his face still void of expression.

"I know he does." She fell back against her chair, a confident smirk on her face.

"He has a funny way of showing it. Leaving you to face all the consequences? Scurrying away in the night?"

That's right, Jude. Keep poking.

"I'm not stupid." Emma sat straight again.

"Never said you were."

"Then don't sit there judging me like I am. Or like I don't know what you're doing. You want to drive me away from Alonzo, pit me against him so I'll turn. But it won't work. True love means sacrificing for the other, and that's what I did. I made sure he could get away." Her hands fisted. "That was always the plan if it came down to it."

"What other plans did you have with Alonzo?" Jude's eyebrows narrowed slightly.

Emma's mouth snapped shut.

"Come now. You obviously have an endgame here. Why are you in Last Chance County?"

She ignored him and took a drink of water.

"Where did you get the Glock clips?"

Nothing.

"We know you're working with the militia." Obviously they didn't *know*, but this was one of Jude's techniques. Trying to get a reaction out of her again.

A sliver of a smile slid up her face, but she didn't say anything. Emma sat back, let her gaze scan the room, and avoided making eye contact with Jude.

"It's only a matter of time before we figure this out. Why are you targeting the gangs?"

Emma picked up her water bottle and began to peel off the label. Great. They were getting nowhere.

Jude fired off a few more questions, but she'd shut down. Eventually he stood up. "Seems like you might need a little time to think things over. I'll be back later. In the meantime, I hope you'll consider my offer. Helping us will help you."

"Yeah, right," Emma muttered under her breath as he left the room.

Penny met him in the hall. "Is that it? That's all you've got? We need answers from her."

"You saw her. She was done. But we did get something. A name. I figure we look into Alonzo, and I'll come back with more ammunition. It's more likely she'll cooperate then."

"Fine." She spat the word out between clamped teeth.

"What's wrong with you?"

"Nothing. It's just my career on the line here." She huffed, hoping to throw him off the scent.

"There's something else. Something . . . more." His brows furrowed together as he studied her. "What did Bryce do?"

Penny sputtered. "What do you mean? Nothing! He did nothing. Nothing is wrong."

"Huh. You're usually much better at lying." He turned and walked down the hall to the open office area.

She ran to catch up to him. "Why do you think I'm lying?"

"It doesn't matter. Ah, Anthony. Can we use your desk and computer?" Jude asked the officer. Anthony and Olivia were chatting with their sergeant.

"Sure." Tony led them to his desk. It was neat and organized. If Bryce worked here, he'd probably have piles of paper and leftover food on his. And most likely pictures of his family, his team. He took those things seriously. Anthony had nothing personal.

Jude handed Penny his tablet. "You and Olivia look on this. Anthony, we got a name for Emma's boyfriend. Alonzo. We need a last name and as much information as we can find on him."

"You got it." Tony sat down and started typing.

"What about you?" Penny asked.

"I'm calling the office in California. If there's a Sosa connection, I want to know how we missed it." Jude took out his phone and left the room.

"Might as well get comfortable, Mitchell." Tony grinned and pulled an office chair from the empty desk next to his for her.

After the better part of an hour, they still had nothing. Penny was ready to put the tablet down and pry some answers out of Emma.

"Found it!" Jude rushed back into the bullpen. He picked up the tablet and typed something into it. "This is him." He flipped it back around to show them.

"That's him all right." Penny glared at the picture. Same brown eyes, dark hair, dark skin. She read the name underneath. "Alonzo Jones? No way is that guy a Jones."

"His mother is Lupe Reyes, Diego Sosa's half sister."

"So this is Diego's nephew? And how did we not know he had a nephew?" Olivia asked.

"Lupe grew up with a different father, here in the US. But going back, now we can trace travels to the same area Diego grew up in. They were family. We just didn't know. And it looks like Lupe was only sixteen when Alonzo was born. He lived with the Jones family in California as a child. Recently changed his last name this year to . . ."

"Sosa." Penny folded her arms. "So what is he doing here?"

"That's what we need to find out. But since this is where his uncle died, I can't imagine it's anything good." Jude's brow wrinkled. "He's been in Colorado for the last five years. No record. No issues."

"So are they working with that militia or the gangs?" Tony asked.

"Good question." Olivia Tazwell perched on the edge of Tony's desk.

"Whatever it is, we need to get to the bottom of it." Penny stood. "Ready to go back to interrogation, Brooks?"

"Let's give it another shot."

"This time I'm coming in with you." Penny wanted to look this girl in the eye.

"Leave the talking to me and we have a deal."

"We'll watch from the side room." Olivia pointed at herself and Anthony.

Emma lifted her head off the table as they walked in, but didn't say anything.

"Anything else I can get for you, Miss Kemper?" Jude asked her.

"What is she doing here?" Emma's surprise quickly morphed into a glare aimed at Penny.

"Yup. I'm still alive. Your brother's bomb didn't kill me." Penny sat across from her. Jude took the seat next to Penny.

"So, where did you and Alonzo meet?" Jude asked.

Emma gave them a mean stare and nothing else.

"Looks like he didn't have it easy growing up either. Single teen mother. Raised by another family. The Joneses."

The girl went still.

Jude continued. "Did you bond over that? Difficult childhoods and everything?"

"What would you know?"

Ah. Hit a nerve. Now they were getting somewhere.

" You two obviously have a deep connection. But what you might not realize here is that this isn't going to end well for Alonzo, whether his last name is Jones or Sosa. You would be helping him out by preventing more charges."

"You have no idea what he's capable of."

Jude shrugged. "We already know where he is. Already pieced a lot of the plan together. I'm only giving you a chance to help yourself here."

"Oh, you know the plan?" Emma gave them a look of mock surprise.

"We know enough."

Emma laughed. "You don't know squat. Because if you did, *neither* of you would be here right now."

Jude looked to Penny. "I think we're done." They stood up to leave.

"Darn right we're done." Emma shook her hands in the handcuffs. "Better run home now. Keep your new family close, Agent Brooks."

Her words chilled Penny to the core. Emma knew Jude was recently married.

Which meant that Sosa had Bryce Crawford and his family in his sights.

TWENTY

THE LOBBY OF THE POLICE STATION MUST'VE been designed to be as uncomfortable as possible. The hard bench pressed into Bryce's back while he lay on it. He tossed a nerf football up in the air and caught it again. Background chatter from the other police officers working buzzed in the background. Izan had left earlier, but Bryce wasn't going anywhere until he talked with Penny. He had to show her that he wasn't a playboy. He wasn't a cheater. He was serious. Plus he needed to know what they figured out about the Sosa guy from his girlfriend.

But this was taking forever.

A rush of footsteps made Bryce drop the ball and sit up. What was all the commotion? Anthony, Olivia, Jude, and Penny rushed from the back hall. Jude was on the phone.

Bryce stood. "What's going?"

Penny did a double take and stopped. "You're still here?"

"I told you I—"

"That doesn't matter now. Your family." She grabbed him by the arm and dragged him to the door.

"What about my family?"

"You have your keys?" she asked him.

"Yeah, but—"

"You drive. I'll explain." They all ran out into the night air. "I'll ride with Bryce. Meet you there," Penny yelled to the other three as they split up. Other police officers ran for their vehicles.

This wasn't good. And it had something to do with his family. Bryce sprinted to his truck. Penny hopped into the passenger seat, and he took off. "What happened?"

"Sosa is back."

Bryce squeezed the steering wheel tighter. "That guy is really a Sosa?"

"The man that got away tonight is Diego Sosa's nephew. Alonzo. We weren't able to get a whole lot of information from Emma, but we at least got that much."

"Is he back for revenge?"

"It would make sense that he'd target you guys, since Jude shot Diego."

"That was two years ago. Why now? And is Izan okay?" Bryce's mother had hidden the identity of the child Diego had thought was his heir. Turned out Izan was that child, but Diego wasn't his father. His father was Diego's accountant, who'd run away with Diego's girlfriend and, over the years, siphoned off a few million dollars.

"We don't know exactly. But when we were interrogating Emma, she told Jude to keep his new family close. How else would she know anything about his new family, *your* family, unless they've been studying up on what happened back then?"

At the sound of the threat, Bryce pressed the gas pedal even harder. He swerved around a sedan and SUV. "If that man even thinks about hurting my fam—"

Penny's warm hand cupped his shoulder and squeezed. "He won't. We're almost there."

"He had a head start!" Bryce pounded the steering wheel. "He left the club hours ago. Who knows what he's been doing ever since, and I've been lounging around like—"

"This isn't your fault, Bryce. Emma could've been taunting us just to rile us up. We don't know for sure but wanted to take extra precautions. We'll bring your parents somewhere safe."

"And Andi?"

"Jude was talking to her on the phone. She's at your parents' house already."

That was a small relief. The police cars behind them all had their sirens and lights on. Bryce ran a red light, hoping with the sirens right behind him, traffic would be stopped. Finally he turned onto the road his parents lived on. Just a few more blocks.

The outdoor lights were on, the living room window lit. His tires squealed as he yanked the wheel and skidded into the driveway. He didn't even have the truck in Park before Penny was out the door running. He threw the gear shift into Park and leaped out after her. The other police cars pulled up.

"Mom! Dad!" His pulse roared in his head too fast and too loud. He strained to hear his mom's voice. "Andi!"

Penny had her gun out and was at the front door, pounding. The door opened. "Everything's fine. We're okay." It was Andi.

Bryce grabbed his little sister and wrapped her in a tight bear hug. "You're all right?"

"Yes, we're fine. Jude called. I got Mom and Dad hiding back in their bathroom like he said."

Oh, thank God.

Bryce dropped a light kiss on her head. "Good job, sis."

Other police cars and Jude's SUV filled in the driveway and street.

"Andi?"

At the sound of Jude's voice, Bryce released his sister. She ran to her husband and kissed him in the middle of the front lawn. Bryce looked away. Penny stood by the door, waiting for him. Now that he knew his family was safe, he wanted his own moment. With her. But there were more important things first, so it would have to wait.

He walked inside the house with Penny. "I should go tell Mom and Dad it's okay to come out now."

"I'll come with you. We're going to have to get them somewhere safe for a few days. The cops will need to clear the house. It will be less upsetting for your dad if he's not here."

"I've got a friend with a cabin a couple hours away. Mom can take Dad there."

"What about you? Maybe you should go too." Penny paused in the hallway outside the bedroom.

"I'm not running away from this guy."

She laid a hand on his chest. "Bryce, he's dangerous. Look at what he's already—"

"I'm not going anywhere, Penny." He covered her hand with his own. "You know me better than that."

She rolled her eyes a little and chuckled. "Yeah, I do. You're too stubborn for your own good, you know."

"You were worried about me earlier, huh? Back at the club."

"I thought you'd been shot. Of course I was worried." She started to tug her hand away, but he held it fast.

"You *care* about me."

"It's my job to care. To protect."

"That kiss said it was more. Why are you denying it?"

"Bryce, I can't do this right now."

"Then when? Because I mean it. I'm not going anywhere. I want to be with you. Let's see what we can be together."

He could see all the emotions flashing across her face. She opened her mouth to speak, but nothing came out.

"Give me a chance. Please." If it was wrong for a grown man to beg, so be it.

She looked at him with a soft smile. "I can't promise anything. But let's finish this investigation and talk, okay?"

Now that was progress. "Deal!" He kissed her cheek and then opened the door to his parents' room. "Mom? Dad? It's okay now. You can come out."

His mother peeked out of the en suite bathroom. "Bryce?" He swept his mom up in a big hug, grateful she was perfectly well. "Do we get to know what's going on now?"

"It's a bit of a long story, and I'll tell it to you while you pack. You and Dad need to get out of town for a while."

Within the hour, Bryce's parents were on the road with a police escort and his dad's nurse en route to meet them. Andi refused to leave Jude, but they would stick together until Sosa was found.

With the adrenaline fading, Bryce was ready to leave all the commotion. Cops were still crawling all over the house, poking into every nook and cranny. Penny was talking with Olivia off to the side of the living room. She twisted her body to one side then the other, probably trying to loosen her back. Those tight lines around her eyes meant she was tired, most likely in pain. He should get her home.

He walked over to the women. "Doesn't look like there's much more we can do here, Pen. How about I give you a ride to your sister's house?"

"That would be nice." She waved to Olivia. "I'll talk to you tomorrow."

They walked out into the crisp night air, crickets and cicadas chirping. He held the door for her as she plopped onto his truck's passenger seat. "I'm beat."

"Let's get you somewhere you can rest." He closed her door and walked to the driver's side. He breathed deep, glad to finally do something for Penny, show her that he was more than just a good time. That he could help take care of her and she didn't have to do everything alone. That he was a different man now.

Maybe she would come to see that God wasn't so far off. That He cared about her too. Wanted her.

They drove in a comfortable silence, country music playing from the radio in the background until they were out of his old neighborhood. This was nice, but he wanted more. He wanted this every night, going home together knowing he wouldn't have to say goodbye. Not that he would say that out loud and scare her off. But something inside settled. He knew what he wanted now. He just needed to figure out how to make this happen.

Help her to see You, Lord. And help her to see that we're better together.

She leaned her head back and sighed. "This has been quite the day."

"You're telling me."

"I still can't believe we didn't know about this nephew. I need to figure out where he crossed paths with Emma Kemper. Maybe then I'll figure out what his plan is."

"Let's go over it all. What do we know so far?" Bryce turned down the radio.

"Emma arrives in Last Chance with Glock clips and a bomb— maybe more than one bomb—her brother made."

"They blow up the warehouse, which we believe was a location the Puerto Rican gang was using."

She turned to face him. "Right. Then there was the drive-by. We never did find out who was responsible."

"And there was the fire and shooting at the Honduran restaurant."

"Which we think would be the Puerto Ricans getting payback, but where did they get the automatic weapons from if not Emma's clips?" Penny asked.

"But then why would Sosa and Emma blow up the Puerto Ricans' warehouse and then give them Glock clips? It doesn't make sense."

"Exactly. And then there's the militia. They don't like either gang and have something planned, according to Bobby Prescot."

"That's a lot of pieces to the puzzle. But I'm not seeing how they fit. I feel like we're missing something. Something big." Bryce glanced over at her.

Penny was quiet. He wanted to give her an answer. Of course to help, but also to show her that he was fun and strong, but he was smart too.

So why would a guy like Sosa come here? What was his endgame?

Diego Ruiz Sosa had been a psychopath with a dying cartel looking for his supposed heir and stolen millions.

What did Alonzo want?

Then it came to him. "What if Sosa is driving out the competition?"

"What do you mean?"

"If he wants to set up his own cartel here—and didn't you say that one of the drug dealers is getting pushed out?—wouldn't it make sense to clear out the competition? Not only that, but instead of doing all the work himself, why not get these groups to turn on each other and do the fighting for him?"

Penny sat up straighter. "You know . . . that kinda makes sense. So Alonzo moves here, figures out who the key players are, and has them fighting each other while he swoops in and establishes his own little kingdom in Last Chance. Jude is always talking about how we're so close to the routes between Salt Lake, Vegas, and Denver. A lot of different cargo moves through here."

"Not to mention you can go straight north for a day to the Canadian border, and there's not a whole lot to stop you if you want to go international."

"And in the meantime he targets everyone involved with his uncle's death to prove himself the new leader."

"Now the question is, how do we find him? Because I'm not

about to let this punk take over. And the sooner he's gone, the sooner we can talk about us." He reached over and squeezed Penny's hand. She gave him a light squeeze back.

He let go to turn the steering wheel as he drove down the street Libby lived on. They pulled into the driveway. Bryce turned the engine off.

"I think I can walk to the front door myself. You don't have to wait, let alone turn off the engine."

"I'm walking you to the door, like it or not. Especially since there's no light on." He ran around the truck to open her door again.

She smiled. "I always did like that about you."

Finally, things were looking up. He reached for her hand as they walked to the porch. Her long fingers fit nicely, entwined with his. He would have to—

"Bryce. Look." Penny stopped before they reached the step, her voice strained.

The front door of the house swayed open in the wind.

TWENTY-ONE

PENNY GRABBED HER SMITH & WESSON EQUAL-
izer and shoved the door open with her shoulder. "Libby!"
One of the kids screamed. Sounded like from upstairs.

A deep voice yelled. It wasn't Dan. He was still on his overseas
work trip.

"Harry! Hazel!" She moved toward the stairs, Bryce on her six.

"Get them out of here!"

The sound of the strange man's voice had her tightening her
grip on her gun as they raced up the stairs. She sprinted to Hazel's
room. Gestured to Bryce to check Harry's next to it.

Hazel's room was lit with a nightlight. The purple unicorn cast
an eerie glow. No lump under the frilly comforter. No one waited
behind the door. No one under the bed.

"Where are they?" The words came out a whisper, adrenaline
and panic closing off Penny's voice. She ran and yanked open the
closet doors. Nothing.

Two more rooms to clear. A thump sounded from the other
side of the wall. Penny ran into the hallway.

She paused outside the doorway of Harry's room, listening.

Lord, if You're really there, help. Protect my family. Bryce. Please.

"Bryce?" she whispered.

Gun held in her two hands in standard thumb-forward formation, she stepped into the space-themed bedroom. A force slammed into her, knocking the gun out of her grip as she fell next to Harry's twin bed. She rolled from her side onto her back. A man with a ski mask stood over her. A shadowed lump lay next to her.

It was Bryce, crumpled on the floor.

This man overpowered Bryce. He wasn't tall enough to be Alonzo. Who was he? Not that there would be much of him left if he hurt her sister or the kids.

He towered over her, leering. "This will be fun."

Not tonight. *A little closer, buddy.* She didn't have much room—Bryce on one side, the bed on the other—but it was enough.

Penny coiled her muscles and took aim. As he came at her, she kicked him in the gut with both feet and rolled up to standing. Before he could catch his balance, she lunged at her attacker. He crashed into the wall. Action figurines rained down on them.

The man grabbed her as he fell, pulling her down, his grip around her tight and heavy. She landed on her stomach and couldn't get away.

He rolled her over and sat on her, pinning her to the carpet. Chubby hands found her neck.

Penny jabbed at his exposed middle. Air whooshed out of him. She quickly grabbed him, one of her arms around his shoulder, trapping it, and the other around his waist.

She exploded her hips up and swept her leg around, rolling him over. He cried out. She definitely needed to thank Jude for teaching her that move.

Bryce still wasn't moving. But the Smith & Wesson the man had knocked out of her hands earlier caught her eye. She reached for it only to be shoved off. A mean right cross to her jaw had her seeing stars for moment. She ducked his next swing and met his chin in an uppercut.

He stumbled backward. She quickly rolled, grabbed the gun, and squeezed off a shot.

The man screamed and grabbed his shoulder where she'd hit him.

Darn, too high. She aimed again.

"Penny!"

At the panicked sound of her sister's voice, she froze. Gomez, the same man who'd trapped Penny in the warehouse, appeared in the hallway with a gun to Libby's head and a tight grip on her arm. He stood behind her like a coward. He didn't come in the room but used her sister to block the doorway.

"You don't want to do that." His glare was cold. Heartless. He wasn't Sosa, but she had no doubt he wouldn't hesitate to hurt Libby. The man she'd shot stayed against the wall, leaning, moaning. Bryce stirred slightly. Penny wanted to make sure he was okay, but didn't dare break eye contact with Gomez.

"Where are my niece and nephew?" She ground out the words.

"Being loaded into a vehicle as we speak." He pointed his weapon at Penny. "Now drop your gun."

"Fat chance."

"We already played this game once, and you lost." He swung the barrel of his gun to point at Libby instead. She whimpered, squeezed her eyes shut. Her whole body trembled.

"Put. Your gun. Down."

Penny's jaw clamped tight, her nostrils flared. Was he bluffing? Would he really shoot? She would have more options and less risk if he weren't holding a gun on her sister.

Gomez's eyes narrowed, his trigger finger twitched.

"All right!" Penny screamed. She slowly lowered her gun, waiting—hoping he'd loosen his grip on Libby and she could make a move. But he didn't. She left the gun on the carpet and stood.

"Kick it away."

She did.

Without breaking eye contact with Penny, Gomez spoke. "Ross, get the gun."

The man moaned as he pushed off the wall. It took monumental effort for Penny to not kick him in the teeth as he picked up her Smith & Wesson.

"Call Davis and Ortega and have them come up here now. They can take care of our friends here."

Ross spoke into a radio. Within seconds, another man appeared in the hall. Gomez nodded toward Penny. "Take the girl and the unconscious man over there and lock them in the pantry."

Penny's breath stopped.

"I'd rather shoot them both now," Ross said, still grasping his shoulder, blood dripping down his shirt.

"You know the plan. They need to stay alive. For now."

Penny couldn't have them taking Libby and the kids anywhere. "Take me and leave my sister here. Leave the kids. I'll go wherever—"

"No! I have no doubt you'll find a way out of the pantry eventually, but by then we'll be long gone and our plan will be in place. Meanwhile, you get Emma released for Alonzo, and we'll keep our little insurance policies nice and close."

"I have no authority to release Emma."

"Then you'll have to get creative. And anything that happens to her will be done to your sister and the kids, so you better make sure she's not harmed."

The new guy grabbed Penny by the arm. She yanked it back, ready for a fight. A shot sounded. Libby screamed.

"That was the only warning you'll get." Gomez speared her with a look. The hole was in the ceiling, thank God. Not her sister. Not Bryce.

This time Penny walked downstairs, the cold metal of a gun in her back. Another man showed up and picked Bryce up fireman style. They marched to the pantry, Penny's pulse speeding up with each step. She couldn't fall apart. Libby. The kids. Bryce. They all needed her to be strong right now. The man dropped Bryce on the floor. Bryce groaned, started to move. Penny was shoved down next to him. As Ross started to close the door, Penny yelled at the one in charge.

"How am I supposed to get ahold of you? If I get Emma."

"Don't worry about that. We'll be keeping an eye on things. We'll find you."

The last thing she saw was Libby being dragged away before the door shut, her cries reverberating straight to Penny's soul. Everything that had been holding her together up until that point drained away.

She sank to the tile floor, ice seeping through her jeans. So much like the basement. Her vision blurred.

No. Please, not now.

Flashes of the corpse, a spider crawling over the wrinkly skin—it all rushed back, consuming her. Screaming from her own voice echoed off the wall.

Something near her moved. Bryce?

But she was trapped.

It was just a nightmare. Not real. She couldn't get enough air. Nausea rolled through her. Penny curled up tight, head tucked into her knees. Covered her head with her arms, embracing the blackness. Anything to get that image out of her head.

A warmth cut through the ice that had frozen her lungs shut.

"Penny." The voice was weak, sounded far away. But it called to her, beckoned her out of the dark. Bryce? Was he okay?

"Penny. Breathe, baby. Breathe with me." He was a little closer now, the warmth moving from her shoulder to her elbow to her tingling hands.

The voice helped. Her heartbeat quieted as she listened and breathed the slow rhythm.

"That's right."

Penny lifted her head. She swayed as dizziness overtook her, but eventually Bryce's face came into focus. "Keep breathing. With me."

She followed his breathing sequence. In for a three count. Out for a three count.

"There you are. Good. Tell me three things you see now."

See? "I see your eyes." Eyes that locked in on her, held her safe. The pitching sensation faded.

"Great. What else? Two more things."

"I see . . . blood." Dark-red blood from a cut on his temple. She snapped out of the fog. "You're hurt." She reached out toward his wound. "Are you okay?"

"I've got a killer headache where someone clocked me from behind. Knocked me out cold." He took her hands. "But I'm more worried about you at the moment. How are we doing?"

She took in a longer breath, her lungs thawing. Expanding. "Better."

"Yeah?" He seemed to be searching her face for something. She nodded.

He pulled her to his chest and held her. "Thank God. You had me worried there, Mitchell."

Her ear pressed right at his heart could hear the organ pumping strong and steady. She rested there until her icy bones thawed and she could feel her fingers again. The images of the past hovered, but they didn't consume her. Here with Bryce, she could find firm footing again in reality, in the present. As long as she didn't think about the fact that she was trapped in a cold, enclosed space.

At least this time it wasn't a basement, and she wasn't alone. Bryce was here.

He sheltered her from that haunting past. Her pulse slowed. Her very breath deepened, and the dizziness faded away.

But then reality kicked in. "Libby! The kids! They—"

"Whoa. Hold on." Bryce cradled her face in his hands. "Slowly. What happened? Do you know where we are?"

"We're at Libby's. They took her and the kids."

"Who? Alonzo?"

"No, but it was Gomez and some others who work for him. He wants me to get Emma released. Said anything that happens to her, he'll do to my sister. My niece and nephew." Her voice squeaked. The dark corners of the room started collapsing in again. Cold washed over her, flooded her veins.

"Hey, hey, hey. I'm losing you. Penny?"

She locked onto Bryce's warm gaze. The cadence of his voice drew her. "Come on, baby. You're okay. Take long . . . slow . . . deep breaths."

Right. Bryce was here. He would help.

They needed to get out of here.

"We have to find them," she whispered.

His thumb wiped the salty tracks down her cheeks.

"We will. Let's get your circulation going again."

She allowed Bryce to pull her up to her feet. The room swayed slightly, then righted. Bryce ran his warm hands up and down her arms, melting the ice there.

"I think I'm okay now. Just don't leave me."

"Never."

He pulled her in and hugged her, a slight pressure to her head as he kissed her there. "I'm right here."

TWENTY-TWO

BRYCE HELD PENNY, NEEDING HER CLOSENESS and warmth to calm his own nerves as much as to offer her this safe place. He'd never seen her this shaken before.

And yeah, he could admit he felt it too. Someone had gotten the drop on him. He was supposed to be here to protect Penny and her family. Show her she could depend on him. Instead, he'd been knocked out cold within the first few minutes. Now that he had her in his arms, he wasn't going to let her go.

Lord, be our strength. Be with Libby and the kids.

But there was still so much about this woman he didn't know. Like why he'd woken up to find her rocking and hyperventilating in the middle of the pantry.

"Doing okay?" he asked her.

"I'm ready to get out of here."

"Let's see what we can do about that."

The door was locked. Even with a swift kick to break the locking mechanism, the door didn't budge. "They must've blocked it with something. Any tools in here?"

Penny wrapped her arms around herself. She shuddered as she

176

looked around. "Not that I can see. We need to get word to some-one or find something to break down the door."

Get word to someone. Bryce felt his pockets. "What kind of bad guys are these? They let me keep my phone?"

"Thank God." She leaned into the door, some of the tension in her shoulders relaxing.

"Looks like I missed calls. Jude. Jason Woods. Olivia." He scrolled down the screen. "What's going on?"

"Right now we just need to get my sister and the kids."

Bryce pushed aside the unease about the list of missed calls. "I'll call the rescue team. They'll be here quickly." Bryce made the call to dispatch, explaining the kidnapping, and then gave them the address. "Send the cops out to look for those kids ASAP. You can send the rescue squad here to get us out."

"Yes, sir, I have a squad car on the way. But the rescue squad is out on another call." She was new, someone he hadn't met yet. "Do you need me to stay on the phone with you?"

What he needed was to get Penny out of this pantry ASAP. But it wouldn't help her to get upset, and it certainly wasn't the dispatcher's fault. "We're good."

He called Izan instead. Then tried Jude and Olivia. No answer with any of them. He tried crewmate Zack Stephens next. Thank goodness he answered on the first ring.

"Hey, we need help. Can you get any of the off-duty guys and come help us out?" Bryce explained what had happened.

"I'll grab Izan and we'll be there as soon as we can, but we're out in the boonies. Got called in to help support the on-duty crew with a field fire, but they're sending us back. So it will be a little bit before I can get there. Can you hold out?"

"Believe me, we're not going anywhere. But get here as soon as you can."

He ended the call. Now he just needed to keep Penny calm while they waited.

Her breathing was starting to speed up again. But it was probably better to let her know they were in for a bit of a wait.

He took her hands in his and helped her sit down on the floor. "Stephens and Izan will be here, but they're stuck out in the remote part of the county, so it will be a little bit longer than we thought."

"What?" Her voice squeaked. He'd never seen her this scared. She'd been fearless throughout the whole Diego Sosa thing. Seeing this side of her didn't take away from her appeal though. It only made him care more, deepened the desire to see her safe.

"I'm right here. Not going anywhere."

Her eyes searched his face, pinging back and forth. "You probably think I'm nuts." She released a humorless chuckle.

"I'm guessing there's a really good reason enclosed spaces freak you out. I mean, last time I saw you in a closet, a bomb had just gone off, so there's that."

He gently caressed her hands, trying to massage some warmth back into her fingers.

She closed her eyes, dropped her head down to her knees. "I thought I was over this."

"Over what?" Yes, he wanted to hear what had her so terrified, but he wouldn't push.

She lifted her head. "I keep seeing her body. And the spiders." Her voice sounded small, far away.

"Whose body?"

"She was our next-door neighbor for a short time. She'd make us cookies and bring them over. But I've worked so hard to forget those days that I can't even remember her name now."

Bryce moved next to her, tucked her close to help fight off the chill. She didn't resist. "I'm sure you have a good reason for not wanting to remember."

She sniffed. "I hated that duplex. We had a nice home growing up, but after my mom got sick and died, my dad ended up losing it. Had to move into that rundown rental in the middle of my fourth grade year. But the elderly lady next door was kind. She was the only good thing about that place."

Bryce's heart squeezed. "I didn't realize your mom died when you were that young."

"She died right before my ninth birthday. And my dad . . . he fell apart."

"He really loved her, huh?"

"We all did." Her voice wobbled. "She was everything. The glue that held us together. She was amazing."

"And your dad didn't handle the loss well, I take it?"

"He just wasn't there." There was a sharp edge to her words. "Ever. When he was physically with us, he always seemed like he wanted to be somewhere else. I can't tell you how many times we went to bed hungry because he was too out of it to realize we hadn't had dinner or there was no food."

"He didn't feed you?"

"I think he was so wrapped up in his pain he simply forgot about those basic necessities. I understand it more now, but back then I didn't. And I was an angry kid. Angry that my mom was gone. Angry that my dad didn't seem to care about us girls. Angry that it was up to me most of the time to get what we needed."

He kissed the top of her head, wishing with all his heart he could take away her pain. "So you stepped up and took care of your sisters. Are you the oldest?"

"No, I'm the middle sister. Libby is oldest. Tori is younger than me. But we pretty much raised ourselves."

"So your dad didn't know what to do with three grieving daughters."

He almost felt bad for the guy.

"That's one way of putting it. And it all came to a head that one night."

"What happened?"

Penny scooted in closer to him. "I needed to make a papier-mâché project for school and needed flour. Dad kept saying he'd get it, then wouldn't. Libby tried to tell me not to bother him, but he was supposed to be taking care of us, you know? So when he came home from work late . . . again without the flour, I went off on him. And he just looked at me and said, 'Buck up, Pen. If you need something, go figure out how to get it yourself. Don't ever depend on anyone else. Including me.' So I did. I went next door to borrow some flour. I knocked on the door and thought I heard the old lady inside. She didn't hear very well, so I walked into the house like I'd done before. In the kitchen, the basement door was open. I went downstairs, and there on the floor was the old lady. Dead. A couple of spiders crawling on her. I ran back up the stairs, but someone locked the door behind me. Later we found out the lady had been robbed by her own son. He'd pushed her down the stairs and locked me in with her."

Bryce held her tighter. "You were trapped? With a dead body? How long until you were rescued?"

"Not until the next afternoon."

"You were trapped *all night*?" He was ready to go toe to toe with Penny's father himself until he remembered he'd already passed away. What kind of dad didn't realize his daughter was missing all night?

"When I wasn't there to get on the bus for school, Libby realized something had happened to me. She's the one that called the police. They couldn't get ahold of my father because, surprise, surprise, he'd lost his job and never told us, so they didn't know where to find him. They tried looking for me at school and other places. It wasn't until they knocked on the old lady's door to get the neighbors involved in the search that they finally heard my screaming and found me."

"No wonder basements freak you out."

"And spiders."

"I'm so sorry. But we will get out of here. I promise."

"I know." She squeezed his arm.

"So can I ask . . . what did your dad do after all this?"

"CPS got involved. Threatened to take us away. Dad got his life back on track. Sorta. Found a job. He made sure we had food and clothing. But"—she lifted her chin and sat up, pulling away from Bryce a bit, almost as if in defiance—"that trust was broken. He was supposed to be there for us. Protect us. He didn't even know I was gone. He was that . . . broken. And I decided then and there if that was what true love did to people, I didn't want anything to do with it."

Seeing that resolve in her big green eyes, it became clear. "Is that why you ran away from here last year?"

She scooted away further. "Bryce . . . you have to understand. Before Mom, my dad was a good man. I had no doubt when Mom was alive that he'd fight to the death for us, that he loved us, cared for us. And he was so fun. But when she died, he became a completely different person. Loving her destroyed the man I'd grown up with. And the last man I let myself get involved with wasn't any better."

"Are you still not over the Ashlee thing?"

"I'm not talking about you."

So there *had* been someone.

"What did he do?" And who was he? Bryce was ready to take him down.

"Someone I had no business falling for. He's the reason I left the ATF."

"Was he part of one of your investigations? A suspect?"

She closed her eyes and leaned her head back. Her throat bobbed as she swallowed. "Worse. He was my boss."

Bryce was ready to hunt the man down, but he didn't dare say a thing. He might lose it completely.

Penny opened her eyes, stared blankly at the ceiling. "He told me it would be fine. That he wanted to marry me. And of course

I couldn't tell anyone. Not even Jude, who was my partner at the time, or I would've been fired. I thought Carter had my back though. Would protect me, and once we were married it would be worth it. So I kept waiting. Then one night I walked into his office and found him cheating on me. With another woman in the bureau. An intern." She dropped her gaze to Bryce. "So I left. And I promised myself I wouldn't depend on a man like that again. Ever."

"Not every man is like that. *I'm* not like that."

"But where you see love, all I see is a lot of potential for heart-break and destruction. A weakness someone might exploit."

"But real love makes us stronger. Better. Look at my parents. Jude and Andi. And what about right now? Penny, we're good together. Isn't it helping that you're not stuck here alone? That we can lean on each other?"

"I'm not denying it works out great for some. Just not me. I can't let myself be that dependent. That weak."

"But sometimes when we're at our weakest, we finally see what we need."

"What do you mean?"

He might as well lay it all out there. "I know what it's like to be broken and weak, because when I realized you weren't coming back, I fell apart. Completely. But it was then that I also found I needed someone a whole lot bigger than me to put me back together. My mom, Andi, Logan, and I found that faith Jude had been talking about was real. That man we met at the bakery, John, he leads a discipleship group, a Bible study I go to."

She looked at him then. "You believe that God stuff?"

"Yeah. I do."

Her eyes narrowed and her voice grew soft, almost like she was talking to herself. "That's what it is."

"What *what* is?"

"The change. I knew something had changed in you. I just couldn't figure out what it was."

She saw a difference? Maybe God was working in him after all. But it sounded like it would take more convincing to show her that love wasn't always so self-destructive. Because as far as he was concerned, it was love that beat clearly in his heart for this amazing woman. He wanted a chance to show her that it was worth it. That he was worth it. That God was worth it.

"Penny, I believe that God is real. That He cares. I don't know what's going to happen in the future, but we're going to get out of here and do everything we can to get your family back."

TWENTY-THREE

PENNY STOPPED REARRANGING THE SHELVES. The space was still too small, closing them in. She should be out finding her family.

"Maybe He is real. Maybe He actually does care. But I can't stay here any longer doing nothing." She shoved against the door. Nothing. She tried again, but it didn't budge. She rubbed her sore shoulder. "I need more space. A running start." She gritted her teeth and was about to throw all her body weight against it when Bryce grabbed her and held her tight.

"It's not gonna open that way." His strong arms kept her from falling to the ground.

"I have to try." She tried to pull away from him, desperation taking over.

But Bryce's grip was solid. His voice quiet. "Whatever they did to block this door, they jammed it good. Help is on the way, Penny. We need to sit tight and wait a little longer. You're going to hurt yourself if you keep going."

She shook her head. "I can't do nothing." Her voice came out as a weak whisper. She needed to do something before the panic came back. Her sister and the kids were out there at the mercy of evil men, and it was her fault. She never should've come back to Last Chance.

"Hey, did I ever tell you about the frogs?"

"What?" Her gaze landed on Bryce, his eyes steady, a glint of humor teasing. How could he find anything funny about this?

"I never told you about that?"

He was distracting her. Obviously. But hey, if it kept the panic at bay . . . by all means. "You never mentioned a story featuring frogs, no."

They sank back down to the floor. She sat between his knees, leaned against his chest. His strong arms wrapped around her, sheltering her from the chill.

"Buckle up. This is riveting stuff."

Penny huffed. "Riveting, huh?"

"Oh yeah. See, my buddy and I wanted to be heroes. We knew that meant we had to rescue someone, and in the fourth grade, there weren't many damsels in distress. So we set our sights on animals. Our science teacher, Mr. Hale, had specimens of different animals in jars, which always seemed kinda cruel to me."

"Ugh. Those jars always creeped me out." Penny shivered. Bryce held her closer.

"What did you do?" she asked, settling into his embrace.

"Obviously it was too late for the animals in the jar, but I was determined to make sure Mr. Hale wouldn't dissect any more creatures in the name of science. I wanted to send him a message. So my friend and I spent a week catching as many frogs as we could. We kept them in a couple of big buckets, and one day we cut last hour and filled Mr. Hale's car with all the frogs."

Penny chuckled lightly. "You didn't."

"Oh yes, we did. Got in so much trouble too. I think we had detention for a month."

"You and Logan?"

Bryce froze. He didn't say anything.

It was so foreign for this energetic man to remain this quiet and still.

"Bryce? Are you okay?" She pulled away from his arms, which had gone strangely limp, and turned around to face him. Seeing something beyond the good-time grin he always wore, or the powerful glower when he faced a challenge, was a rare glimpse at a man she'd always suspected was there but had hardly ever seen.

"What happened?" she asked.

He shook his head slightly. "Oh, nothing. Just... remembering. I haven't thought about him in a long time."

"About what? Your friend?"

"Yeah. Luke."

"Did something happen to him?"

He looked at her, a sorrow in his gaze she'd never witnessed before with him. "Yeah. Luke died. And even worse, it was my fault."

"What are you talking about? How was it your fault?"

"Because I didn't do enough to stop it."

The heartbreak in his voice almost wrecked her. "What happened?"

"Luke was my best friend. It was just him and his mom, and she worked a lot, so he was at our place all the time. Enough that I noticed bruises and stuff. When I asked about them, he'd get really quiet. He never said anything, but I suspected his mom. He admitted she got pretty mad sometimes, but he didn't want me saying anything."

"Did you?"

"Not at first. Then he missed a few days of school, and I got worried about him, told my teacher what I thought. She told me I didn't know what I was talking about, that I shouldn't accuse innocent people. His mom was simply an overworked single parent. She had already contacted our teacher and said Luke was on a trip, so of course my teacher wasn't going to believe me."

"Did he come back?"

"Yeah. And when I asked how his trip was, he had no clue what I was talking about."

"So his mom lied."

"And when I tried to talk to him about it with the teacher, *he* lied. Said I was just being typical Bryce, class jokester. He laughed at me, said no one could ever believe what I said. Then I got in trouble for taking a joke too far. And after the frog incident, who was going to believe me? The teacher even called my parents and told them I had a problem, that I wasn't taking my classes seriously enough, was causing issues."

"What did they say?"

"They were mad I was failing reading, and so I don't think they really heard me when I tried to explain."

"And Luke?"

Bryce squeezed his hands, tucking his thumbs into his fists. "He died not long afterward. They said it was an accident. He fell and hit his head. And I tried again to tell my parents, that they needed to go to the police. But they thought I was trying to deal with the death by making up a story that gave me someone to blame."

"They didn't take you seriously?"

"Not that time." Bryce shrugged. "Most people don't."

"That's not true."

"Sure it is. In school, people liked hanging out with me, playing sports with me, partying with me, but no one expected anything more than just a good time. I barely graduated. Even my high-school girlfriend broke up with me right before she left for college because she needed to grow up and be with someone serious."

"There's a lot more to you than a good time, Bryce. You know that, right?"

"I know I can be impulsive, and I do love having fun and going out, but sometimes, yeah, I wish people would realize I'm not stupid. I even looked up Luke's mom later. She had a record of allegations of child abuse before they moved to Last Chance. It wasn't just me."

"Did they ever reopen the investigation into Luke's death?"

"No. His mom left soon after his death and ended up dying of a drug overdose."

"How sad." Penny reached out for Bryce's hand. "You know I always saw you as more than just the life of the party, right?"

He looked at her with a question in his eyes, not convinced.

"You're a loyal and courageous man. They way you jumped in to help protect your family with Sosa, the way you run into burning buildings to rescue people—do you know how rare that is? And you're still the only guy I've ever dated that would hold open doors for me."

He gave her a sad smile. "Then why did you leave without letting me explain? I wasn't serious enough?"

"Uh . . . no. Probably because you were too serious . . . about us. And that's not a bad thing. Any other woman would probably be thrilled to have someone as committed and loyal as you. I'm just not sure I'm cut out for the kind of long-term relationship you deserve."

He squeezed her hands, tugged her closer. "Can't we give it a shot? Penny, we're good together. And I'm willing to try if you are."

Oh, she could so easily fall for this man. The intensity in him, the way his touch steadied her and ignited her at the same time. The way he would give his all for family. And as a package, there was nothing lacking in this cowboy firefighter.

Before she could vocalize anything, a scraping noise sounded from the other side of the door.

"Bryce? Penny?" voices yelled.

They stood and banged on the door. "In here!"

"Hey, guys. Hang tight. We gotta move this cabinet and you'll be home free."

Within moments, Penny and Bryce walked into Libby's kitchen to find Izan and Zack Stephens.

Finally, Penny could breathe. But she couldn't rest. Her family was out there. And until she could find them, she didn't have the headspace or time to worry about her heart and everything circling there.

"Sosa has my sister and her kids," Penny told the guys. "And we haven't been able to get ahold of Jude."

Zack nodded. "Most of the police force and emergency services are out at a raid. I bet Jude is there too. But they sent us back. Maybe things are wrapping up."

"Try calling him again." Bryce handed Penny his phone. She called, put the phone on speaker, and set it on the dining room table.

"Hey, do you know where Penny is?" Jude answered. "I've been trying to call the both of you."

"I'm here. You're on speaker with me and Bryce. What's going on?"

"The militia just issued a statement. They kidnapped the governor's wife and son."

"The militia? What do they have to do with this? And why would they kidnap the governor's family?" Bryce asked.

"We're still trying to figure that out. In the meantime, you need to get here. The task force has been called in. All available law enforcement is being pulled in to find them," Jude said.

It was on the tip of her tongue to tell him.

We had it wrong. It wasn't your family they were targeting. It's mine.

She could hear Emma in her head.

You don't know squat. Because if you did, neither of you would be here right now.

But Jude's job was to protect the governor and figure out what was going on with the militia. If she said anything about her sister and kids, Jude would be there in a heartbeat.

And he'd probably lose his job because of it.

She couldn't let him do that. Besides, they could split forces. He could keep looking for the governor's family. She would get her sister and the kids back.

Emma Kemper and Alonzo were *her* case.

Bryce opened his mouth to say something into the phone. To shut him up, she quickly pressed her finger against his lips. Lips she'd kissed tonight. Lips that tempted her to do crazy things like give her heart away and put down roots in Last Chance.

But that was way too much to unpack right now. First . . . Libby and kids. And keep Jude out of it.

"I can't be there to help. I'm working another angle of my own." Penny spoke into the phone. "That's why I called."

"What is it?" Jude asked.

"I'm gonna need you to trust me." Jude didn't have to know how she got her intel. Many times it was better when he didn't.

"I don't feel right about your pursuing it on your own. And it's the governor's wife and child missing. Are you sure this lead is worth your time?"

"I'm not alone. Bryce is here. And believe me, the life of a woman and any child isn't something I'd take lightly." Her sister was a wife too. Her niece's and nephew's lives mattered very much.

"I'll try to put off Woods. He's breathing down our necks, demanding every resource we have be spent on this, but I don't know how long I can hold him back."

"We'll be there as soon as we can." That's all she could promise.

"Stay in touch. Don't do anything stupid."

"You know me better than that, Book. Bye."

Penny ended the call.

Bryce glowered. "Why didn't you tell him?" Izan and Stephens looked confused.

"What do you think he'd do?" Penny faced them, arms folded across her chest.

"He would come help us find them," Bryce said, as if it were obvious.

"Right. And he'd lose his job for doing it when he's been called in to the investigation with the governor's family. Then where would he be? Anthony and Olivia are probably out there too."

Bryce lost some of his bluster. "I suppose you have a point."

"So it's up to me." Penny needed him to understand.

"I'm sure as heck not gonna let you go alone. You already told Jude I was coming with you." Bryce straightened.

"Not just you. We're here too. And we'll do whatever we need to help." Izan pointed at himself and Zack.

"You guys will help?" Bryce asked them.

"Of course. We're family. What do you need?" Zack leaned over the table.

Penny looked the men in the eyes. Each was ready to face who knew what. "Thank you."

"Okay, so where do we start?" Bryce was ready for action as always.

"I don't know why Sosa would target my family, but I'm going to call my brother-in-law before we do anything else. He needs to know."

"Do you think they planned this? Your sister and kids taken the same time the governor's family is kidnapped?" Izan asked.

"I don't know, maybe they wanted the distraction. But I have to call Dan. Why don't you do a quick search of the house. See if Gomez and his goons took anything. Left anything. You get the idea. Bryce and I can start upstairs after I call. You guys go through the main living area."

After Penny called Dan and told him what was going on, Bryce and Penny quickly searched through the kids' rooms together.

"Nothing here. You?" Bryce asked as he righted the rocket lamp that had been knocked over in Harry's room.

"Just my phone. It must've fallen out of my pocket earlier. Let's try Libby's room."

The blankets on the king-sized bed bunched up in the middle. A novel lay on the floor next to a pillow that had been knocked off. They'd probably grabbed Libby as she was winding down for the evening. The kids as they slept. They must be terrified. Penny couldn't think about that too much. She had to focus on finding them.

On the nightstand next to the bed, Libby's phone charged on a wireless charger. Another cord next to it dangled off the edge.

"Her watch!"

Bryce paused his search on the other side of the bed. "What?"

"We can track her smartwatch with her phone."

"Doesn't the watch have to be near the phone for that to work?"

"Libby doesn't like to take her phone when she runs, so she has a cell plan just for the watch. It should give me her exact location." Penny snatched the phone off the charger.

"You know your sister's password?" Bryce came and looked over her shoulder.

"You know Logan's?" She gave him a look.

"Point taken."

She opened up the app, clicked on the map icon and zoomed in. "Do you know where this is?"

"Looks like a trailer on the outside of town."

"This is where they must be keeping her and the kids."

"Let's go," Bryce hollered as he ran downstairs. "We got 'em."

They showed the location to the others.

"Do any of you have a weapon?" Penny asked them.

"I've got a pistol in the truck," Zack said. Izan shook his head.

"We need more firepower. Dan must have something around here." Penny spun around the living room where they stood.

"There's a 12-gauge with a box of ammo on top of the hutch over there," Izan said. "I saw it as we were searching." He pointed toward the dining room.

"We'll take that. I have my backup weapon in the guest room." Penny grabbed the shotgun and handed it to Bryce. "I assume you know how to use that?"

"Does a cowboy know how to two-step?" He winked at her.

And after his story, she knew. The wink wasn't a sign that he didn't care or wasn't taking this seriously. He would do everything in his power to save her sister and the kids. He really was a hero.

"Good. We'll need to park farther away and scope things out when we get there. But let me make one thing clear: nobody shoots anything if innocents are nearby. Understood? And we need Sosa alive. He's got something going on, and we have to find out what it is. If he's not there, we'll need his henchmen."

She waited until each man nodded understanding before they left. Soon they were jogging through a tree line that ran around the outside of the lot the trailer was parked on. The trailer had seen better days. Coyotes barked in the night. Lights were on inside, but all the windows were blocked with blinds or drapes. Straw bales surrounded the outside of the trailer, most likely used for winter insulation to keep the pipes from freezing.

"What's the plan? We can't go in blind with guns blazing," Izan said.

"We need to draw them out and get eyes on what's going on inside." Penny peered at the trailer, trying to best guess where her sister and the kids would be.

"Why don't we go knock on the front door?" Zack asked.

"Seriously?" Bryce balked.

"I play a good drunk guy. I can pound on the door, pretend it's someone I know. Try to push my way inside." Zack made it sound easy, but there were too many ways that could go wrong.

"Too risky," she said.

"What about the TIC? I have one in the truck I was repairing." Bryce used his thumb to point toward his vehicle.

Izan stared at him. "You know how to fix a TIC?"

Bryce froze for a second. "It wasn't a big deal. The screen needed replacing."

Zack looked confused. "And you knew how to do that?"

Bryce shrugged like it was no biggie. "There's a YouTube video for everything."

"Focus, boys. Yes, the thermal imaging device will help. We should be able to distinguish where the kids are at least. And I'll use Libby's watch to see if we can figure out where she is in the building."

Bryce jogged away and soon came back with the thermal imaging device. Thankfully, with the cooler night air settling all around them, the ninety-eight-degree bodies stood out in red and orange on the TIC's screen.

"There are the kids, on the south side of the trailer." Bryce pointed to them. The orange blobs were significantly smaller than the others.

"It doesn't look like anyone is guarding them. There's three adults on the other end of the trailer. Is that where your sister is?" Izan asked.

Penny used Libby's phone app. "Yeah, she's over there."

Bryce pointed at the TIC screen. "She's probably the one sitting down on the ground while the other two people are standing. That must be a kitchen. Looks like there's heat coming from a coffee pot too."

So all three of them were alive at least. That brought the nerves down a smidge. "First, let's grab the kids. If we can get them out while they're not guarded, and without alerting Sosa, we can focus on getting Libby next. And we'll take away their leverage."

Bryce looked at the other two. "Izan, you stay here. You have a clear shot at the back door. Watch our backs and give us a signal if you see anything. Zack, you take the front yard. If anyone else approaches from the driveway, take them out."

Zack moved away silently, and Izan hunkered down among the shadows of the trees. Penny and Bryce approached the room on the south side. The window was boarded up with a piece of plywood.

"Let's try the room next to them. It's empty, right?" Penny asked.

Bryce checked the TIC again. "So far. But I think it's a bathroom. Look how small and high that window is."

"It's our best shot for getting in there undetected. Give me a boost." Penny tugged a long straw bale out from under the trailer and stood on it. She removed the window screen without a sound.

Bryce stood next to her on the ground. She easily slid onto his shoulders. "Step up here onto the bale, and I'll be able to reach," she whispered.

Bryce held on to her legs and stepped up. Once Bryce was stable, she used the side of the trailer to brace herself and moved to kneel on his shoulders. The flimsy window didn't take much to wiggle open.

She shimmied her body through the small opening and quietly stepped onto the toilet situated right under the window. Peeking around the door, she saw only dark outlines of frames hanging on the walls of the hallway. A light from the opposite end of the trailer glowed, but the coast was clear.

She tried the door next to the bathroom. Locked.

Of course it couldn't be *that* easy. She quietly tapped on the door—the secret code she'd taught Hazel and Harry when they had a clubhouse. Nothing.

She tried it again.

"I'll check on the kids. I'm telling you, you're hearing things. No one is out there." A deep voice came closer.

A noise like bedsprings squeaking sounded on the other side of the door.

Penny tapped the sequence one more time. She laid her ear against the thin wood of the hollow door.

"Aunt Penny?" a young voice said. Hazel!

"Yes, it's me. Unlock the door," she whispered, hoping Hazel could still hear.

Noise from the other side of the trailer, the deep voice of a man—was it Alonzo?—reached Penny. They were coming this way.

The jostling of the knob creaked, and soon, the door cracked open, Hazel's scared face on the other side. As soon as their eyes locked, the door swung wide open and a whimper escaped. Heavy footsteps from the other end of the hall sounded louder, the man getting closer. He would see her soon. Penny engulfed Hazel in one arm and quietly closed the door behind her. She relocked the door, then scooped Hazel up and held her close.

"I knew—" the little girl started to say.

Penny pulled away quickly enough to cover Hazel's mouth and scanned the room. A queen bed took most of the space, and the little body curled up on it about broke her heart. But the rise and fall of Harry's chest meant he was alive. Thank God.

"Listen carefully. The man is coming to check on you. Lie down next to your brother and pretend to sleep. Be super-duper still. Quick!" Hopefully the whispered words conveyed how urgent it was. "I won't let anything happen to you."

Penny laid Hazel next to Harry, who thankfully was already asleep, though tears and sweat ran down his forehead and cheeks. She had barely enough time to slip under the bed before the door-knob jiggled again and the door opened.

Heavy breathing from the doorway. A grunt. Then the door closed again. Penny waited for a ten count and slowly rolled out from under the bed.

"All right, Hazel. Let's wake up Harry and get you two out of here."

Hazel popped up and fell into her auntie's arms, crying. "I knew you'd come," she squeaked out between sobs.

TWENTY-FOUR

FIRST STUCK IN A PANTRY AND NOW THIS. WAIT-ing outside doing nothing was torture. Bryce about broke down the wall as he watched a big bulky body approach the room where the kids were on the TIC screen, especially when he saw how close Penny's outline was to what had to be a man's body. Bryce could hear the heavy footsteps from the bathroom window.

Please Lord, protect them. Don't let them be seen.

From the open bathroom window, he listened. It sounded like the man opened and then quickly closed a door. A deep voice sounded right outside the bathroom. "I told you the brats are fine. They're asleep. You're hearing things." The footsteps faded as Bryce watched the blob on the screen move away from Penny and the kids and back to the other side of the trailer where Libby was.

He breathed easier. Soon Penny and two little outlines moved toward him. She hoisted Harry up through the window first. Then Hazel. Bryce grabbed them and helped them down to the ground, a finger to his lips reminding them to stay silent. Once Penny was back outside, they each grabbed a kid and ran for Izan in the tree line.

In the shadows of the tree trunks, Penny looked each child over. "Are you guys okay? Did they hurt you?"

He'd never heard such tenderness, such raw emotion in her voice.

Harry sniffed but held his chin high. So much like his aunt. "I told Hazel that you would come save us."

"Nuh-uh! I told you—"

Penny cut her niece's argument off with a swift hug. "It doesn't matter because you were both right. I'm here and we're going to keep you safe. No one will ever hurt you again!"

Harry held tight to Bryce's neck. "And you came too, Coach?"

"I told you I was here for ya." Bryce gave the kid a big grin. They had to have been scared out of their minds. "You guys are so brave."

Hazel's lip trembled. "But what about Mommy? Those bad men have her. They hit her. And they said if she didn't do what they said, they would hurt us."

"We're going to get your mom, but first we need to make sure you two are safe. We're going to bring you to Bryce's truck, okay? And you're going to have to be really brave and wait there while we get your mom."

"You can't leave us!" Hazel squeezed Penny's neck tight.

Penny looked at Bryce, raising her eyebrows as if asking him for help.

"You guys already did the really hard part," Bryce told the kids. "But you want Penny to be there to rescue your mom so she'll be safe too."

He felt a shudder go through Harry's little body. "I don't want to be alone."

Izan sneaked up to them. "I can stay with the kids."

Good idea. "Remember Izan? He helped coach." Bryce pointed at his buddy.

Harry lifted his head. "And he came to school with you. He's a fireman too."

Penny smiled at her nephew. "Right. So he knows how to keep you both safe. Can you wait with him in Bryce's truck?"

Both kids finally nodded. The five of them wound their way around the trees and ditches and came back to the truck. Penny hugged each kid and set them together in the passenger seat. "I need you two to duck down and stay out of sight. Izan is going to watch over you so nothing happens, okay?"

The children still looked scared, but they both agreed. Tears slid down Hazel's cheeks. Bryce let Penny talk to them while he walked over to the driver's side with Izan. He handed him the keys to the truck. "If anything happens, you get these kids out of here. Take them to fire hall. Keep them safe."

"You know I will."

Yeah. He did. So maybe his brother wasn't around anymore, but Bryce had his crew, friends that were quickly becoming a lot like family. Once the kids were somewhat settled, Bryce and Penny jogged back toward the trailer. They met up with Zack in the front yard.

"I think now would be a good time for a distraction. There's only two men guarding Libby. If we can draw one away, we'll have a better chance at securing her," Penny whispered.

"So I get to pull out my acting skills after all?" Zack wagged his eyebrows.

"No, we need a ruckus outside, something that won't alert them that we're here but that they'll still want to check on." Penny looked back at the trailer as if studying it for any weakness.

"Or we could smoke them out," Bryce said.

"What?"

"If we start a fire in the bedroom where the kids were, they'll be forced outside."

"A fire would be obvious that we're onto them. They might retaliate and hurt Libby. Or she could be trapped in the fire." Penny counted on her fingers all the reasons his plan wouldn't work.

But Bryce wasn't ready to back down quite yet. "They want her for a reason. I don't think they'll kill their bargaining chip."

"We're not going to risk it. And remember, we have a secondary motive here. We need these guys alive so we can figure out what Sosa's endgame is." Penny stared him down.

"What if we start the fire outside?" Zack asked.

Bryce looked at all the dry grass in the yard and the field next to it. "It's too dry. We can't risk starting a wildfire. It would be out of control so fast."

"All right. Drunk neighbor it is." Zack nodded as if it were a done deal.

Penny's brows furrowed. "It's too dangerous."

"Yeah, but this guy knows you and Bryce. So who else is left?"

Her shoulders sank. "Guess that's our best option." She looked behind her. "I'll go inside through the bathroom again and text you when I'm ready. When you get my text, go knock on the door. Bryce, you cover him. See if you can lure him outside. You two subdue that guy, and I'll get the one with Libby."

"Who's going to cover you?" Bryce demanded.

"I'm used to working alone. Don't worry." She brushed off his concern like it was no big deal.

"But—"

"We don't have time to argue." Penny walked toward the bathroom window again.

Zack's eyes went wide. "You've met your match there, buddy. Let's go."

She'd at least need a boost. Bryce jogged quietly up to her. "Penny!" he hissed. She whipped her head around, finger to her lips. They reached the straw bale under the bathroom window again.

"I don't like this," he said.

"It's the best we've got. Are you going to help or not?"

That stubborn streak in her was going to be the death of him.

"Fine." He boosted her up and waited until she was back through the window. He ran around to the front of the trailer.

Zack waited in the shadows, watching his phone. Bryce gave him a thumbs-up. He held the shotgun, but how could he actually use it? If this guy got close to Stephens, there was too much of a chance his friend would be hurt. He kept the barrel pointed to the ground and crouched behind a bush at the corner of the trailer. At least here he had a clear view of the front door as Zack approached it.

Penny's text came through. Bryce was poised, ready for action. Zack sang loudly and obnoxiously as he approached the door.

"Hello? Helloooooo?" He laughed and pounded on the door. "Anybody home?"

Bryce checked the TIC screen. One of the men left the area Libby was in and moved closer but didn't open the door. Bryce made a circular motion with his pointer finger at Zack, indicating he should keep going.

"Yo! I need some help. Hello?" Stephens pounded on the door again and then leaned against it.

After more seconds of silence, the man inside finally opened the door.

"What do you want?" The man cracked the door open but didn't come out.

"Hola, amigo!" Zack laughed. "I uh . . . I kinda ran out of gas. Could you—"

"Get out of here." He tried shutting the door, but Zack's work boot was in the way.

"No, really, I will. I just need a leeeeetle gas-o-line." He held up his thumb and forefinger close together. Bryce crept closer.

The man must've heard him. He opened the door wider.

"Who else is out there?"

"No one but me. Well, and a little Jimmy Walker." Zack snickered. He *did* make a good drunk guy.

"I'm giving you one—" The door opened wider. Wide enough for Zack to grab the front of the man's shirt and yank him outside. "Hey!"

Bryce sprang from his spot. Stephens had the man down on the grass. They rolled in the lawn. Bryce couldn't risk using the shotgun, so he set it down and was about to jump in when a glint of metal flashed in the moonlight.

"He's got a knife!" Bryce yelled.

Zack grunted. He rolled and popped up onto his feet, just beyond the other man's grasp.

Bryce moved behind the stranger. He tried to approach from the right while Zack covered the left. The man between them swung a deadly arc with his blade when either of them got close. One of them was going to have to grab him to get that knife away.

Bryce waited. Watched. As soon as the man looked at Zack and his focus diverted for a split second, Bryce grabbed the arm with the knife. But the bulky man was faster than he looked. His arm slipped out of Bryce's reach, and in a split second, the blade sliced into Bryce's thigh.

Pain seared. Bryce groaned. But it was the distraction Zack needed. He lunged at the man, and they both fell to the ground. Bryce grabbed his thigh and moved closer, ready to jump in. In the dark, he couldn't tell who was who as the two men wrestled. Warm moisture seeped between his fingers. Suddenly the two men stopped.

"Stephens!" Bryce yelled.

The shadowed clump separated, one man slowly moving to his feet. "It's okay, boss. I'm fine." Zack's voice was strained, but the other man didn't move. Bryce stepped closer, his eyes glued to the man in the grass with a knife sticking out of his chest. He wasn't going anywhere.

"Go get the girls!" Zack said as he bent over.

Bryce didn't need to be told twice. He ran to the front door and paused. Anything could be on the other side of it. He opened it cautiously. A scuffle sounded from another room, grunts and groans, and from the sound of it, punches being thrown.

A particularly feminine voice screamed.

Penny! Bryce ran in, the toe of his boot catching on the pistol lying in the middle of the hall. He scooped it up and rushed in.

Libby lay on the floor, but the man with dark hair had Penny in a choke hold. He also held a gun and was in the process of bringing it up to her head. Bryce didn't hesitate when he saw the clear shot. He pulled the trigger once.

The man's grip around Penny's neck loosened. He fell to the linoleum.

Bryce leaped over to catch Penny. "Are you okay?"

She pushed him away and instead grabbed the man by the lapels of his jacket. "What is the plan? What are you doing here?" her voice screamed. Libby roused.

But the man's stare went from panicked to vacant as the life drained out of him. A pool of blood spread below his body.

Penny lowered him and looked up at Bryce.

"We needed him alive!"

Seriously? She was mad at him? "He had a gun. He was about to kill you."

"I had it handled." She stood up and glared at him.

She hadn't had it handled. She probably knew she hadn't. But if he'd learned anything tonight, it was that Penny desperately needed to feel a sense of control. So he'd bite his tongue for now. Saying anything would only push her away.

"Penny?" Libby's weak voice sounded. She sat up.

Penny ignored Bryce and knelt next to her sister. "Are you o—"

Her words were cut off as Libby grabbed her in a tight hug. Bryce didn't want to intrude on the sisters' private moment. He moved and stood over the man he'd shot.

It wasn't Alonzo Sosa.
Obviously this wasn't over.

TWENTY-FIVE

HER WORLDS WERE COLLIDING AND NOT IN A good way. Penny couldn't keep the walls up between work and family and . . . whatever Bryce was. She swung from wanting to strangle the man to remembering that kiss in the nightclub parking lot, wishing for more moments like it.

What was wrong with her?

At least Libby and the kids were physically okay. Penny paced the wide hospital hallway, the utilitarian linoleum polished to a harsh shine. After being trapped in the pantry, she would gladly pace as much as she wanted with plenty of space to move while she waited for Libby to be discharged.

Bryce and Jude walked toward her. Both men looked a little haggard. Bryce's pants were torn and bloody. One leg of his jeans was cut off completely from where he had been stitched up from a knife wound. Jude's clothes were rumpled, sweat-stained.

"They okay?" Bryce asked.

She nodded toward the closed door where the doctor was still with Libby. "The kids are fine. Libby has a bump on the head and a black eye, but she'll be okay. Dan is on the way home."

Jude stood in front of her. "So that was the lead you were following? Tracking down your sister and her kids?"

She shrugged. "I told you I didn't take the kidnapping of women and children lightly."

"You could've told me." He stared her down.

"And you would've come."

"No doubt."

"And lost your job."

His gaze narrowed. "You're right. But—"

"You had another family to look for. I'm just sorry we weren't able to get another lead on Sosa. The one cell phone we found was smashed in the guy's pocket from when he hit the floor. But what about you? Any leads on the governor's wife and son?"

"We'll get Sosa. And we're still looking for the governor's family. But you are family too. I'm just glad you're safe. And for the record, I think you made the right move blowing off Jason Woods."

"I doubt he would say so."

"Your family has to come first. Maybe it's for the best that you left the ATF. You couldn't do that as a fed."

She stuffed her hands in her pockets. "That's what I keep telling you. Private sector is where it's at."

He chuckled as he leaned against the wall, exhaustion etched into his features, in the fine lines framing his eyes.

"How'd the raid at the militia compound go?" Bryce asked.

Jude sighed. "A bust. I mean, we seized some weaponry and explosives, but no sign of the governor's wife and kid."

"What now?" Penny needed to get her sister and the kids settled first, but then she would do whatever it took.

"The governor is on his way. While the others keep the search going through the night, I've been commanded to go home to get a couple hours of sleep. We've been ordered to be back at six a.m. for debriefing." He pushed off the wall and faced Penny. "And before you ask, until we get their house cleared, you and your family will be staying with Andi and me. I've got some friends from the police department that will be on watch outside twenty-four seven."

Penny was about to protest when Libby came out of the hospital room, a child on each side of her. Jude looked to her. "Your husband should be here tomorrow. I'll have someone waiting to escort him here from the airport."

"Thank you." Libby gave him a tired but grateful smile. She was worn out. They all needed rest.

Penny took Hazel's hand. "Let's get you guys settled for the night. You get to have a sleepover at Jude and Andi's."

"Pen." Bryce grabbed her other hand. "We need to talk—"

"I know. Later."

His jaw clenched tight, his brown eyes smoldering as they gazed at her. But he nodded and let her hand go, his fingertips brushing hers until the very last second she pulled away.

There was too much to figure out right now. Maybe with space she could think clearly about what to do with her growing attachment to Bryce Crawford. But she needed to see Libby and the kids settled first. Of course, there wasn't much space, since he followed them to Jude and Andi's.

Before long, the two kids were in the guest room at the Brookses' house.

Bryce Crawford was impulsive. Reckless even. But it was in his arms where Penny'd felt the safest she'd ever been. Her nephew adored him. Hazel was half in love with him too as they both cuddled up on either side of him, his long body stretched out on the guest bed as he read them a story. The kids' eyes drooped, each little blond head resting on Bryce's capable chest and little hands tucked around his arms.

"He's the reason you left, isn't he?"

"Shhh!" Penny spun around to see her sister in the hallway, watching her with a peculiar smile.

Penny walked past her to the living area. Sounds from the kitchen, where Andi was brewing coffee and tea, drifted over.

"Pen, why are you pushing him away? I heard the way you talked to him at the hospital. But he saved your life." Libby looked at her with an unspoken "duh."

"You mean when he killed my witness? The one shot I had at finding Sosa and closing this case?" Yeah, it sounded petty, but she needed a handle on this. Something to push back on. Something to remind her she had some semblance of control over her defiant heart.

"I know I was knocked out for a while, but I saw it. That man was going to kill you. Bryce *saved* you."

It was on the verge of her tongue to deny it, to restate that she'd had the situation in hand, but Libby would see through it in a heartbeat. As the internal walls crumbled, everything was leaking out. Maybe this habit of going at it alone was one she needed to break. Because she was definitely seeing more potential in sticking around. And yeah. He had saved her.

"What's important is that you and the kids are safe," she finally managed to say. Who could argue with that?

Libby moved in and hugged Penny. Not one of their awkward pats on the back or anything. A real embrace. That made twice in one day. It was strange. And . . . rather nice.

"I never did thank you for that." Libby pulled back, wiped the tear that slipped down her cheek. "So thank you. You know, for saving us. I knew you'd come."

"You did?"

Libby nodded. "Yeah. I prayed, and even though I was terrified, there was this . . . peace. Like, I knew we were going to be okay. And I knew you wouldn't stop until you found us. Maybe I shouldn't get on your case so much about your dangerous job."

Right. Her job that had gotten them into this in the first place.

Libby didn't deserve what'd happened tonight. Penny looked her sister in the eye. "I'm so sorry."

Libby whipped her head back. "Sorry? Penny, you saved us."

"But if it weren't for me, none of this would've happened."

"What are you talking about?"

"It's because of *me* they took you in the first place. That's why I don't visit much or stay in one place. I have to separate my work from my personal life to keep *you* safe."

"Us? I think you do it to keep your heart safe. That's why you push him away too." Libby tilted her head toward the room on the other side of the wall, where Bryce and the kids were. "But who is going to rescue you when you need it, Pen? Say what you want, but that man in there showed up for you. Don't push him away when he so clearly cares about you."

TWENTY-SIX

RATHER THAN SLEEP ALONE IN HIS APARTMENT, Bryce stayed overnight at the fire hall with Izan and Zack. It was too quiet in his own place, and there was no way he would be able to sleep with Penny nearby if he stayed at his sister's house and crashed on the couch as she'd offered.

He hated having everything so up in the air with her. He wanted another chance. A future with Penny Mitchell. Maybe, someday, their own kids to read bedtime stories to. He just had to show her he wasn't like her dad or her boss. At least with the crew nearby and knowing Penny was safe, Bryce could relax enough to get a few-hours doze in before the meeting. His leg throbbed where he'd been knifed, and his head didn't feel so hot either, but it only fueled his desire to catch these guys.

He grabbed a quick shower and triple espresso drink before he rode to city hall, where they were meeting the governor. The conference room was quiet for as many bodies as they'd crammed in there. Jude and Penny and Anthony sat at the table. Even after a harrowing rescue and little sleep, she looked amazing. Strong.

She met his wink with a slight smile as he moved to stand at the back of the room, where he could stay more alert. Olivia stood next to him. The chief of police chatted with Allen Frees quietly at the other end of the room.

What was taking so long? Bryce checked his watch again. 6:05.

Finally Jason Woods, Governor Noble, and another woman walked in. Not that Bryce knew the governor personally, but even he could tell the man had aged overnight. There was no friendly smile, just gaunt cheek bones, a tic in his jaw, and a wrinkled suit. Bryce didn't think the room could get any quieter, but somehow it did.

The governor stood at the head of the long table and made eye contact with each person around it before speaking.

"I used to think Last Chance County was one of the safest places a family could go. I'd spend summers out here with my grand-parents, my cousins"—he gestured toward Jason Woods—"and friends. I was excited to show my son all the places I'd frequented."

Wait. Woods was the governor's cousin?

Bryce missed something the governor said, but he focused on the man once more.

"Obviously things have changed. This isn't the same county I knew as a boy."

No one said a thing.

"Find. My. Family." With each word, a sharp finger stabbed the table top.

"Sir!"

"If I may—"

"We've already—" Voices interrupted and spoke over each other from all over the room.

"Enough." The governor sliced the air with his hand. "I don't want excuses. I want them found. Now."

"Yes, sir." The mayor tugged at his collar. "We are doing every-thing we can. But I still advise you to cancel the ball tonight. If we could just take this news to the public, they could—"

"No! This militia wants the publicity. The attention. They want to make a spectacle of my family. I will not give them the satisfaction. And there is no need to cause the public to panic. We will go on with the events as planned."

With that, the man turned and left, Jason Woods and the mayor right behind him.

Small conversations erupted around the room. Jude and Penny joined Bryce and Olivia.

"Gutsy move on his part to keep this quiet," Olivia said.

"He's not wrong though. These groups want the glory and frenzy. If people knew the governor's wife and son were missing, do you know how many false leads we'd be sifting through right now? At least keeping it quiet will help us focus on the leads we already have," Anthony said.

"What leads?" Bryce asked. "As far as I can tell, we've got nothing."

"Not exactly." Olivia hooked her thumbs through loops on her uniform vest. "You said Sosa was behind the kidnapping of Libby and the kids, but we know he has some tie to the militia too. We have the two dead bodies from the trailer. One of them was Arturo Hernandez. The other we're still identifying, and we're processing the scene. That will take time."

"And we have Emma," Anthony said.

Penny turned to face Jude. "I want a crack at her."

Jude paused a moment. "We've got nothing to lose. Let's give it a try. She'll be transferred to the federal prison soon."

"I'm going with you." Bryce didn't want to let Penny out of his sight, even if she was going to the police station and accompanied by his federal agent brother-in-law.

"You can watch through the one-way glass with me," Olivia said as she nudged his arm.

Penny stared at his arm where Olivia had made contact. Her eyebrow twitched.

"You good, Pen?" Jude asked her.

"Great." She flashed a fake smile. "Let's find our lead."

Before long, Anthony was sent on a call, but Bryce and Olivia stood behind the one-way glass window, staring at a stark-gray room with a worn table and old wooden chairs. Penny leaned against the wall, picking at her cuticle. She didn't look up when the door opened and Jude escorted Emma inside.

But Bryce noticed the slight narrowing of her eyes. She was a lioness on the hunt. He almost felt sorry for Emma.

Almost.

"You're on a sinking ship, Emma," Penny said, still focused on her nail beds.

"Whatever."

Jude pulled out Emma's chair since she was still handcuffed. He took a seat across the table while Penny circled the small room.

"Why are you wasting my time?" Emma speared Penny with a look. "You wouldn't have me here if you didn't need something."

"Oh, we have everything we need. We're just nice enough to offer you one more chance to lighten your sentence. I'm sure you think you're protecting Alonzo, but it's only a matter of time. I doubt he'd be so kind to you. I bet he'll cave as soon as he's in custody and leave you holding the bag."

"Nice try, but you won't get me to turn on him. He loves me." Emma didn't look too worried as she leaned back in her chair.

"Pretty confident words for a woman he left behind." Penny rounded the table and leaned in Emma's face.

Emma's only response was a sharp intake of breath and deadly glare.

"Oh, she's good." Olivia chuckled.

"Yeah, she is." Bryce leaned his forearm on the frame of the glass, taking a little pressure off his injured leg.

Jude sat back watching the exchange, letting the women talk. Penny pulled out her phone and set it on the table in front of

Emma. "This guy gave us everything we needed to know. Before he died."

Emma sat up and looked at the screen. She laughed. "Ramos? He was a low-level dealer. He knew nothing. You're bluffing."

"I know Arturo Hernandez is dead."

Emma went still. Penny circled the table once more, probably letting her words soak in. "We're closing in on your boyfriend as we speak. I thought, woman to woman, we could level with each other. So I'm gonna tell it to you straight. He's not worth the multiple life sentences you're facing." She leaned over the table on both hands, looking right at her prey.

"Alonzo would never let that happen." Emma got right back in Penny's face.

"How does an intelligent girl like you even get caught up with a lowlife like him? You had a 4.0. A full-ride scholarship to school. Is he the reason you left in the middle of your junior year?"

"You don't know anything. He has a plan. I'll be free soon enough. I can't say the same for your loved ones." Emma smirked.

"Oh, my family is fine. Just chatted with them before I came in here. Which means your plan didn't work. No one is busting you out, Emma. And you, Jude?"

"Everyone is great."

"See? Everyone is peachy." Penny sat in the chair by Jude. "I mean, except Hernandez. Oh, and Ramos. He wasn't a smart pick for a kidnapping attempt. Very sloppy. But you saw how that ended up. And tonight we'll have the Governor's Ball. I'm really looking forward to meeting Cindy and Adam Noble." Penny leaned back, looking perfectly relaxed against the chair.

Emma's brows turned in. Her smirk faded.

Maybe she was finally catching on. Penny was going in for the kill. Bryce swelled with pride for her. Emma would do best to stay out of her way.

"So Alonzo can do whatever he wants with the militia. But

I don't see him busting down doors to get you out of here. He's letting you rot like yesterday's garbage. He had one shot, and that 'low-level dealer' blew it."

"You know nothing," Emma hissed. "What would a stuck-up pig like you know about true love? Alonzo is his own man. The militia thinks they're using him, but *he's* the one in control. All the pieces are in place. The gangs already turned on each other. The militia owes Alonzo everything. And he *will* free me. It's only a matter of time. There's nowhere the governor can hide his family that's safe. He'll bow to Alonzo eventually."

"You think your man is going to rule? And what? That you'll be the queen beside him?" Penny scoffed.

"Why not hold the strings and let someone else do the heavy lifting?" Emma's smirk was back.

Penny popped off her chair and stretched. "Ah. Well, lovely chat, Emma." She tilted her head, a finger to her chin as she studied the woman in cuffs. "I bet you'll look good in orange." She winked and left the room, leaving Jude to escort a slack-jawed Emma out.

Bryce and Olivia met Penny in the hall. Emma hurled expletives as Jude led her away. Other officers in uniform scurried past in both directions. The chatter and radio noise from the bullpen down the hall was muffled.

But it was Penny's green eyes sparkling with victory that captured Bryce's attention.

"So that's his endgame," she said. "Sosa wants to set up his own little kingdom here. He's already scaring the gangs away, pushing his own product. He must've supplied the militia for favors in return."

"What does he want with the governor's family?" Olivia asked. "There still hasn't been a ransom set yet."

Bryce had an answer for that. "I'm guessing leverage."

Penny nodded. "The militia is antigovernment. They've been very outspoken about wanting a change in the capital. I bet Sosa is just using them to do his dirty work. He gets a few politicians in his pocket, it becomes a lot easier to do shady business and organize a network across the whole state with direct access to three major cities."

Not if Bryce and this team had anything to say about it. "But we're not going to let that happen."

"I certainly hope not."

Bryce spun around to see Jason Woods staring them down. He walked toward their group. "What's being done here to find the governor's family? Does this look like a good time to stand around and chat?"

Woods's job was on the line, and technically the governor was family to Jason, so Bryce tried to overlook the implications. "We're doing what we can to find them. Penny just got some valuable intel on Sosa's endgame."

"Are you sure he's the one behind the kidnapping? My cousin's wife and child are out there somewhere. You better not be wasting time."

Penny stood, hands on her hips, and had no problem facing the man before them. "We know Sosa kidnapped *my* family. We got them back. We'll get the governor's family too."

Bryce stepped up to stand beside her. "And they *are* connected. Sosa and the militia must have a common goal or at least a mutually beneficial understanding. Believe me, we're not wasting anyone's time."

Jason didn't say anything for a moment. "Good. Keep at it. Ms. Mitchell, if you don't mind, I'd like to hire you to keep an eye out for Sosa at the ball this evening."

"The ball is still going on?" Olivia asked. "That will be a lot of police coverage for the event when we could be out looking for the family."

"I don't like it, but the other agencies believe Sosa will show if we continue on as planned." Jason turned toward Penny again.

"Brooks said you have some protection detail training and you can recognize Sosa by voice, so the governor wants to add you to the crew tonight. Wear evening dress. If you come with me, we can go over particulars."

She glanced over at Bryce and Olivia before facing Woods once more. "Anything to be of service."

Bryce didn't like the sight of her walking away with Jason at all, but it wasn't like he was a threat. The man was more wind than substance. But Bryce wanted to be the one at her side. Too bad he wasn't a bodyguard for hire too.

Olivia nodded toward the flurry of activity in the bullpen. "Come on, Bryce. Let's look into the militia members and see what we can find before the ball."

TWENTY-SEVEN

YOU LOOK SO PRETTY!" HAZEL SAID AS SHE stared at Penny in the full-length mirror in Andi's bedroom. The red beaded gown with the halter top was surprisingly comfortable for formal wear. The slit up the side went high enough to easily access her holster there but not reveal the weapon. She needed to blend in with the crowd tonight and still do her job to keep the governor safe and find Sosa.

Libby appeared in the doorway. "All right, munchkin, why don't you help your brother in the kitchen. He's making cookies with Andi, and I hear they need a taste-tester."

"Cookies? Bye, Aunt Penny! Have fun at the ball!" Hazel was already out the door and down the hall.

"That's one way to occupy her so you can lecture me." Penny put the finishing touches of red lipstick on.

"You make it hard to get you alone. I had to be creative." Libby fixed a stray lock of hair that had escaped the updo. "But I didn't come to lecture you."

"Sure you did. You have that look."

"I just want to see you settled and happy, Pen. Put down some roots. Maybe even get married someday. Is that so bad?"

"Weren't you the one that always told me to never find my happiness in a man? And then you went and married one. Talk about mixed messages." Penny reached for the earrings Andi had left out for her. "Besides, wasn't too long ago you and Dan were on the verge of splitting up."

"Yeah. Moving here was my last-ditch effort to save our marriage. I hoped a less stressful job, a small-town vibe would give us more family time."

Penny studied her sister in the mirror. Despite the stress and trauma of everything that had gone on, she'd never seen her so at peace. Content. "You seem better now. Guess it worked."

"It wasn't the new job or the move. It was God." Libby watched her put the earrings in.

"Ah. So this is the part where you tell me I need Jesus." Penny swiped her clutch off the bed and dropped her lipstick into it. "But I need to leave soon."

"I just hope you'll give Bryce a chance. He's one of the good ones."

"I'm not denying that Bryce is a good man. But I've seen what loving someone can do. Two isn't always better than one."

"No, but three is." Libby looked down at her wedding ring a moment. "You want to know what really saved my marriage? A verse from Ecclesiastes that said a cord of three strands is not easily broken."

What was she talking about? "You and Dan have an open marriage? I'm not religious, and even to me that doesn't sound right."

Libby laughed. "The third strand is God. When we both came to understand who He is, what He's done for us, everything changed."

Penny wanted to swat all the words away, but something she'd never heard in Libby's voice stayed her. "What changed?"

"For the first time in my life there was something—no, Someone bigger than us. I found hope and purpose and love in God."

"And that magically fixed everything?"

Libby sat on the bed. "There wasn't anything magical about it. It's still hard work to keep our marriage going. But as Dan and I went through counseling and read the Bible and got to know the Lord on our own, priorities shifted. I wasn't looking to Dan or our marriage to fulfill me in ways it was never meant to. Things that used to be so important to me didn't mean as much anymore."

"Things like what?" Penny picked at the beading of her clutch, not necessarily ready to reveal how much she wanted what her sister seemed to have already found.

"For one, I didn't need the stability and recognition from my job or Dan or the kids. I found that all in Christ. I never realized how much I worried about how other people saw me. How I had this image of having it all together that I felt pressured to maintain. I still struggle with that, but it's better. And I went from asking 'What do I need from Dan, what is he not giving to me, and why won't he just pick up his dirty towels in the bathroom and make my life easier?' to 'What can I do for Dan? How can I show him love today?' I'll tell you, that's not marriage advice or life advice you'll find in a magazine article or most of the psychology podcasts I listened to, but it's made all the difference for us."

"And what if the worst thing happens to Dan? Or the kids? What happens when you lose them? God's gonna pick up all the pieces and make it better?" Penny stared right at Libby, daring her to speak truth.

"I can't imagine my life without them, but yeah, if something happened and I lost them, I know I'll see them again. And I'd grieve. My heart would shatter. But I know God would hold me together, because I've realized I never had it together in the first place. I've tried. I spent a lot of years that way, and now that I have the freedom to let that worry go, I want it for you too."

"I'm not going to deny that I've been thinking about it, but"— Penny sat next to Libby on the bed—"I'm doing fine on my own. Don't you think?"

"Until you're not. Penny, letting others in, letting God in, doesn't make you weak the way Dad told us. It makes you stronger. Remember, a cord of three? The verse goes, 'Though one may be overpowered, two can defend themselves. A cord of three strands is not quickly broken.' You can't deny a braid is stronger than a single strand. Please, just think about it?"

She was right. She couldn't deny the imagery, but she needed to leave. "I will. But I have to go now."

Penny tried hard to put all the things Libby had said out of mind as she drove to the big hotel venue for the ball. But they stuck in her brain rather annoyingly. She had a job to focus on though. This wasn't time for personal matters.

So why did the words beckon her?

I'm doing fine on my own.

Until you're not.

Like when she'd fallen apart in the storage closet. Or at the thought of going into that storm cellar. Those moments were coming more frequently. Why now? She was older. Stronger now. But the panic attacks were coming more frequently.

Not only that, but the way she was drawn to Bryce was evidence too . . . the ultimate weakness. She was falling for him.

Maybe it wouldn't be so bad to spend a little more time here with Libby and the kids. She could certainly do a better job visiting.

And Bryce? Well, she didn't quite know what to do about him. But that was a problem for another time, because right now she had a job to do.

She slipped her Sig into the thigh holster under her dress. Thank goodness Andi had one she could borrow. Libby had some cute slingbacks she would still be able to run in if need be.

Penny went through the security at the door, showed her identification, and was led back to the meeting room where the governor and others from his office waited.

Governor Noble shook her hand. The classic tux and well-groomed brown-and-gray hair didn't hide the lines of worry around his eyes and across his broad forehead.

"Thank you for coming, Ms. Mitchell. Since you seem to know who all the players are in this game, I'm grateful to have you on our security team tonight." He quickly introduced her to the others in the room, mostly security protection, assistants, and staff members from his office.

"It's my pleasure to be here. I'll keep you safe."

"I appreciate that." His tight smile was sad. Obviously the worry about his family weighed it down.

"Sir, forgive me for saying so, but are you sure you don't want the citizens to know that your wife and son are missing? What if they could help? What if someone saw something?"

"Believe me, I've been through it all. I wanted to show up here tonight and prove to these cowards that I'm not going to roll over and play dead."

"What is it they want? Has there been an official demand?"

"They want me to step down. They're not happy with the changes we've been making at the capital. But they'll see soon enough. I don't cower to bullies."

He turned as another man in a suit gestured to him. "Excuse me, Ms. Mitchell."

"Of course." She stepped away, giving them privacy as the two men put their heads together, deep in conversation.

Tony walked into the room looking rather dapper in a black tux. He checked in with the guard at the door.

She waited for a hint of attraction or warmth. Nothing.

He wasn't Bryce.

But he did walk right up to her, mouth firm.

"What are you doing here?" she asked him.

"They needed extra security." He didn't give her his typical flirty smile. In fact, he seemed annoyed or something.

"What's wrong?"

"I thought we were on the same team."

"We are."

"Then why didn't you call me the second your family was kidnapped? I would've been there to help find them."

Ah. That.

"Do you not trust me?" he asked.

"That has nothing to do with it."

"Then what is it about?"

"Tony, all I could focus on was finding Libby and the kids. I wasn't really thinking straight. And I admit, I'm not the greatest at depending on others. I'm sorry. But for now, we need to focus on finding the governor's family."

"No more of this leaving me in the dark?"

"I'll do my best. Are we good?"

He gave her a short nod. "Okay." He looked around the room. "Where are the others on the task force?"

"Jude is here somewhere. Olivia too, I think. Bryce had a work shift."

"You two figure anything out?" Tony's smirk was back.

Penny rolled her eyes at him. "Wouldn't you like to know."

Jason Woods clapped. The chatter around the room immediately died. "All right, people. Let's keep eyes open. You know what to do."

Penny took her place behind the governor as he left the room. They made their way to the stage, where a podium stood. Officers situated around the room guarded every angle. Penny stayed in the spotlight, scanning the crowd, ready to move if need be.

"Welcome, friends and neighbors. Who's ready to boogie?" The governor spoke into the microphone.

Cheers and clapping rose from the crowd.

Penny studied every inch of the room, not really listening to the governor's speech. She didn't know how he was holding it together with his wife and child missing. But she'd make sure nothing happened to the man on her watch. The governor's security had ensured the corners of the room were well-lit. Caterers came and went as they filled plates and trays of hors d'oeuvres on the back table. None of them stood out or paid much attention to the man on the stage.

Before she knew it, Governor Noble was waving and leaving the podium. His countenance changed as soon as he was offstage. His shoulders dropped and he ran a hand through his hair.

A woman handed him a tablet as soon as he reached the wings. "Here's a list of the people you wanted to touch base with tonight."

"Thank you, Reba." He scrolled down the tablet, then handed it back to her. "Let's get this over with." He rolled his shoulders back as if bracing himself and walked a few steps. He paused and pulled out his phone. His whole body went rigid.

"What is it?" Penny asked.

He shook his head. "Nothing." He gave her a tight smile.

"Are you sure? If you know something—"

"No, no. I'm fine. I'm just not really in a dancing mood. But let's go out there, make our appearance, and leave."

"Whatever you say." Penny stepped back behind him, watching the shadows as they navigated the dark spaces at the edges of the stage and wound down to the dance floor. The governor mingled with guests, shook hands, smiled. Penny stayed on his tail and watched for her target.

The governor bent over the table and looked at something a man with a jacket and bolo tie was showing him. Penny took a moment to study the outskirts of room. It had been a lot easier from up on stage.

A man in a black Stetson, standing at the coffee station by the desserts, caught her eye. His back was to Penny, but he was the right height and build. He spoke to a woman and then left the room. Just before he did, he turned, and she caught his profile.

Sosa!

TWENTY-EIGHT

USUALLY BRYCE LOOKED FORWARD TO HIS WORK shift. But then again, he wasn't usually left out of a once-in-a-lifetime Last Chance party like the Governor's Ball. And it didn't help that Penny was there too. Probably looking gorgeous in the red formal gown he'd caught a peek of when Andi had pulled it out of her closet and handed it to Penny.

But like it or not, law enforcement and emergency services were spread thin, and someone had to work the rescue truck tonight. Maybe he wouldn't feel so useless if he and Olivia had found something when they'd knocked on doors of known militia members and canvassed the area earlier. The whole day felt like a bust.

He stared at the computer on the desk he shared with the other lieutenants. He was about to check his phone for a message when the rescue tones went off. He sprang off the chair and jogged to the bay. Zack met him there.

The dispatcher's voice called out over the speaker system. "Rescue Squad 5, please respond with extrication for nine-year-old child trapped in a railing. They are conscious and breathing at this time."

Zack grinned. "What do you think, stairs or playground equipment? I'm guessing playground."

"Let's go find out." Anything to be doing something. Bryce hopped behind the wheel and started the engine. He drove to the address sent to their truck. It was on the outskirts of the town, down a dirt road. The small farmhouse was freshly painted, the yard tidy.

Bryce looked at Zack. "Stairs. Definitely stairs."

They walked up to the front porch. A woman in a sleek black dress and high heels met them at the door. "Thank you so much for coming. I don't know how—wait. You're Coach Bryce, right?"

"That's me."

"I'm Gloria." She showed them inside. "My son is on your baseball team. Martín."

"Martín is caught?" The little guy was a bundle of high energy. But he was a smart kid too. "How did he do that?"

"You'll have to ask him. We were on our way to the Governor's Ball, and the next thing I know . . . this." She led them through the entry into the living room, where sure enough, Martín's head stuck out between elegant iron posts halfway up to the second floor.

No sign of Martín's usual grin or mischievous smirk today. In fact, Bryce had never seen the boy looking so glum.

"Hey, bud, don't worry. My friend Zack and I will get you right out." Bryce set down his toolbox.

"I hoped it would be you, Coach," Martín said.

"Guess it's your lucky day." Bryce winked.

"It wasn't luck. I know you have Tuesdays off for ball, and I figured out your schedule." His big brown eyes were starting to show a bit of their usual glint.

Zack chuckled. "You're smart all right. So how'd you get your head stuck?"

Martín's mouth clamped shut.

His mother wrung her hands together. "Can you get him out?

I don't care what you have to do to the railing. We'll get that fixed. Just set him free."

Within a few minutes, Zack and Bryce pried the bars far apart enough for Martín to slip his head back through. As far as rescues went, this was one of the easiest.

As soon as the boy was back on the first floor, Gloria looked him over and hugged him. "Are you okay?" She kissed his cheek, leaving a bright pink lipstick mark.

"Sí, Mamá. I'm fine." He wiped his cheek.

Maybe it was embarrassment that had him so quiet. Zack packed up their tools while Bryce tried to reassure his friend. "Everyone gets in a pickle sometimes. I'm glad I was here to help. And that your mom called us right away."

Martín nodded but didn't say anything.

Even Gloria looked worried. She knelt in front of her son. "*Mijo,* are you sure you're all right?"

Martín looked from his mother to Bryce and back again. Something was definitely off.

"Why don't you take these out to the truck. I'll be right there." Bryce handed his tools to Zack. As soon as he left, Bryce got down on his knees to be eye level with Martín.

The stitches in his leg pulled, but he ignored them. "It's okay. You can tell me anything. Did something happen?" He could see the boy getting in trouble and not wanting to tell his mother.

His mother spoke in Spanish. Bryce picked up the gist of it. She was encouraging him to talk.

Releasing a long sigh, Martín finally looked up at Bryce. "Remember how at school you said we should tell someone if we see something dangerous or someone hurt?"

"Yeah? Did you see something?"

The boy nodded. He glanced at his mother, his eyes shimmering as if holding back tears.

"What is it, mijo?" his mother asked.

"I can't say. He said he would hurt you," the boy mumbled as he looked at his mom.

"Who?" His mother squeezed his hand.

Martín shook his head.

Bryce laid a gentle hand on the kid's shoulder. "Hey, no one is gonna hurt your mom. We will do whatever we need to protect you both. If you saw something, I need you to be really brave now and let us know."

"I saw a bad man hit a boy and a mom."

Bryce froze. "Where?"

"When I road my bike to Billy's house. His older brother saw me. He said if I kept my mouth shut I would be fine, but if I said anything to Billy or anyone else, he would hurt my mother. Kill my sister."

Bryce stood and looked at the mom. "Who is Billy and where does he live?"

"He's a neighbor," she said. "By road, you have to go around the fields and their house is a couple miles away, but the boys have a shorter path cutting through our backyard." Her voice shook. "His older brother Tyler was dating my daughter. Do you really think he would hurt us?"

They both looked at Martín. "Was the boy there, at Billy's house?" Bryce asked him.

Martín gulped. "A big man—he was bad—he dragged them out of a car and he hit them and put them in the old barn. Their hands were tied up. That's how I knew he was bad. And sometimes Billy says he's sick, but I know he isn't. His dad hurts him."

Bryce pulled out his phone and found a picture of the governor's family. "Was this the boy and woman you saw?"

Martín nodded.

Bryce quickly got their address. "I need to call this in right away. Until we know what's going on, it's best that you two stay here."

"Of course." Gloria's face paled.

He held out a fist for a bump from Martín. "You did the right thing."

And then it hit him. "Did you get stuck on purpose?"

The boy paused, nodded.

His mother gasped. "Martín!"

"Don't come down on him too hard. He's a hero tonight." Bryce thanked them and ran outside. He and Zack climbed into the truck.

"What's going on?" Zack asked.

Bryce told him. "I need to call it in. But Jude, Penny, and the others are busy guarding the governor."

"Call the governor's line. See who picks up. Then we can call the cops."

"Good idea." Bryce searched online for the number and called.

"This is Jason Woods."

Guess that would make sense that he would take Governor Noble's calls. Bryce explained where the Nobles were being held. "Can you read Penny, Jude, and the others in, so they know what's going on?"

"I'll take care of it. And . . . good work, Crawford."

"Thanks. I'll call the police and—"

"Don't bother. I'll get it set up. If you can, why don't you try to get eyes on the place while you wait for the police to show up. Don't be a hero or anything, but if you can get visual confirmation that would help. Then stand by for support."

"Sure." Bryce hung up with Woods and turned to his partner. "Time to go find Governor Noble's wife and son. They want us to scope it out and be there for additional support."

"Maybe we should use the bike trail you mentioned. They'll see us coming if we approach from the road."

"Good point."

Bryce and Zack shrugged out of their reflective turnout gear and grabbed their black jackets from the back of the truck instead.

They followed Gloria's directions through the fields to find the narrow bike trail. With the sun setting, the colder air settled down over the grass, causing a misty haze. Soon the top of a barn poked above the hill ahead.

They came to an outbuilding on the far edge of the field. A cluster of trees hid them as they watched the open area in front of them. The big barn stood to the right, a smaller shed and a corn crib beside it. The house sat on the other side of the driveway from the barn. It was an old farmhouse style like Gloria and Martín's, but it wasn't nearly as neat and tidy.

Cows bellowed from the barn structure. Piles of junk and old vehicles were scattered around the property as well as more sheds and a detached garage. Plenty of places to hide. But not a soul in sight.

There were no lights in the windows of the house, but a white van with a floral logo sat in front of the house under the big pole lighting up the barnyard. No one milled around. They'd have to move in closer to find the wife and kid.

"I'll head this way and check out the garage and shed over there by the house," Bryce whispered. "Why don't you see if you can find anything in the barn and on that side. Hopefully by the time we're back the cops will be here."

Zack nodded and slipped away. Bryce moved from a junk pile of old tires to the shadows of a pickup truck. From there, he scurried to the corner of the garage. He pressed an ear against the side door. Nothing.

He tried the knob. It turned easily in his hand. He slipped in. The smell of motor oil and grass clippings hit him. There was a car covered with a tarp in the middle of the space. Enough light shone in through a high window to show the wall opposite him held shelves full of tools and sporting equipment. No people though. Bryce went back outside.

A noise like footsteps sounded.

"Zack?" Bryce kept his voice low.

After a moment of nothing but lowing cows, Bryce moved toward the house. At the sound of rocks scuffling, he spun around again and came face-to-face with the barrel end of a shotgun.

"What are you doing on my property?" The man holding the gun stood in the shadows, but he was tall and brawny and smelled like he spent his days mucking out the barn.

Before Bryce could answer, the back of his head exploded with pain and everything went black.

TWENTY-NINE

NO DICE. PENNY HADN'T FOUND SOSA AND WAS starting to believe she hadn't really seen him. She stood outside the banquet hall and looked both ways in the hotel hallway. Caterers, guests, and a family with twin toddlers moved throughout. No sign of the man in the hat.

Jason Woods walked toward her from the lobby.

She jogged up to him. "Hey, did you see a man in a black Stetson in that direction? It's Sosa."

Jason shook his head. "I saw a guy in a black hat a second ago, but it's not Sosa."

"You're sure?"

"He kinda looked like Sosa, but it's not him. How well did you see him?"

"I saw his profile. It was only for a second but—"

Jason gave her a patronizing smile. "Maybe you're becoming a little too vigilant."

Woods tried to take her by the arm, but she pulled away from him. "I can walk fine on my own."

He lifted his hands in surrender and backed off. "Only trying to be a gentleman. But remember, we hired you to do a job."

"And I'm doing it." She went back through the doorway, aware Jason's eyes were on her. She did a quick scan of the banquet room. The governor shook another hand as he left the table of businessmen and women he'd been visiting with.

Couples danced on the parquet floor set near the stage. Jason left the room again and turned toward the meeting room they'd been in before the event started.

She wasn't sad to see him go.

Penny made eye contact with Anthony and Olivia on the other side of the room. She signaled to them, and they both came over. They stood off to the side of the table while the governor continued his conversation. Sounded like he was talking to cattlemen.

"Did you two see anything suspicious? I thought I saw Sosa, but I guess it wasn't him."

Olivia shook her head. She wore her uniform, like some of the other on-duty cops.

Anthony looked around. "I haven't seen anything. And believe me, I've been looking."

"Me too." Penny brushed back the lock of blonde hair that once again escaped her bun.

"How much longer will the governor be here?" Olivia asked quietly.

Penny checked her watch. "No idea, but I can't imagine he'll want to stay too long. He's already pushing it as it is."

She studied the governor. His smile went nowhere close to reaching his eyes. He nodded at the man talking, but she got the impression he didn't really hear what was being said.

Olivia clucked her tongue. "I don't know how he's holding up like he is. But I have to go do a perimeter check. I'll see you two after." She walked away and joined one of the other uniformed cops by the door.

"You holding up okay?" Tony asked her. "You couldn't have gotten much sleep last night."

"I'm good."

Jude approached them with a glass of punch he didn't drink. "You two enjoying the party?"

He wore a suit and tie to blend in, but his eyes didn't stop studying the room.

Penny turned to keep the governor in her view as he moved to the next table. "I've been better. And I heard your wedding reception was quite the shindig. Rumor has it you were seen doing the Macarena."

Tony's jaw dropped. "Brooks doing the Macarena? Now that I gotta see. Think if I request it, the band over there will play it?"

Penny chuckled. "We could always try."

But even that wouldn't quite make this feel like a real party. Sure, there was music, jazzy and soft, and couples danced near the stage, but without Bryce, it all fell flat.

She missed him.

Desperately. And it hadn't even been that long since she'd seen him.

But she wished he were there. Even though he probably would've been a complete distraction. Better to stay focused.

"Any new leads?" she asked Jude.

He moved closer. "I'm working with an FBI team. We're waiting for a warrant on the governor's phone records. I find it hard to believe the captors haven't made contact."

Anthony matched the low tone of Jude's voice. "You think he's hiding something or in on it?"

"We'll know soon. I don't think he's in on it, but I do think the kidnappers have reached out. They must have specific demands." Jude took a sip of his punch. "I'll keep you posted."

As soon as Jude left, Anthony's phone buzzed. Multiple police officers in the room grabbed their phones. Something was happening. Tony moved a few steps away and put the phone to his ear. Penny followed him.

"What's going on?"

He listened a minute longer. "Someone called it in that they found the wife and kid. A farm right outside of town. They're setting up a perimeter."

"Then we should go." Penny grabbed his arm and dragged him over to the governor. She whispered that they had a credible lead on his family.

The governor stiffened. "By all means go. I'll be right behind you. My team will take care of me."

Penny and Tony sprinted to the hallway and out to the lobby. The two-storied room was busy with groups of people loitering and visiting. The duo scooted around a group of ladies in formal wear and ran to the main entrance of the hotel, the double glass doors parting for them. The parking lot was full of vehicles. A black sports car peeled out of the parking lot.

"They're in a hurry." Penny peered, trying to catch a license plate, but it was too far away.

"So are we. Let's go. I'm parked over—"

Tony's words were cut off when a wave of heat knocked them to the ground. An explosion tore a large hole in the outer wall of the hotel and lit the building on fire.

THIRTY

BRYCE SLOWLY OPENED HIS EYES. HIS WHOLE body ached. He lay on a cold slab of cement and slowly pushed his way to sitting, waiting for the room to right itself. This whole getting-knocked-out thing was getting old.

"It's about time. Are you okay?" Jason Woods sat against a pole in the middle of the room. Bryce looked around. The spider webs in the corners, the dank air, the tiny transom window at ground level . . . they were definitely in some kind of basement. Good thing Penny wasn't here.

"I'd be better if people would stop knocking me upside the head." He felt the back of his head. A big bump was there, a scab where he must've bled. "How long was I out? And how did you get here?"

His vision blurred for a moment and then cleared.

"How should I know? One minute I was at my car. The next I'm waking up here."

"Where are we? Any sign of the Nobles?" And where was his partner, Zack?

"I haven't seen anything."

Besides the loosened tie, Jason had lost the suit jacket, but he didn't look too worse for wear. Bryce stood, using another pole, when dizziness and nausea almost overtook him. "We need to find a way out."

Voices and footsteps sounded above their heads. "Do you know who they are?" Bryce pointed at the ceiling.

Jason shook his head. "You were the one who said you knew where the wife and kid were. How did you know?"

"You sent the cops, right?"

"Crawford, how did you know? Who told you?"

Was Jason actually angry with him? Why would he be mad? On closer inspection, he didn't look too beat up either. No signs of pain or soreness. Heck, the man's hair still looked gelled to perfection.

"Why do you want to know?" Bryce walked over to him.

Jason stood up. "We should know if your intel was good. Because I get the feeling you led us straight into a trap. So how did you know the Nobles were here?"

"The intel was good. Besides, if you sent the cops like you said, they'll be here any second." Bryce studied Jason's facial features. "Why are *you* here?"

"I told you. Someone jumped me from behind." Jason's brows furrowed.

"Yeah, but why do they want you? I was poking around, so I get why they have me. But why did they go out of their way to find you?"

"How am I supposed to know? Now, for the last time, how did you figure out where they took the Nobles?"

Something was off. Jason was way too fixated on that when it didn't really matter. Or maybe it was the natural instinct to protect, but no way would Bryce expose Martín and Gloria. "I, uh, followed Sosa."

"You followed him?"

"Yeah." Bryce left it at that.

Jason rolled his eyes and turned. He climbed the wooden plank staircase.

"Where are you going?"

Instead of answering, Jason pounded on the door. "Let me out."

Seriously? He thought they would just let him—

The door opened. A man that looked familiar stuck his head in. "What does he know?"

"Nothing. Clear out and burn the place down."

"Not until I'm through with him," another voice said.

The door swung completely open, and the man let Jason pass.

"Hey, wait!" Bryce rushed for the stairs, tripping on the bottom step when a wave of dizziness hit him again. He held the railing.

"Wish I could say nice knowing ya, Crawford, but that would be a lie." The man at the door laughed.

Bryce remembered that laugh. Conner Reynolds. He'd played football with Woods back in the day. Now, apparently, they had a different kind of team.

The militia. Conner's had been one of the names on the list Olivia and Bryce had tried tracking down a few days ago.

The door opened wider, and Alonzo Sosa appeared with three different men. Men Bryce didn't know, hadn't seen before. But he knew from their glowers this wouldn't end well. They moved down the steps like an army.

"Why don't you make this fair, Sosa? You and me." Bryce fought to clear his vision as he stood tall and balled his hands into fists.

"I'm not interested in fair. I'm interested in information. And if you don't want to give it to me, then you'll no longer be useful to me, and I'll move on to your sister. Maybe your mother next. Your father I'll kill just for fun though. He won't know anything useful."

Bryce lunged at Sosa, but the three bodyguards ganged up on him, wrestled him to the ground. Two men held him down while the other kicked him. Breath whooshed out of him. The hits came, one after the other to the face, the ribs, the side. It was all he could do to hold back screams of pain. He didn't want to give Sosa the satisfaction.

"That's enough. Pull him up." Alonzo watched as the men yanked him off the ground. He stepped closer.

Bryce stared him down. As soon as Alonzo was close enough, Bryce spat in his face. "You think you're something because you can have your lackeys beat me up? You're a coward. Do what you want to me, but leave my family alone. I guarantee you will regret it if you mess with them."

"You don't like it when someone messes with your family? I know how you feel." Sosa removed a pure white handkerchief from a jacket pocket and wiped the blood-tinted spittle off his face. "But everyone here will learn. You don't mess with my family either. You killed my uncle. Stole his money, my birthright. And one by one, I will take you down. The question is, are you going to tell me what I need to know and die quickly, or will you drag this out and make me take my time with the rest of the Brookses and Crawfords?"

"I ain't telling you squat."

"I knew you'd pick the hard way." Sosa came closer, patted Bryce on the cheek. "All the more fun for me."

With a grunt, Bryce strained against the hold on him, ready to pound the man into the ground and never let him rise. But the men restraining him didn't break.

"Smile." Sosa held up a phone and took a picture. "Don't worry. I have a feeling you won't be here alone for very long." He tilted his head toward the pole to the right of them.

The men dragged Bryce to it. They duct-taped his feet together, then his hands behind his back and around the pole. No biggie. As soon as they were gone Bryce could break through—then they pulled out zip ties. Over the duct tape, the heavy-duty plastic restraints were zipped tight.

That was bad. One or the other he could handle. Not both.

Sosa and his men marched back up the stairs and shut the door.

Once the sound of it clicking reached his ears, Bryce leaned his head back and sagged against the pole holding him up.

What do I do here, Lord?

The more Sosa focused on him, the more time Jude and the others had to figure out where they were. It kept his family and Penny safe. Gave them time to find the governor's family.

And Zack must still be out there somewhere. Hopefully he'd sent for the cavalry, because obviously Jason Woods was a low-down sleaze who was in bed with Sosa. There's no way he'd actually done what he'd said and called the cops.

Bryce strained to listen to the voices above him. He had to figure out what was going on and how to get out of here. They had to have the Nobles nearby, right?

The voices all mumbled together. There was a group of them, though. That much Bryce could tell.

"Are you sure he doesn't know anything about the Nobles?"

That was Sosa.

"He has no clue where they were moved to. Now tell me, why didn't you stick to the plan?" Woods sounded furious.

Bryce stilled his ragged breath, trying to hear Sosa's response.

"*You* want to tell *me* what to do? Let's remember our deal. I provide the weapons and the explosives. We get you into office. You need me so you don't get your little hands dirty!"

Jason was in on this for his own political career? The creep.

"If you would've stuck to the plan, we would've been fine. You were supposed to wait on the kidnapping until yesterday. You made no mention of the bomb at the hotel. If you hadn't given me the heads-up, I would've been there. Caught in the blast. You—"

Bomb? But Penny was at the hotel! Bryce pulled against his restraints. He had to get out of here.

"You're lucky I gave you any warning. You told me the man would fold and have Emma released. You lied. There are consequences. And the governor needs to pay. He needs to know I'm serious."

"He will pay. If you would—"

"He has no intention of releasing Emma, or he would've done so already. I held up my end of the bargain. Our deal is off, and apparently, I have to take matters into my own hands." A pause. "Don't worry. If he didn't die in the blast, he'll be dead by tomorrow and the office will be yours. But so you know just how serious I am—"

A gunshot sounded, followed by a thump, like a body falling to the floor.

"Reynolds!" Woods screamed. "That's my friend!"

"*Was* your friend. You're lucky it wasn't you."

Their voices faded away and were lost in a shuffle of noise.

Bryce leaned against the pole. A bomb at the hotel. That maniac Sosa walking free. His body didn't hurt nearly as much as not knowing if Penny was okay.

Lord, please let her be okay. Keep her far away from here.

THIRTY-ONE

PENNY RUSHED TOWARD THE HOTEL ENTRANCE, Tony behind her. Sirens screamed as emergency vehicles pulled into the parking lot. Firefighters already on scene scrambled to set up hoses. Police officers tried to move people away from the danger. But nowhere in the crowd was the governor or any of his staff.

And they couldn't push through the raging stream of people pouring out of the building.

"Back entrance!" Penny yelled over to Tony.

They turned and ran around the other side of the hotel—the side that wasn't engulfed in flames. More people trickled out of the exits, but not as many as at the front of the building. Penny slipped through the doorway. Water showered down from the sprinkler system, immediately dousing them. Alarms blared. Emergency lighting was limited to dim red glows from the exit signs and small lights on the ceiling.

Penny grabbed the first police officer she saw, a cut on his chin bleeding. "Did you see the governor?"

He shook his head as he held the door and ushered people out. "This way! Carefully!" He tried to contain the crowd of people rushing toward the door. Penny and Tony fought against the flow and made it to the banquet hall. The chandelier in the middle of the room had crashed to the floor. Tables and chairs were toppled. People were everywhere. Still no Governor Noble.

"Where is he?" She searched the people as they streamed toward the exit in the corner of the room. "I don't see his closest security team either."

"He would've been on his way out. What exit would he have used?" Tony yelled over the alarms and panicked cries around them.

"The one closest to the meeting room."

They ran for the hallway. Broken sections of ceiling and a collapsed wall blocked the way to the lobby, but they could pick their way around rubble in the other direction, going deeper into the building. Tony offered a hand and helped her climb over a chunk of plaster and wood. "Almost there."

They reached what had been the meeting room. The door had fallen away completely, the chairs knocked over. Reba and one of the security guards were sprawled on the floor against the wall. Penny ran and checked their pulses. Both began to rouse.

"Over here! I found Noble!" Tony called from the other side of the table. "We need help."

Jude appeared in the doorway, dirt or soot smeared across his face. Another man Penny recognized as one of the FBI agents stood behind him.

"We need to move quickly and get him out of here. This building is unstable." Jude moved to help Tony. Together the men pulled the governor out from under the broken table and wall that had caved in.

Reba and the security guard woke. Penny and the FBI agent helped them up. They were all able to walk out and follow Tony and Jude, who had the governor propped between them.

Once they moved far away enough from the building, Tony

and Jude set the governor down in the parking lot. Tony's radio immediately went off, and he stepped away to listen.

"Where's my family?" The governor's voice was scratchy and raw.

"Why don't you tell us what you know first." Jude stood above him. "And you two"—he pointed to the security guard and Reba—"go get medics and bring them here."

The guard nodded and jogged away. Reba looked back at the governor. "Sir?"

"It's okay. Go find the rest of the staff. Tell me they're okay."

After she left, Governor Noble dropped his head to his hands. "What do you want to know?"

"Have the kidnappers been in contact with you?" Penny asked.

He nodded slowly. "The text said they would meet me at the airport."

"That's over an hour away." It didn't make sense. "How were you planning to ditch your security team?"

"They don't mean that airport. There's a secret airport here in Last Chance. It wouldn't have taken much for me to sneak away."

"And what did they want?" Jude asked.

"They would take me in exchange for my family, and that's all I cared about. We were set to meet tonight after I left the ball. But then you"—the governor lifted his head and looked at Penny—"you said you'd found them. I called to say the deal was off, but they told me whatever lead the cops had was a trap. That's when the bomb exploded."

Tony tapped Penny on the shoulder. "You're gonna wanna hear this."

They moved away but kept Jude and the governor in their sights. "What is it?"

"That callout we got about finding the Nobles was the wrong address."

"What? So whoever the governor talked to was right?"

"Yeah, but get this. Zack Stephens called in. He and Bryce apparently are the ones that figured out where the Nobles really are. The firefighters and police were supposed to show up and didn't. They were sent to the other side of town."

"Because of the whole wrong address thing?"

"That's my guess. Zack found the wife and kid, but he can't do anything. There's too many people guarding them, and somehow he lost contact with Bryce. When no one showed up, he called again. He gave dispatch the right location, a barn just outside of town. But no one knows where Bryce is. He's disap—"

Penny's phone rang. Pulling it out of her holster pocket, she checked the screen.

Blocked number. She let it go to voicemail. The phone immediately dinged with a text message. Penny opened it up to see an address.

Another ding.

It took a moment for a picture to load.

Penny's breath caught. Her body seized.

It was a picture of Bryce, bruised and bloodied. The words underneath made her blood run cold.

Get me Emma if you want him to live. Involve the police and he's dead.

THIRTY-TWO

BRYCE BOUNCED AROUND IN THE DARK, TIGHT space. He probably shouldn't have risked it, but a broken tooth was a small price to pay for getting a punch in. Even with his hands tied together, he'd managed a good hit. Sosa would be sporting a nice shiner.

But Bryce wasn't nearly satisfied. And if the man hadn't had his goons surrounding him when they'd pulled Bryce out of the basement and stuffed him in the trunk of this car, Sosa would've been out cold.

But no. Here he was, hands once again taped and zip-tied together as well as fastened to his feet, which were also taped and tied together. Bryce yanked his arms up once more, trying to break at least one of the zip ties. His head slammed against the side of the trunk.

Ow !

Clearly he wasn't going to get anywhere like this. He'd have to wait until Sosa opened the trunk before trying to make a getaway and hopefully getting a couple more good licks in.

Because he desperately needed to get away. He still didn't know if Penny was okay after the bomb they'd talked about at the hotel. Jason Woods was still out there, probably on the rampage after what'd sounded like Sosa killing Conner Reynolds. And who knew if they'd ever found the governor's family? He could only pray Zack got to them and was okay.

The car finally stopped.

Bryce waited for the trunk to open. Footsteps on gravel sounded right outside the car. Any minute now . . . But nothing.

Where were they? And what were they waiting for?

"Think she'll show?" That sounded like Sosa's guy, DaNeal Gomez. Like he was right on the other side of the trunk lid. He was another one Bryce wouldn't mind going toe to toe with. He and Sosa had watched while the other two used a taser on Bryce before throwing him in the car.

"She'll be here. The question is whether or not she'll have Emma with her," Sosa said.

Emma? Who did Sosa get to break Emma out of jail? The smell of cigarettes seeped in.

"Penny Mitchell is enough of a loner and a rebel that she'll do what needs to be done." Sosa sounded like he was sucking in a long breath, probably inhaling on his cigarette of choice.

But he didn't know Penny. She would never break Emma Kemper out of jail. Not for Bryce. She would find another way.

Tires spitting gravel and a diesel engine approaching alerted Bryce.

But Penny didn't have a diesel truck.

The trunk lid lifted, the light from a street pole above blinding Bryce. But the gun pressed against his temple was a clear enough sign to prevent him from trying any wild moves. The diesel engine was getting closer though.

"One wrong move and I won't hesitate to shoot Penny. And after you watch her die, you'll join her. Understood?"

Bryce answered Alonzo with a glare.

"Understood?" Sosa pressed the barrel harder.

"Fine!"

"Cut the tie that links his hands to his feet, but nothing else," Sosa told Gomez.

Gomez reached in with a box cutter and sliced the zip ties.

Sosa didn't release any of the pressure on Bryce's temple though. "Help him up."

Gomez did as bid. Bryce hated that he needed the help, but with the blood rushing into his cramped legs and the duct tape still wrapped around his ankles throwing off his sense of balance, it took a moment to stand on his own.

Gomez held a taser and a gun of his own and kept them aimed at Bryce as Sosa turned to watch the approaching truck. The dusty black Dodge Ram pulled up across from them and stopped under the glow of the streetlight.

That was definitely Penny behind the wheel, but the face of the person beside her in the cab was hidden by a black hood.

Penny hopped out of the truck. "I'm here. Let him go." She came around to the front of the truck and stood in front of the headlights with one hand on her hip and the other holding her Smith & Wesson, pointed at the ground. She wore a fancy red dress that showed off her toned shoulders and had a slit that stopped midthigh. Her hair was kind of wild and messy as it tossed on the wind. The combat boots on her feet made Bryce smile.

She was gorgeous and she was fierce.

And he was head over heels in love with this woman.

"Show me Emma and we have a deal." Sosa's voice was cold and calculating.

Penny moved to the passenger side, pulled the person out of the seat, and guided them out of the truck. They stood right outside the door. It was definitely a woman in

an orange jumpsuit, but the hood still covered her head. Handcuffs dangled from her wrists. Both women stayed there to the side, standing in the shadow of the truck.

The hood was a smart move. The female prisoner was probably a decoy. Maybe Olivia?

"Good to see you, Pen," Bryce called over. She must have a plan of some sort. Maybe if he could converse a little she'd let him in on it.

"You too." She winked at him.

A wink? That's it? What did that mean?

He'd have to try again. "Heard you had an eventful ball. Fireworks and all. Everyone o—"

"Enough! Emma?" Sosa called out. "Are you okay?"

"Alonzo?" The hooded woman stepped forward.

What?

The voice under the hood was muffled, tentative, but it sure sounded like the woman from the club.

No . . . she wouldn't have.

Penny yanked off the hood.

It *was* Emma Kemper. Curly brown hair. Glasses.

Bryce strained against Gomez's hold on his arm. "You broke Emma out of jail? What are you thinking!"

Penny didn't look at him. Her green eyes were laser focused on Sosa, her hand gripped firmly around Emma's upper arm as she dragged her back into the headlights. "Let. Him. Go."

"Not until you release her." Sosa didn't waiver.

"I came alone. Unlike you. How can I trust you'll release Bryce?"

"Enough games!" Sosa yanked Bryce over toward him, but with his feet bound together, Bryce fell to the rocky ground. His shoulder took the brunt of it, hitting the ground in front of Sosa.

Everything else seemed to move in slow motion. Lights flooded from all directions. Someone screamed.

Emma lunged for Penny's weapon. "Run, Alonzo!"

Gunshots rang out. Alonzo ducked and ran along the side of the car. Gomez hit the ground shooting. His body jerked as a bullet hit him in the chest. Then another. Police swarmed, blocking

Penny and Emma from Bryce's view. Another gunshot, somewhat muffled, sounded.

"Get out of the way!" Bryce yelled.

The uniforms moved in on Gomez, clearing the space between Bryce and the black truck. Penny leaned against the hood gasping, eyes closed. Emma stood in the headlights.

"Penny!"

At the sound of his voice calling her, Penny stood.

Emma crumpled to the ground. She didn't move.

And the car behind Bryce sped away.

He rolled over, watching the brake lights glowing red and the dust cloud grow smaller and smaller. Black combat boots appeared by his head.

Bryce looked up at Penny. "He's getting away!"

"We'll deal with it, but first things first." She kneeled down and fisted his shirt, hauling him up to a sitting position.

Instead of helping him to his feet, she leaned in and kissed him.

Oh, did she ever kiss him. She held nothing back. Raw passion mixed with a sweet tenderness that was all Penny. She rested her forehead against his, her blonde hair creating a curtain—one dancing wildly in the breeze.

"Don't you ever do that again," she whispered.

"Kiss you? But I really enjoyed that part."

"Shut up." She sniffed, pulled back enough for him to see the dirt streaked across her cheek and chin and caked into the fine lines around her mouth. She smelled like smoke and ash and vanilla. But it was the love and worry in her eyes that had him choking up. Just a smidge.

"I mean, don't ever get hurt again."

"I didn't expect you to organize a jailbreak to save me."

She chuckled. "Obviously I had some help."

Bryce looked around at the police and his rescue team surrounding them. "Good thing she wasn't in federal custody yet."

Penny helped him to his feet. Jude walked over, his grim expression softening into something lighter for a moment. He pulled out a pocketknife and freed Bryce's hands and feet.

"I'm sorry, Brooks. He got away." Penny wrapped her hand around Bryce's biceps.

" This wasn't how it was supposed to go down. Emma's dead. Gomez too." Jude nodded to Bryce. "But I'm glad you're okay."

"Only because you know my sister would kill you if you didn't find me." Nothing like a little gallows humor to stave off the reality of two dead bodies and an escaped criminal.

"There's that." Jude looked around them. "But we're not done yet. We have one more rescue before we can look for Sosa."

Penny lifted her chin, ready for another battle. "Governor Noble's family."

THIRTY-THREE

P ENNY CLAMPED HER JAW TIGHT AS SHE GLANCED in the rearview mirror as they loaded Emma Kemper's body into a body bag. Jude was right.

This wasn't how it was supposed to go down.

But she didn't have time to think about that as they bounced down the dirt road to where Tony and Olivia were waiting for them. She wasn't sad to have Bryce pressed up against her in the middle of the bench seat of Zack Stephens's truck.

Jude sat in the passenger seat, on the phone. At least driving, she had one hand free to drop down and squeeze Bryce's fingers, relishing his strong hands and gentle touch.

She might never tire of having him close. Not after the scare he'd given her. For a moment, as he fell to the ground at Sosa's feet with all the chaos and shooting, she'd been certain he'd been hit.

But he wasn't. Even beaten, one eye purple and swollen, a fat lip that was split, his handsome face had the ability to make her melt. But right now, it was the fact that with him by her side, they were stronger and better.

And they needed that to rescue Cindy and Adam Noble.

"You gotta be kidding," Jude grumbled from the passenger seat and dropped his phone into his lap.

"What?" Bryce asked.

"They can't find the governor. Or Jason Woods."

Bryce had already told them of Woods's part in all this. "I still can't believe I didn't see through him earlier." Bryce sighed. "No wonder I never liked that punk. How low do you have to go to resort to kidnapping an innocent woman and child?"

"Let alone your own family," Jude added.

"Do you think Noble could be dirty? Is he working with Sosa and Jason?" Bryce asked.

Penny slowed down to take the turn she needed. "We can't rule anything out, but I don't think so. He might be coerced into doing something with his family held hostage though."

Look at what lengths she'd gone through to free Bryce. Yes, she'd had permission. She'd gone out on a limb to get the team behind her and ask for help. But if Jude and the chief of police hadn't given her the permission, she might've pulled off a real jailbreak herself if it meant she could save Bryce. Who knew what a desperate husband would do for his family?

Because, yes, *she* would do just about anything for the people she loved.

But that didn't make her weak. It made her motivated. Focused. There would always be those who exploited. But there were also others, like Bryce and Jude and Elizabeth Crawford, who were motivated by truth and love, and that's the kind of person she wanted to be. Running away from Bryce was a coward move. So who was the weakling there? It took a lot more guts to stay in the game.

A picture of Jesus hanging on the cross, that used to hang in her mother's room, came to mind.

It wasn't weakness that had kept Him there. It was love.

So maybe God wasn't so far off as she thought.

Maybe Libby was right. A cord of three was stronger. Instead of going on instinct and breaking Emma out herself, Penny had asked for help.

And low and behold, it hadn't killed her. Together they'd rescued Bryce. So really, there was no "maybe" at all.

So, I think I see what all the hubbub is about, Lord, what Libby and Bryce and Jude have been trying to tell me. And I'm ready. I'm ready to admit I need You. I want in. And I want to stay. And we could really use Your help and protection with what we're about to do.

Please keep the innocent protected tonight, and help us fight the injustice and make this world a little safer by capturing these men so bent on power and destruction.

Something settled over Penny in that moment and seeped down to her core. Something warm and comforting. Like that feeling of peace Libby had talked about when she'd said she'd known she would be okay, even while she was captured by Sosa's men.

Like that moment in the mountains with Bryce, looking at the stars. Only stronger.

Is that You, Lord?

Bryce squeezed her hand. He leaned over, dropping his voice. "Just in case I don't get a chance to say this later, I'm glad you came back. It hasn't been the same without you. And I just want you to know that I love you."

Penny couldn't tell if they were Bryce's words or the answer to her question, but they filled her heart to overflowing and brought tears to her eyes. Maybe it was both. Because she could finally see. The God Libby talked about, the God Penny had learned about so long ago in Vacation Bible School, would've said the same thing.

I'm glad you came back. It hasn't been the same without you. And I just want you to know that I love you.

She didn't have the words, so she squeezed Bryce's hand back and smiled at him.

Okay, Lord, lead on.

Before they reached the farm site where the Nobles were being held, Penny killed the lights on the truck and slowed to a crawl. She rolled off the side of the dirt road and into the ditch. They jogged down to the tree line at the edge of the property, where Tony and Olivia were.

"It's about time you got here." Olivia fist-bumped Penny as she stepped out from the trees.

"We had a few hiccups at the other end." Penny took the ponytail holder from her wrist and pulled her hair back. "Sosa got away."

"Again?" Tony whispered. "That man needs to be in a maximum security prison."

"He didn't show up here?" Bryce asked. "This is where he had me before. And where's Zack?"

"No Sosa since we've been here." Olivia pointed to herself and Tony. "We sent Zack back with the rest of the rescue squad. They're down the road, about half a mile away for support if we need them."

"And the governor is now missing along with Jason Woods," Penny said.

"No sign of them either." Tony rubbed his hands together. "Now, what exactly is the plan?"

"Where are the Nobles?" Jude asked.

Olivia pointed through the trees. "In the barn. Zack was able to get a visual, and we confirmed it when we arrived with the drone. They have Cindy and Adam in the middle of the barn. Hands are bound. They're sitting on hay bales. Oh, and they have a bomb strapped to the boy's chest. Six men are in there guarding them."

"So we can't go in guns blazing. We need another tactic." Jude looked over at the barn as if studying it.

"We need to convince them to take the bomb off the boy." Penny paced between the pine tree trunks. "I can do it."

Bryce bristled. "Go in there? Alone? Are you nuts?"

"It could work," Jude said.

"Aw, come on. Tony? This is crazy, right?" Bryce asked him.

"I dunno, Crawford. I think it's our best shot."

"Think about it. As far as they know, I broke Emma out and brought her to Sosa. They might believe me if I tell them I turned. That I'm working with Sosa now. And I've got the most experience with explosives. I can disarm that vest. Once I get that bomb off Adam, you guys can storm the castle."

"It's too dangerous." That brooding look on Bryce's face said he wasn't convinced. And she understood. But they were running out of time.

She tugged Bryce a few steps away from the others.

"Look. I know you're scared—"

"For good reason!" he hissed. "I'm not a little scared. I'm *terrified* of something happening to you."

"Yeah, a little like how I felt when I got that picture of you from Sosa. I almost fell apart."

"Then you get it. How am I supposed to let you do this? You'll be walking into the enemy camp. Alone."

"But I won't be alone."

Bryce stilled. "What do you mean?"

"I mean . . . I know I'm not alone. I get it now." She looked up through the branches at the stars for a moment. "I know God is with me, Bryce. Just like you've been trying to tell me. Like my sister has been praying for me. I know He's here." She laid her hand over her heart.

"You believe that?" Bryce's voice was so soft she almost didn't hear. He reached for her hands, and she easily slid them into his.

"I do. And you are here too. You guys will be right outside the barn, ready to help if I need it. I'm depending on you. But you know this is our best shot at saving that kid and his mom. It's a risk we have to take."

He tugged her close and laid a whisper-soft kiss on her temple. "I hate it when you're right."

She chuckled. "I know. And I know how hard it is to see me

walk into a dangerous situation. But I think we both better get used to that. It's the kind of lives we live. The jobs we have. And I know you. You wouldn't want it any other way."

"Maybe."

She framed his face with her hands. "Maybe?"

"All I know is I want a life with you."

"Good, then let's get on with it." She kissed his bruised cheek, and they walked back to the others hand in hand.

Once everyone was in place—Tony and Olivia by the back entrance of the barn, Jude and Bryce crouched by the tractor outside the front doors—Penny knocked on the main entrance and walked in.

Bobby Prescot jumped to his feet along with three other men and Moira. "What are you doing here?"

The other three men and Mo trained their weapons on Penny.

She smiled, her own Smith & Wesson in hand, and walked farther in. There wasn't much in the way of cover. The back of the barn was sectioned off as a corral, where three Holstein cows munched on hay. In the middle, Adam and Cindy sat on hay bales, just like Olivia had said. The sixth guard stood behind them with a shotgun. The rest of the barn had been cleared of all clutter and machinery.

"Hey, Bobby." Penny smiled up at him. She kept her gun out where everyone could see.

"The man asked you a question. What are you doing here?" Mo aimed her own SBR at Penny.

"Sosa sent me. You can release the prisoners."

"We don't answer to him." Mo's gaze didn't flinch. "And we certainly don't answer to you."

Penny continued to walk until one of the men blocked her way. She needed to get that bomb vest off Adam.

"Look, I know the plan. Jason and Sosa told me everything.

I've been involved with this before any of you guys knew what was going on." Penny tilted her chin up and popped a fist on her hip.

Bobby was the first to soften. "You did? But at the bar, you said you was looking for that girl. But then later we heard you was working with the law."

"Yeah. That was the plan. How else do you think Jason knew what was going on? I kept him informed every step of the investigation."

"We have orders, and we'll follow them until we hear otherwise." Mo didn't look like she was gonna back down.

"Then you're wasting time. Sosa and Emma already left the county until things cool down. Who do you think broke her out of jail and helped her escape? Jason doesn't need these guys anymore. He has what he needs."

Bobby's gun drooped lower. He was buying it. Penny looked past Mo and the other three. Cindy had her arms wrapped around her son.

"Look at these guys! What have you been doing?" Penny skirted between Bobby and Mo and stood in front of Adam and Cindy. She studied the vest. It wasn't Vince Kemper's work, thankfully. This would be simple. She looked for the detonator.

Wait. She almost laughed. The whole thing was fake. There were no blasting caps. The wires were just for show.

Penny took the knife out of her boot and cut the strap on Adam's shoulder.

"What are you doing?" Mo pointed the SBR at Penny. She stepped back just so Adam wouldn't be hurt if the gun went off.

"I already told you. Jason said to let these guys go." Penny stared her down. She put herself between Mo and the Nobles. "You should probably go check the perimeter or something. These guys are coming with me."

Bobby looked at the others and shrugged. They were caving. Penny turned back to Adam. She cut the other strap of the vest.

Cindy's shoulders relaxed. She let out a long quiet breath.

Penny indicated for Adam and Cindy to stand up. "Let's go."

"You really think you're gonna walk on out of here? I think we should give Jason a call." Mo tightened her grip on her gun.

"Go for it." Penny resheathed her knife. "Tell him I'm on my way. I might stop for coffee though. I'll grab him one."

Penny gently pushed Adam and Cindy toward the big barn doors. Just a little farther . . .

Mo dropped her gun and pulled out her phone. But while her head was down and the others dropped their guard, Penny picked up the pace.

A few more steps. Adam was practically running at this point. He and Cindy reached the door.

As soon as they opened it, Jude and Bryce rushed in, guns drawn. Penny spun, taking aim directly at Mo. Olivia and Tony snuck in from the back while everyone stared at Penny, Jude, and Bryce.

"Looks like you're outnumbered, princess." Mo smirked. "I knew you were lying."

"Not so fast. You're all under arrest." Tony and Olivia quickly disarmed the man in the corral.

More cops followed, and within minutes, the militia members were all face down on the ground with their hands behind their backs.

Penny walked over to Bobby Prescot. "Do yourself a favor and tell me where I can find Sosa."

"Why would I do that? You think I'm some dumb hick?"

"I think you're a good guy, and you care about people and want to do the right thing."

"She's trying to manipulate you, Bobby. Shut up," Moira yelled from the ground.

"Aren't you tired of being bossed around?" Penny asked him.

"Be your own person. The *good* person I know you can be. Tell me where Sosa and Jason are."

Bobby sneered as he looked Penny in the eye. "I don't know. And if I did, I wouldn't tell you."

So much for that.

Penny walked back to Jude and Bryce. They were talking to Cindy and Adam outside in the barnyard.

"They're not speaking. But I don't think they know where Sosa or Jason are. I get the feeling they kept things compartmentalized in their operations."

"I think we might know." Cindy spoke up. "I overheard Jason's voice on the phone when he called that lady. Mo. He said something about getting a plane ready."

Jude looked at Penny. "Remember what the governor said? He was supposed to meet Sosa at the airport. The secret one on the other side of town. I think it's our best shot."

"Can we see my dad now?" Adam asked.

"Soon. But first we have to make sure he's safe. I need you and your mom to wait a little longer." Jude called Olivia over. "Can you bring these guys to the police station? You can call Andi if they need medical attention."

"Sure thing."

Olivia escorted them to the squad car.

Penny faced Jude and Bryce. "Let's go find Sosa and Woods."

THIRTY-FOUR

AFTER ALL THE DESTRUCTION, ALL THE PAIN, and everything the people she cared most about had gone through, Penny was ready to end this. Sosa and Woods could not get away. She let Jude drive the big diesel truck this time and took the middle seat.

"Do we have a plan?" Penny asked.

Bryce reached for her hand, gave it a light squeeze. "We have no idea what we're walking into. No idea how much the governor is involved or a victim."

"Guess we're gonna have to play this one by ear." Jude's gaze stayed fixed on the road.

"Never thought I'd hear you say that, Book." But he was right. They were going in blind.

Jude adjusted his grip on the steering wheel. "Believe me, I don't like it."

They parked at the edge of the airport field, keeping it hidden along a tree line. Zack met them there. "With the hotel bomb, your takedown at the barn, and everything else, there aren't enough cops to go around. But we should have more support on the way."

"Should we wait?" Bryce asked, although the way his thumb

tapped against his leg, that probably wasn't his first choice. He was a man of action.

"That's a plane engine. Someone is getting ready to leave." Jude jogged toward the hangars.

It helped that there was little moonlight tonight. The four of them ran alongside the building until they reached the corner. Light from inside the hangar spilled out onto the tarmac. They stayed in the shadows, trying to peek around the corner and scope it all out. A midsize Beechcraft King Air plane sat on the runway, the twin turboprop engines roaring. A man climbed the steps.

"Is that the governor?" Zack asked.

"Looks like it. But where is Sosa?" Bryce clenched his jaw tight.

This was their chance. "We have to stop him!" Penny ran past them.

"Wait!" Bryce chased after her. "Go check out that hangar!" he yelled back to Zack and Jude. "Make sure there's no one there."

Penny reached the plane just as the stairs were rising. She grabbed the bottom step and used her weight to pull it back down. Penny and Bryce climbed in.

The governor sat on a plush leather seat, lifted his head off his hands. He closed the door of the plane and then plopped back in his seat. "No more delays, Gary. Take off."

The cushy commuter plane moved, turning until its nose pointed to the long stretch of runway.

"Wait. Stop!" Bryce called toward the cockpit.

"I suggest you buckle up, Mr. Crawford. Gary is under explicit instructions to stop for nothing."

The plane quickly picked up speed.

"Where are you going?" Penny fell into the seat across from the governor. "And where have you been? You left your security detail. No one has heard from you or seen you in hours."

"You had the wrong address! They have my family. What did

you expect me to do? Once I'm in the air, they'll give me coordinates to their location."

Bryce glanced at Penny, a question so clear in his eyes it was impossible for her to miss. How much should they tell Noble?

But they really *didn't* know how much to trust him. He'd been gone for hours. She wanted to believe him an innocent victim, but it could be an elaborate act. She gave Bryce a slight shake of the head.

He couldn't stand straight in the cabin. Instead he leaned toward the governor. "You need to stop the plane. There's probably a bomb on board. Alonzo Sosa is working with Jason Woods. They're the ones responsible for kidnapping your family. You can't believe anything they say."

The engines grew louder.

The governor stared out the window, no expression. No acknowledgment that he'd heard anything.

"Tell the pilot to stop!" Bryce caught himself as the plane moved forward. He slid into the seat across the aisle.

"I won't sacrifice them." Noble didn't bother to look at them. "If they want me to step down, I will." His voice was hollow, sounding more like a bereaved husband and father. Maybe he truly was a victim in all this.

The plane lifted. They were airborne.

"Did you hear me? This is probably a trap." Bryce couldn't seem to get through to the man.

"Stop the plane!" Penny turned and yelled at the pilot behind her. "We need to go back."

"He doesn't want to do that." A small door in the back of the plane opened. Sosa stepped into the tiny aisle, holding a Glock 19. His windbreaker and backpack made him look like he was out for a casual hike rather than a hostage situation. "You are right, Crawford. This is a trap. And while this wasn't part of the plan to have you two joining us, it will work out rather well."

That low-down dirty weasel. Penny's muscles coiled, ready to pounce.

Sosa swung the end of the gun to point at her. "Uh-uh, darling. One move and the governor or your boyfriend dies. I won't be picky."

Penny glared at him, hand curled into a fist on the armrest.

Sosa slapped papers down in front of the governor on the small tray. He held the gun against the governor's temple. "Crawford was almost right. There *is* a bomb. But not on this plane. Your son is wearing it. And he's sitting right next to your beautiful wife. And all you need to do to ensure that bomb doesn't go off is to sign these papers releasing Emma Kemper and offering her a full pardon."

Sosa didn't know she was dead? Penny looked at Bryce.

That worked in their favor, right? An element of surprise they could use?

But should Penny tip their hand and tell the governor that his family was safe?

It was probably best that she stay quiet. Signing the paper would mean nothing since Emma was lying in the morgue. And if Sosa lost his only bargaining chip, he might be even more dangerous. She didn't relish the thought of a gun going off in these tight quarters.

But if she had a clear shot, she'd take it.

"Pick up the pen and sign them." Sosa stood over them, his finger on the trigger.

"I thought you wanted me to step down from office." The governor looked up, genuine confusion in his expression.

Sosa paused and then shrugged. "Sure, that too."

The plane banked to the right, but Sosa didn't let up on the trigger or lose his balance. The space was too small to make any sudden moves. Penny seethed to watch the criminal tower over them, his gun to the governor's head.

But he wasn't all-powerful.

Lord, I've seen some pretty miraculous things today that make me believe You really do hear us and care. Please get us out of this alive and protect the innocent.

Noble studied the papers in front of him. "How do I know you'll let them live?"

Finally the gov was showing a little backbone.

"Don't do it, sir." Bryce's hands gripped the armrests until his knuckles were white. He was probably dying to do something. She got it. It was everything she could do to stay seated and not pounce on Sosa herself.

"Is that something you want to risk?" The sneer on Sosa's face was too much like his uncle's. Penny wouldn't put it past the evil man to have the papers signed and still kill an innocent kid if he could.

The governor must've thought so too. He picked up the pen and signed the paper. Penny didn't miss the slight tremor in his hand though.

Sosa kept the gun trained on him while he tucked the paper into an inside pocket of his jacket. "Gary, are we high enough?" he asked the pilot.

"Yes, sir. Eight thousand feet."

"Is there anyone on my staff you *haven't* corrupted?" Noble's voice sounded more like a growl. "Now have them release my wife and son!"

Sosa laughed. "Release them yourself." He backed up to the cabin door.

Penny had one chance. She had to stop him. She sprang off the chair and aimed for the gun.

A boom sounded. He managed to get a shot off before she kicked it out of his hand. Sosa roared, but rather than go for the gun, he yanked the handle on the side door.

"Are you cra—" Bryce's voice cut off with the wind that rushed in. Penny fell in the aisle, grabbed the gun, and pulled the trigger as Sosa was sucked out of the plane. The whole aircraft listed hard to the left.

Penny looked past her feet dangling out the door and caught a glimpse of a white parachute floating in the night sky.

Sosa! The scumbag had a parachute! The plane flew at a weird angle, though not completely spiraling, so it was probably on autopilot. But it was the human pilot that worried Penny. His head slumped to one side.

"Bryce! The pilot!" Penny nodded toward the front of the plane. She still lay in the aisle, hanging on to the bottom of the seat. The governor and Bryce grabbed her arms and pulled her farther into the plane. Bryce helped her up to the chair while Noble wrestled to close the door, straining to pull the cable in and lift the stairs. Bryce had to help him to finally secure the door and latch it once more.

Once it was closed, he turned and walked past the four other passenger seats to reach the cockpit.

"Well?" she asked him.

Bryce leaned farther over the pilot's seat, probably checking the man for a pulse.

He looked back at Penny. "Buckle up. See if you can call Jude. Anyone. We need someone to tell me how to land this thing." He had to yell over the wind and engine noise.

Her eyes went wide. "What?!"

Rather than take the time to explain, Bryce wiggled into the open seat in the cockpit. He yanked the spare headset on, situated the microphone near his mouth.

Oh my word. The pilot was dead? Did Bryce know how to fly a plane?

She looked over at the governor. He looked like he was going to be sick. She couldn't sit here and do nothing. She stood and moved toward the cockpit. She had to hold on to Bryce's seat to keep her balance.

Oh man.

The pilot was dead all right. Sosa's shot had gone right through his skull.

"Mayday, Mayday. Anybody hear this?" Bryce spoke into the microphone. He studied the lit screens and knobs in front of him.

"Have you ever flown before?" she yelled over the wind and engine noise.

"Took one lesson with a friend who flew crop dusters. One."

"Well, that's . . . something."

"Nothing about this looks familiar." He adjusted the mic again. "Hello? Mayday!"

Penny grabbed the pilot's headset and slipped it over her ears.

"Crawford? Is that you?" The voice was a little crackly but unmistakable.

Yeah, there was *definitely* a God out there.

"Jude. Man, you gotta help me. The pilot is dead. We're losing altitude." Bryce somehow kept his voice steady.

"I know. I'm in the airport control tower. We have someone coming. Tell me what you see."

"A lot of blinking lights on these panels." Bryce grabbed the two-handled joystick. He seemed to struggle to steady out the plane and pull it out of the big circle they were making. "I'm trying to steady her out, but it's fighting me. We're down to six thousand feet."

"We need to slow you down." A new voice came through the headset. "Can you see the altimeter?" The guy on the other end walked Bryce through the panel. "Now pull back on that lever a bit. Try to keep those rudders steady."

Bryce took a moment to buckle himself in. "Penny, you should go back and sit. Please."

She hated to leave him, but there was nowhere else to go. She couldn't move the pilot. She could at least keep an eye on the governor and let Bryce focus on trying to land this plane. Because they were going to need another miracle to walk away from this.

THIRTY-FIVE

BRYCE, THE GOOD NEWS IS YOU'RE ALREADY headed back toward Last Chance. We see you on the radar." The voice in the headset was steady and calm. Thank goodness one of them was, because Bryce sure wasn't feeling all that calm at the moment.

But wait . . . he said *the good news.* "What's the bad news?" Bryce asked.

Silence.

"Dude, what's the bad news? I need to know what's going on."

"Uh, there's a mountain in the way and no good place to land."

"You've gotta be kidding me." Bryce's pulse spiked. "Okay . . . what we do?"

"I'm going to walk you through this every step. We already have rescue crews and a chopper heading toward you."

Guess that was something. But at this point it was up to God and him to land this plane. He yelled back to Penny and the governor to buckle up and brace for impact.

Bryce couldn't let the panic take over. He repeated every line the stranger on the speaker said and followed each direction. Maybe it was a blessing he couldn't see much except the black night sky outside the window.

"You're doing well, Bryce. Now lower those flaps. It's going to decrease the speed even more."

The altimeter continued its countdown. Three thousand miles. Two. One.

He could see the outline of trees, a rugged terrain. The ground rushed toward them too fast. "Now, Bryce, now! Pull up! Keep it steady!"

Bryce braced himself, feet pressed hard against the floor. "Hold on!" At the last second he threw his hands around his head as the ground rose up.

The impact took his breath away. Penny screamed. The engines whined. Metal clashed. Time hung in the air as Bryce was slammed by a force like the hand of God Himself pressing him against the seat.

Then silence.

Bryce breathed again, slowly moving his body, beginning with his fingers. They worked. He didn't wait for pain or anything else to register. He found his buckle and released the latch.

"Penny! Governor?" He climbed out of his seat and turned. A tree branch dissected the cabin. The branch and pine needles blocked the way. He couldn't see them.

"Penny!" He dropped to the floor and crawled under the thick limb.

Oh God. Help.

The governor stirred. Groaned. But Penny lay crumpled in the aisle and wasn't moving. Bryce crawled over to her. Her chest rose and fell. Breathing. That was good.

But that branch. Oh, that was bad. So bad. A thin branch of the tree had impaled her abdomen. Blood seeped through. The branch had already broken away from the limb dissecting the plane. But they needed to get her help. Fast.

Bryce moved over to the governor. "Hey! You okay?"

He opened his eyes, blinked. He slowly roused.

"We need to get off the plane. Can you move?" Bryce asked him as he came to.

"I think so." The governor unbuckled himself, looked down. "Oh no."

"Yeah." The governor's seat swiveled completely around. He turned it to get behind Penny. "What do we do?"

"We need to keep her as steady as possible. Is there anything strong, flat we can use for a backboard?"

While Noble checked the luggage compartment, Bryce took her pulse. It was weak but steady.

The governor came back with a garment bag. "This was all I could find."

"Lay it down best you can next to her. When I roll her toward me, you slip it under."

He nodded. On the count of three, Bryce rolled Penny onto her side as smoothly and gently as he could. Noble slid the bag under, and Bryce rolled her back down. She stirred a bit.

"Penny, baby, you need to stay still, okay?" He whispered near her ear, kissed her scraped and dirty cheek. They'd been through so much already. "I'm going to get you home."

Please, God. Save her.

They used the garment bag to slide her toward the large opening where the door had been and laid her on the ground outside. The governor sank to the dirt, resting against a tree.

"We can't stay here. The plane could ignite at any time." And Bryce needed to keep moving. He had to get Penny home.

He'd promised her, and he was going to keep that promise.

"It's sparking!" The governor stood and backed away.

And the smell of fuel meant—"Back away!"

Bryce scooped up Penny and ran.

They ducked around trees, climbed the incline sloping away from the plane, but the explosion still knocked Bryce down to his knees. He cradled Penny against himself, letting his own body take the brunt of the fall. The governor helped him up. They turned and watched the wreckage burning.

"That should at least make it easier to find us." The governor looked over at him. "Do we keep moving?"

The sound of a helicopter stilled Bryce. "I think they found us."

The next hours were a blur of rescue workers, questions, medical assessments, and chaos.

Penny was immediately whisked away and taken into surgery. As soon as Bryce and Governor Noble stepped out of the rescue helicopter, a kid with dark hair and braces sprinted and launched himself at his dad.

Cindy Noble embraced her husband with a wobbly smile and tears streaming down her face. She looked over at Bryce. "Thank you for saving him." Her voice cracked with thick emotion.

"I don't know that I can take much credit, ma'am."

The governor shook his head. "You're a hero, Mr. Crawford. No doubt."

He certainly didn't feel like one. Not with Penny fighting for her life on an operating table.

Not even when Jude grabbed him and told him, "They tracked down Sosa. You coming?"

But at least that gave him something to do.

An army of black SUVs drove to a remote cabin in the mountain forest outside Last Chance. The other federal agents didn't question Bryce's presence after Jude told them all "He's with me."

Bryce slipped on the Kevlar vest handed him. "We know how this guy operates. He's slippery. He'll have an escape plan."

"Then we'll take the back," Jude said.

Good, because Bryce needed to end this.

Jude adjusted the straps of Bryce's vest. "Just remember, you're here to observe more than anything."

"You know I'm not great at the watching and waiting and staying out of it, right? I can't promise anything."

Jude kept his deadpan expression. "I'm counting on it. Just stay safe." The slightest glint of humor poked through.

Huh. Go figure. Maybe his by-the-book brother-in-law was loosening up a little.

He and Jude took watch over the back of the cabin at the northeast corner, closer to the tree line. Others were set at the opposite back corner. Within seconds of the agents breaching the front, Sosa was crawling out a back window. As soon as his feet hit the ground, Bryce shot off from his position, ignoring the yelling he heard from somewhere behind him.

Not. This. Time.

With everything in him, Bryce propelled himself and flew at the blur moving away from the cabin. He tackled Sosa, wrestling him to the ground.

Jude pulled Bryce off as two other agents lifted Sosa off the dirt.

Bloodied and dusty, the man wasn't nearly as cocky as he'd been on the plane. "This isn't over!"

Desperate cries from a desperate man, considering Sosa could hardly stand. It might have had something to do with the blood still trickling down his arm from where Penny had shot him.

"Oh, it's over, Sosa. You've got nowhere else to run." Bryce glared at him.

Sosa whipped his head to address the agent dragging him away. "I demand you release Emma Kemper. I have documents signed by—"

"It doesn't matter. She's gone." Jude, steady and calm as always, faced the criminal that had caused so much destruction.

Sosa paled. "What do you mean *gone?*"

"She's dead. Killed in the shootout when you left her there to save your own hide."

"No. You're lying. It's a trick, right?" He looked at the other agents. "You're lying!"

They didn't bother to speak and instead led him away while he continued to demand answers and medical attention. Through it all, Bryce grew numb. He didn't remember the ride back to the hospital. Once they arrived, there was still no word on Penny.

Bryce sank into a chair in the empty hospital waiting room.

He didn't know if it was minutes or hours later when Jude sat next to him and forced a cup of coffee into his cold hands.

"Hear anything yet?" Jude asked.

Bryce shook his head. "Find Woods?"

"He's still on the run. But the governor's family is safe. Settled at a secure location."

Good. Bryce dropped his head back, rested it against the wall. His mom came at some point with Libby and sat next to him. She took his hand but didn't say anything. Andi rested her head on Jude's shoulder. Izan and Zack and some of the crew trickled in, offering encouragement and assurances. He had so much to be thankful for.

But all he wanted was Penny.

He went ahead and let the tears fall as Jude prayed out loud for her.

THIRTY-SIX

PENNY COULDN'T BE DEAD WHEN SHE WAS IN this much pain. She tried to open her eyes, but her lids weighed a ton. Each breath hurt, but she would thank God because it meant she was alive. For one glorious moment, she'd been with Him. The light. The peace. The joy that'd filled her, she would never forget. She hadn't wanted to leave. But even without words, she'd understood. This wasn't her time.

And so now she was here. The stinging smell of antiseptic. Beeps and blips and muffled voices.

And breathing. Someone was in the room. Bryce?

Oh, Bryce.

She wanted to see him, assure him that God was real. He had heard them. She wanted to build a life, a cord of three strands, with him.

Warmth flooded her, giving her strength. It was enough to help to lift those heavy eyelids.

But the room was dark. She wanted to speak. Call his name. Something in her mouth, going down into her body, prevented her. She must be intubated.

She blinked, trying to clear her blurry vision.

A shadow moved closer. A man.

But this man didn't smell like ocean breezes or summer baseball games.

He stepped closer to the bed. He wore scrubs, a mask. Was he a doctor? A nurse?

She couldn't move. Who was this?

A swath of light spilled in, illuminated his face as he raised a pillow above her head. Jason Woods?

"Leave her alone!" The voice roared like a lion, a mighty and beautiful sound. Bryce lunged from the doorway. Knocked Woods to the ground.

Penny could only see the shadows rolling. They grunted, punched, the sickening sound of flesh hitting flesh. The door opened wider. Jude and Olivia rushed in, light from the hallway falling on the wrestling men. They quickly pulled Bryce off Jason before he could get another punch in.

"Don't worry. We got him." Jude handcuffed Woods and passed him off to Olivia. He reached down and offered Bryce a hand. Bryce stood, wiped his face. Then his eyes landed on hers.

Penny cried to see the shimmer of tears in his own gaze as he approached her.

"These eyes are the most beautiful eyes I've ever seen." He cradled her face in his hands and graced her forehead with a featherlight kiss.

For such an impulsive and strong man—hadn't Andi once called her brothers the thunder twins?—his touch was incredibly gentle. The tenderness in his gaze undid her. How had she ever run away from him?

This man that would tackle any obstacle that threatened her. The man that cherished her, had rescued her more than once, and had pursued her even after she'd tried to run away.

More people in scrubs came in. They checked her eyes, the machines, the numbers. Through it all she didn't lose sight of Bryce.

Finally a doctor looked down at her. "It's good to see you awake, Ms. Mitchell. Would you like for us to get that tube out of you?"

She could only nod, but it couldn't happen fast enough. She had something she needed to say.

Within moments, it was out. Her throat hurt, but so did every other part of her body. As soon as two of the other nurses left, leaving room on one side of her bed, Bryce came closer, grabbed her free hand while a nurse messed with her IV on the other side.

"Would you like some water?" she asked Penny. "Here. Sip slowly." She held a straw up to Penny's mouth. The cool water soothed as it slid down.

She set the cup down and looked at them. "I'll give you two a minute, but I'll need to come back and check your incisions and drains later." She winked and left the room. Finally.

Bryce kissed Penny's hand. "You had me worried, Pen."

She swallowed, trying to get enough moisture to say what she needed to say. She didn't want to wait another second.

"I love you."

He kissed her parched lips. "I love you three."

EPILOGUE

PENNY RESTED HER HEAD ON BRYCE'S SHOULder. The lazy sway of the wooden swing was the most vigorous movement she could stand with her aching body still healing. She soaked in the sunshine beating down on them, grateful for fresh air and a cloudless sky. After a week in the hospital, she wanted all the breezes and sunshine she could get. And the barbecue smell wafting over from the grill was nice too.

She never wanted to see another cup of gelatine or applesauce ever again.

Andi walked over, her light-green sundress catching the wind and flowing behind her. "Food is ready."

"You feeling okay, sis?" Bryce asked as he helped Penny stand. "You look a little pale."

"I'm fine, ya big lug. Now let's get Penny to the table before the food cools off."

She walked in front of them, pushing a lawn chair out of Penny's path. Harry and Hazel burst out the open French doors of the house and onto the patio where a table was set.

"Kids, find your seats," Dan called after them. He sipped his drink as he stood with Jude at the grill.

Bryce's father already sat at one end of the table. Elizabeth and Libby carried trays, one piled high with sweet corn and the other with watermelon, and set them in the middle of the spread.

"I hate not helping them," Penny whispered over to Bryce. She leaned on his arm far more than she liked to admit.

"You'll be there soon enough." Bryce squeezed her hand. "Then I'll be fighting to keep up with you."

Jude set down a plate piled high with grilled chicken breasts and hamburgers. After Bryce gave up his place next to Penny so the kids could each sit by their auntie, everyone was finally situated.

The meal was a loud affair—lots of laughter, lots of chatter. Penny loved it all.

"Excuse me, everyone." Andi pushed her chair away from the table and stood, tugging Jude up too. "Jude and I have an announcement."

"Are you having a baby?" Hazel asked.

"Hazel!" Libby's cheeks grew red.

"What? You said when I was curious about something I should ask."

Everyone chuckled.

Andi gave Hazel a mock glare. "Since someone is just too smart for their own good, I guess we don't have anything left to say."

"What?" Elizabeth pressed her fingers to her lips. "A baby?"

Andi nodded, tears welling in her eyes. Jude wrapped his arm around her.

Bryce and Elizabeth took turns hugging the happy couple. The kids lost interest and went back to the swing set in the shady corner of the yard.

"Are you glad you came back to Last Chance?" Libby asked Penny quietly as she moved to the seat Hazel had vacated.

"If I say yes, does that mean you will forever be gloating?"

"Probably."

Penny grinned. "I guess I can handle that."

Bryce came and sat on the other side of her. "I'm gonna be an uncle. Can you believe that?"

She could. He would be an amazing uncle too. And it was early yet, but maybe someday they'd have their own announcements to make.

"We need to celebrate. I have just the thing!" Elizabeth left and came back with bottles of sparkling cider and an angel food cake drenched in strawberries.

Libby took over the serving of the cake while Elizabeth poured the cider.

"Wait until Logan finds out. Then maybe he'll finally come back home for a visit." Bryce took a big bite of strawberry.

Andi shook her head. "I doubt he'll be coming anytime soon."

"What does he do again?" Dan asked.

"Remember, I told you, honey. He's a smokejumper. He fights wildfires, like Tori, but he's in Montana, was it?" Libby looked to Elizabeth to confirm.

"Actually, he called me this week. He's still smokejumping, but he moved."

Bryce set down his fork. "He's only done one season in Montana. Don't tell me—"

"He's gone to Alaska. They had an open spot." Elizabeth's smile dimmed a bit. "He assures me he's doing well and is excited for a new adventure."

Bryce muttered, "More like excited to track down Jamie."

"What a coincidence. Tori is in Alaska too." Libby sat straighter in her chair, shooting Bryce a look. "It will be nice to know they both have family here. Praying for them."

"Let's just hope Logan finds what he's looking for," Andi said.

"Good idea, sis." Bryce looked at Penny, love shining in his brown eyes. "I know I have."

BONUS EPILOGUE

Thank you for reading *Rescued Faith*. We hope you loved this story. Find out what happens next for Bryce and Penny with a **Bonus Epilogue**, a special gift, available only to our newsletter subscribers.

This Bonus Epilogue will not be released on any retailer platform, so get your free gift by scanning the QR code below. By scanning, you acknowledge you are becoming a subscriber to the newsletters of Michelle, Lisa, and Sunrise Publishing. Unsubscribe at any time.

Gear up for the next Last Chance Fire and Rescue
romantic suspense thriller, Rescued Heart
by Lisa Phillips and Megan Besing.

Dive back into the danger—and the romance—of the bestselling Last Chance Fire and Rescue series...

Actress Bianca "Bia" Pearl has finally landed the headlining role that could help leave her scandalous past behind—a role that may even earn back her parents' respect. All she has to do is stick to the script, both on and off camera. Bianca is determined to prove to the press that she's not who they say she is...an overrated gold digger.

Firefighter and former foster child Eddie Rice has always drawn the short straw in life. Now, he's determined to help kids in need have a better future than he did. And when Eddie is selected to represent the fire station at Last Chance County's masquerade ball, he realizes it's the perfect opportunity to secure the mayor's signature on a grant for a much-needed rec center.

But when a case of mistaken identity and a bribe lead to Eddie and Bia being trapped together in a fire, the pair must team up to escape—and protect their futures in the process.

Rescued Heart is a heart-pounding romance that celebrates the power of second chances, the resilience of the human spirit, and the transformative power of love.

Keep reading for a sneak peek...

ONE

THIS MIGHT BE A PARTY, BUT BIA PEARL WAS here to play her part—just like any other scene. All that mattered was the chance to smile for the cameras. If only the dress code allowed sweatpants and flip-flops.

At the opened double front door stood a woman wearing an expression darker than her charcoal knee-length dress. Her peppered hair was slicked back in a bun so tight it seemed to lift her thin brows while her frown deepened. Not exactly the expected welcome at a fundraiser event.

Bianca picked up the front of her dress and pressed on a smile. Her heels clicked on the gold-and-black swirled marble just off-beat to the jazz music playing somewhere beyond the narrow hall.

The woman adjusted her grip on the leather folder pressed against her chest. "Invitation?"

Bianca opened her clutch and produced the shiny golden ticket. Invitation, phone, and black-tie-appropriate attire. Check. See? She didn't need Hollywood's top-tier agent. But someone on her side would be a plus for a change. "I'm so glad the rain held off. Knowing my luck, I probably would've broken a heel in a puddle."

The woman raised one of her penciled brows. "Yes, well, most of tonight's invitees arrived by chauffer."

Bianca secured her clutch under her arm. Everything accounted for minus the whole tardy thing and chauffer. Still a win. As long as she found her costar, Carter Cane.

The woman placed Bianca's offered golden ticket inside a folder on the table. "Enjoy the evening, Ms. Pearl."

Bianca stepped around the woman. "Please tell me I haven't missed the mayor's welcome speech."

Even if she had, there would be time for someone to take pictures of her and Carter. Her contract and movie depended on it. So did her wallet and promises.

The woman slid in front of Bianca. "I'm afraid I can't let you in."

Bianca glanced behind her. But no one else was there. "You can't let *me* into the auction?"

Was this some kind of hidden test? The tabloids had been labeling her with all kinds of lies for years. However, a hot-tempered actress she was not. At least, not normally. "Is there another volunteer I could speak with? I think there's some confusion."

The woman bristled. "I'm Janice Nelson, the mayor's new assistant. There is no confusion. You will not be entering on my watch."

Bianca pushed back her should-have-been-more-curled hair. "What exactly did that ticket I gave you do? If it's because I'm late, I promise you, none of the people on flight 412 enjoyed the unexpected seven-hour layover. And having to change into this dress at a gas station down the road wasn't exactly on my itinerary; however, I would recommend their homemade peach turnovers."

Plus, she may or may not have gotten lost trying to find a town she'd never heard of. Last Chance County wasn't exactly LA.

Janice lifted her chin. "Tardiness, though frowned upon, is not the reason. I'm afraid you are not dressed for this event."

Bianca ran her hand down the front of her dress. Velvet may not yet be back in style, but when fashioned into a flowing floor-length, off-the-shoulder dress stained the color of rubies, it was very much appropriate for a formal evening. Even if her outfit cost less than the dinner plate during tonight's fundraiser auction. "I guess I missed the memo about wearing our cat pajamas. Or were we supposed to wear our puppy ones? And I'm really bummed about missing out on wearing my flip-flops."

Not even a twitch of a smile. Apparently, it was a good thing Bianca's current movie wasn't a comedy.

Janice checked her watch. "You're missing your mystery mask."

Bianca rubbed the spot between her temples. If she grimaced any longer, there would be talk about her worry lines over her ex instead of what kind of budding relationship she and Carter might be forming on set. "I'm sorry. I don't know what a mystery mask is."

Janice drew in a long inhale through her pointed nose. "Your event mask for the masquerade auction. Part of the mayor's requirement for the evening's event."

Bianca swatted her forehead. "Oh, *masquerade*. Somehow, I heard *mystery*." Only Bianca found this laughable. The red-eye flight here was supposed to have created more time to rest. Not what the day had become.

Janice heaved a sigh and threw open her folder. "Here." She handed over a white domino mask with a single row of tiny pearls that ran parallel with the rounded edges. "Don't take this off until the grand live reveal."

Now, the grand live reveal Bianca *did* know about, and she wasn't looking forward to kissing Carter—pretend or not. But the movie's success depended on a social-media takeover, which would ignite tonight with one perfectly timed photo op.

Lord, please let me not have made a mistake by accepting this role.

Bianca slipped the mask on over her eyes. Just another season of pretending. Then the world would see who she really was, and she'd have the money needed to prove to her family that she kept her promises. That she had changed for the good.

Janice scrutinized her for two more of Bianca's heartbeats before finally stepping aside and opening the doors behind her. "The mayor thanks you for your support for his reelection campaign, and remember, half of tonight's proceeds go to a worthy cause."

Supporting a campaign? "Actually, I'm only here because the director arranged—"

"Step inside, Ms. Pearl."

Right. Bianca picked up the front of her dress. It was probably wise she hadn't joked about where the other half of the money went tonight.

Dimmed chandeliers hung from beamed rafters. Tables dressed with black tablecloths and white flower arrangements made an S shape in the rectangular room. It seemed black tie applied to all, decorations included. The stage was in the center, surrounded by a tile dance floor over the carpet. Music drifted from the band, and Bianca tapped her finger on her purse to the beat.

A windowed wall led out to a patio larger than Bianca's current apartment. That was now the only thing she missed about her ex—his house. But looking back, she should have known Nathan hadn't been truthful about who even owned his house. Right now, she'd settle for the court to find the money that had disappeared when they had frozen her account. And for Nathan to stop trying to contact her.

The judge may have exonerated him, but Bianca knew the truth. Too bad no one believed her.

The women at the table nearest to the door had enough feathers on their masks to stuff at least three pillows. Servers in all white carried trays of drinks or food that didn't look big enough to even be one bite. The air smelled like sweet citrus, either from the appetizers or the combination of perfumes swirling about.

Security guarded each of the exits, and they were the only ones whose identities weren't hidden by masquerade masks. Flowers and feathers and decorations made it difficult to find which tables had open seats.

Good thing she and Carter had exchanged numbers at the cast reading. Bianca sent off a text.

Bianca

Where are you seated?

She checked the tables in the first two rows. No open seats. No lone, tall, broad-shouldered men.

Wait. The far corner table contained an open seat. And a masked man in a navy suit with his arm around an empty chair. With the right styled hair and a magazine-worthy jawline.

Had to be Carter.

Bianca wound her way past the other tables and nodded at those already seated. As she slipped into the open chair, she placed her hand on Carter's shoulder. "So sorry I'm late. You will never guess what happened. The—"

"Did it have to do with the sunshiny doorkeeper? Because Janice made me park in the back parking lot. If I had to guess, she's allergic to vehicles not made in this decade. Either that or maybe people in general. And I'd bet she's probably related to the puppet who lives in the trashcan." The man's deep voice had Bianca locking gazes with a dark-eyed stranger.

A quick intake of breath, and then Bianca slid her hand away. "You're not Carter."

The man placed his palm over his heart while a toothpaste-ad-worthy smile stole all of her focus. "Somehow, I'm disappointed now too. I'm only Eddie."

"Shh!" The older woman to his right leaned into Bianca's space and sent them both a glare. "We're not supposed to use our names until the reveal."

Yes. That was the biggest problem here.

Bianca's cheeks heated under her mask. Could this day get any worse? First the layover. Then Nathan had tried to call her. The media had posted again how she'd been a liar at his trial. Plus, being late to meet Carter for their orchestrated kiss and photo. And now . . .

Lord, when are things ever going to be easier?

Eddie touched her elbow. "Do you need help finding this guy?"

What she really needed was about seven more hours of sleep and for God to answer a few more of her prayers. "I—"

The room erupted into applause. Bianca faced the stage, where the man she assumed was the mayor of Last Chance County stood. A mustache framed his wide smile as he waved in his black pants and charcoal suit jacket, complete with a red bow tie.

He was handed a microphone. "Thank you, everyone, for coming. I appreciate your support for my reelection and the youth of our great city in this masquerade auction."

He pointed to his face. "As you've noticed, I'm not wearing a costume mask. But you are, and boy will the social feeds go crazy when we go live and announce all of my wonderful guests. I bet I'll even be surprising some of my dear friends here tonight. With Last Chance County hosting a movie crew, you never know who might be in the chair beside you."

The mayor took a red piece of paper from the grouchy door lady, who now stood beside him. He held up the paper. "You will find one of these tucked inside your napkin. If you can guess everyone who is sitting at your table tonight, there will be a special prize for you after the close of the auction." His grin grew. "Trust me, you want to win it. For now, let's open the night up with some dancing. Take the nearest hand and come join me on the dance floor to celebrate a night of priceless art."

The band on the stage took the cue, and the drummer joined in with the rest of the piano and jazz sounds. The mayor kept his steps to the beat as he exited the stage, heading to the center of the dance floor.

Bianca stood with the crowd. Eighty percent of the men wore black suits, while the others wore gray. Stupid masks.

She checked her phone. Still no reply from Carter. In its place was a picture text from her sister, Madeline. She was surrounded by their mom and grandma and her bridal party while Madeline held a sign that read: *Found my dress at Crystal's Bridal.*

Bianca gripped her phone. She kept missing so much. Things had to be resolved with her family before her sister's wedding.

Her mother's voice popped into her head. *Honey, if you came to your sister's wedding . . . people would look at you, not Madeline. You wouldn't want to steal her day, would you?*

No, she didn't want to steal the spotlight. But feeling a part of the family again would be a nice change.

Eddie cleared his throat. He squinted at her under his mask that barely covered the space around his eyes. The chandelier hanging above their table highlighted the sparkle in his gaze. He had a clean-shaven jawline and wide shoulders. He could star in a movie. Maybe he was one of the extras? Or one of the financial backers for a luxurious resort rumored to be coming to the town.

He slipped his hands into his pants pockets. "Might I suggest a deal? I help you find this Carter guy while you help me dance close enough to the mayor to ask him a question."

Bianca straightened her back. "What kind of question?"

She wouldn't lead an undercover tabloid reporter to swoop in on anyone. No, she was here for a restart. Not to repeat the past.

Eddie tilted his head toward the swarmed dance floor. "I need to make sure he's still going to sign off on an important grant for some inner-city youth."

"Oh." Not connected to the media, the movie, or even the resort. She glanced at her phone. Still no reply from Carter.

Eddie held out his palm. "What do you say? Teammates for the night?"

Carter lived for the spotlight and would not miss an opportunity to be among those dancing.

Bianca slipped her hand into Eddie's. "One song."

His grip sent a warmth through her. "I'll take what I can get."

She could offer him nothing more than teammates, each needing something from the other. A simple exchange.

So why did her heart flutter as if this was a start to something more? Love had left her misguided and at rock bottom. She could not let it happen again. This time, she would seek the qualities God wanted for her future relationship.

Eddie stepped forward. "I'm assuming we're looking for a man in a mask."

She laughed as she followed his lead to the dance floor. Finally, someone with a sense of humor. "However did you guess that?"

Her teammate for the song pulled up beside a woman in a purple dress and a white sequined mask and her dancing partner. The man's lack of enthusiasm did not remain hidden behind his pointy-beaked mask.

Eddie clasped Bianca's hand in his and held it out in a waltz form. He rested his other hand on the middle of her back. His attention scanned the crowd, but his whisper tickled her neck. "And I suppose this Carter also looks sharp in a suit? Since you assumed I was him and all. A fellow strapping lad in his prime."

Bianca rolled her eyes. "He's also as humble as you as well."

Eddie's chuckle harmonized with the melody of the keyboard. "I feel like you have the advantage since I already gave you my name."

Bianca took in the movements of those dancing around her. No one seemed as practiced as Carter would be with his ballroom training. No one except the man she'd mistaken for her costar. "My friends call me Bianca."

Not that she had many of those lately. Except Frances, the waitress who had not only listened to Bianca's woes caused by the situation with her ex but shared the true Hope with her. However,

Frances was currently thousands of miles away in California and thirty-plus years Bianca's senior.

"Well, Ms. Bianca, it's good to know that we've gone from teammates to friends."

Bianca lifted on her toes to gain a better view over the sea of feathers before her. "We can be best friends if you spot Carter."

He spun her in a counterclockwise rotation. "Is that him? Beyond the woman with the red glitter mask?"

Bianca squinted. "I don't see . . ."

A camera light flashed to the side of her, and the mayor walked in front of the man in question.

Bianca tilted her chin. "I spot the mayor, though. He's heading across the dance floor toward my right."

Eddie whipped his head around. "You up for some more spin moves?"

She tightened her hold on his hand. It was a better plan than tramping through all the dancing pairs. He sent her twirling across the dance floor to the thump of the drum. On her fourth spin, nearing the edge of the dance floor, he caught her against his chest and glanced around. "I've lost him."

Just over Eddie's shoulder, a security guard held a door open for the mayor.

She pointed her finger. "There."

The mayor disappeared behind the door just as Eddie turned. A man with a dimpled chin, dressed in a black suit and corresponding mask, jogged over in front of the same security guard that had opened the door for the mayor. Both the guard and the man glanced at the nearest security guard stationed at another door. Then the suited man pulled out what looked like a roll of bills from his pants pocket and held it out to the guard.

Bianca gasped. *Not this again.*

Nathan had taken a handoff the day before the police had stormed their home.

The guard tucked the bills into his palm and opened the door enough for the man and himself to slip through with no one else the wiser.

Bianca squeezed her fingers around Eddie's. "Did you see . . ."

Another bribe. No one had believed her last time.

Last Chance County was supposed to steer her to her happily ever after. A renewed career. Restored family. The actual truth about her character. Looked like this party had just become her most challenging scene yet.

LAST CHANCE COUNTY

• LAST CHANCE FIRE AND RESCUE •

Expired Return

Expired Hope

Expired Promise

Expired Vows

Rescued Duty

Rescued Faith

Rescued Heart

Rescued Dreams

• LAST CHANCE COUNTY SERIES •

Expired Refuge

Expired Secrets

Expired Cache

Expired Hero

Expired Game

Expired Plot

Expired Getaway

Expired Betrayal

Expired Flight

Expired End

ACKNOWLEDGMENTS

There are many people that make me sound smarter, wittier, and helped bring these characters to life. Here's to those I rely on!

Thank you to my editors Lisa Phillips and Susie May Warren. As always you helped me dig deeper and take this story to a higher level than I could ever reach on my own. As editors and fellow writers you are a fountain of ideas and so encouraging throughout the process. I love working with you both.

Thank you to my brainstorming/story-partner/true friend Mollie Rushmeyer for all the coffee and lunch dates and...everything.

A shout out to my Deep Haven sisters Andrea Christenson and Rachel Russell: it was different to write in a series without you two, but you've been there still every step of the way.

Many thanks to Matt Hoffman (and our go-between Karen!) Your help and expertise on planes and flying helped tremendously. Chalk up any and all errors on the subject to me and my creative license. ☺

To my local ACFW-MN NICE group, I love brainstorming with you all.

To my peeps Karen, Bethany, and Angela, your encouragement and prayers are priceless! We need another game night.

To Linda who was always quick to respond to my crazy texts with questions about dispatching, law enforcement, medical emergencies, etc. I know you loved helping me and have celebrated every release. This whole writing journey will look very different without you cheering me on.

There are not enough words of appreciation for my family. Jesse, Anders, Evie, Lucy, and Trygg you are at the heart of everything I do. You get the raw end of the deal so many times when I'm deep in my writing cave in deadline-mode. And yet your encouragement never waivers. I love you all so BIG!

And most of all, thank You, Jesus.

After growing up on both the east and west coasts, **Michelle Sass Aleckson** now lives the country life in central Minnesota with her own hero and their four kids. She loves rocking out to 80's music on a Saturday night, playing Balderdash with the fam, and getting lost in good stories. Especially stories that shine grace. And if you're wondering, yes, Sass is her maiden name.

Visit her at www.michellealeckson.com.

Lisa Phillips is a USA Today and top ten Publishers Weekly best-selling author of over 80 books that span Harlequin's Love Inspired Suspense line, independently published series romantic suspense, and thriller novels. She's discovered a penchant for high-stakes stories of mayhem and disaster where you can find made-for-each-other love that always ends in happily ever after.

Lisa is a British ex-pat who grew up an hour outside of London and attended Calvary Chapel Bible College, where she met her husband. He's from California, but nobody's perfect. It wasn't until her Bible College graduation that she figured out she was a writer (someone told her). As a worship leader for Calvary Chapel churches in her local area, Lisa has discovered a love for mentoring new ministry members and youth worship musicians.

Find out more at www.authorlisaphillips.com.

RESCUE. DANGER. DEVOTION

THIS TIME, THEIR HEARTS ARE ON THE LINE...

The skies over Alaska's vast wilderness are ablaze, not just with wildfire but with the flames of a dark and dangerous conspiracy. Join the Midnight Sun Fire Crew in another heart-pounding adventure as they find themselves fighting not only fires...but for their lives. Old romances reignite and new attractions simmer, threatening to complicate their mission further. Now, the team must navigate their tangled emotions and trust in each other's strengths as their fight for survival becomes a fight for justice in another epic, best-selling series created by Susan May Warren and Lisa Phillips.

Get your romantic suspense fix from Sunrise!

Elite Guardians: Savannah

Safety. Secrets. Sacrifice.
What will it cost these Elite Guardians to protect the
innocent? Discover the answers in our
Elite Guardians: Savannah series.

A Breed Apart: Legacy unleashed!

Get your hands on all of Ronie Kendig's
A Breed Apart: Legacy series.

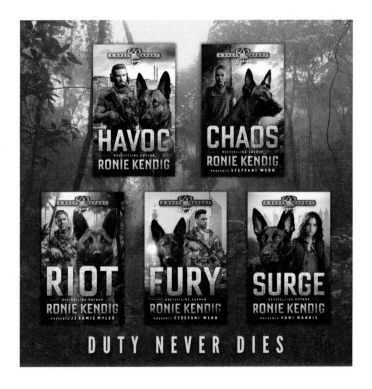

Available Now!

Follow the Montana Hotshots and Smokejumpers as they chase a wildfire through northwest Montana. The pages ignite with clean romance and high-stakes danger—these heroes (and heroines!) will capture your heart.

This exciting series is available in ebook, print, and audiobook. What are you waiting for?
Read the complete series now!

FIND THEM ALL AT SUNRISEPUBLISHING.COM

Connect With Sunrise

Thank you so much for reading *Rescued Faith*. We hope you enjoyed the story. If you did, would you be willing to do us a favor and leave a review? It doesn't have to be long- just a few words to help other readers know what they're getting. (But no spoilers! We don't want to wreck the fun!) Thank you again for reading!

We'd love to hear from you- not only about this story, but about any characters or stories you'd like to read in the future. Contact us at www.sunrisepublishing.com/contact.

We also have a regular updates that contains sneak peeks, reviews, upcoming releases, and fun stuff for our reader friends. Sign up at www.sunrisepublishing.com or scan our QR code.

Made in United States
Cleveland, OH
15 April 2025

16123000R00182